OMEGA

THE SERIES BY

JAN DOMAGALA

THE
GLO🌍
BAL
— *EDIT* —
The international division of PENGUIN

Omega

Copyright © 2021 by Jan Domagala

All rights reserved

Published by Red Penguin Books

Bellerose Village, New York

Library of Congress Control Number: 2021905791

ISBN

Print 978-1-63777-040-5

Digital 978-1-63777-041-2

No part of this book may be reproduced in any form or by any electronic or mechanical means, including information storage and retrieval systems, without written permission from the author, except for the use of brief quotations in a book review.

This is a work of fiction and any resemblance to any person, institution or organisation alive or dead is purely coincidental.

I would like to dedicate this, as always to my Dad who sadly is no longer with us, my Mum, my two kids, my big sis and my best friend and partner Joy, who have given me all the loyal support required to keep me going through the bad times as well as the good, thanks guys I love you all.
I would also like to thank all the writers who have inspired me to put my ideas down – Jack Higgins, Matthew Reilly, Clive Cussler – to name but a few, the list is endless. Thanks guys for the hours of pleasure I've had reading your work. I just hope I can impart some of that to anyone who reads this. Hope I don't let you down guys and keep up the good work.

CONTENTS

THE COL SEC UNIVERSE

COL SEC PERSONNEL

Kurt Stryder: Main character. He was born on Celeron and, when not on duty, still lives in his family home overlooking the coast. Stryder joined Col Sec because his father instilled within him a strong sense of necessity to do the right thing. He remembers his father telling him that for evil to triumph, all that is required is for good men to do nothing. That was his motivation for joining the military and later volunteering for the programme. He has blonde hair, cobalt blue eyes, and a warm smile accentuated by high cheekbones that give evidence of his Nordic ancestry. He's tall, just over 6ft, and has a lean, hardened physique from years in Recon Delta— the Special Forces of Col Sec (Colonial Security).

General Sinclair: Head of Col Sec. The general is in his fifties but still stiff as a ramrod from his years in the military. His brown hair is receding with age, creating a high forehead topped with a sharp widow's peak, and he has deep brown eyes were unfathomable. His resting stoic expression gives nothing away, and his thin lips rarely spread into a smile. It has been said that if he ever played poker, he could have made a fortune from his deadpan expression.

Doctor Baxter: Programme Head. In-charge of the experiment that would change the military forever—and the same one that Kurt Stryder volunteers for. He stands at 5'10 with a reed-thin body and razor sharp mind. The doctor also wears spectacles that he pushes up his nose when nervous.

Zara Hardy: Recon Delta Marine. She was born on Earth and sent to keep an eye on Kurt. Zara is tall and athletic with mocha skin and long black hair usually worn in a plait down her back. Her deep brown eyes and mischievous sense of fun bring her closer to Kurt, and they find a common sense of purpose.

Captain Anthony (Tony) Storm, callsign Guardian: Recon Delta Marine Captain. Captain Storm leads a team guarding Kurt on Research Station Five. He is 6'4 with close-cropped dark brown hair and steely grey eyes. His broad shoulders and chest are proof of his physical strength, but his real strength lines in his drive to put the needs of his men first above his own, hence his callsign: Guardian.

Private John Wayne, callsign Cowboy: Recon Delta Marine in Captain Storm's team. Private Wayne is as strong and reliable team member and friend to Captain Storm, Private Ives, and the other team members. His callsign "Cowboy" was chosen because of his father's love of 20th century western movies that starred John Wayne.

Private William Ives, callsign Hacker: Recon Delta Marine.

He is less physically imposing than his team mates, but with the unique ability to hack into any computer—a skill that earned him the callsign "Hacker." He is somewhat of an enigma because, despite his speciality being computers, he has the heart of an adrenaline junkie. In his free time he loves nothing more than base jumping, rock climbing, and anything that gets the blood pumping.

Matthew Hawk: Recon Delta Marine, on secondment to Colonial Intelligence. Being born and raised on a planet with gravity slightly greater than that of Earth gave him slightly thicker bone density and muscle mass than that of anyone born on Earth. That, coupled with his broad shoulders, 6'6 frame, and well-muscled torso, arms and legs, make him quite the force to be reckoned with. He also has cold, ice blue eyes that sparkle with a mischievous quality often mistaken for indifference.

Colonel Abraham Gemmell: Reckon Delta Marine and General Sinclair's right-hand man. The Colonel towers at 6'5 and is as fit as soldiers half his age due to the regular exercise routines he undertakes with those under his command. He is the type of officer who would not ask a soldier to perform something he is not prepared to do himself. His sharp grey eyes shine with a fierce intelligence and laser-like focus that he directs at every challenge he faces. His black hair has not lost any of its lustre, despite being in his late forties.

Joanne Watkiss: General Sinclair's aid. She is a physically plain and unattractive woman with a short, stocky build and dark hair. As such, she is unaccustomed to attention from the opposite sex.

ELYSIUM ALLIANCE PERSONNEL

Captain Pavel Norsky: Captain of the Alliance's Special Forces unit, the Black Knights. Captain Norsky is in his early thirties and known as a fast-track officer who wants to become a Major by the time his present mission comes to an end. Currently stationed on Celeron, his mission is to capture Kurt Stryder.

Captain Pavel Tchercovic: "Security Chief Captain James Howard." He is sent to stop the programme Kurt volunteered for. He is an undercover agent, seconded from the Black Knights, acting on intelligence gained from a mole inside Col Sec.

Captain Pavel Temic: Black Knights Captain. He is an undercover agent working under the guise of "David Grant." Tall and good looking, he is well-suited for his role.

Captain Nokorovic: Black Knight Captain. He is an aide to General Solon, the head officer in charge of black ops in the Elysium Alliance's Black Knights.

General Solon: Black Knight Officer-in-Charge. General Solon is the highest ranked officer and most decorated officer in the Alliance military. He is a staggering 6'6 with the body of a weight lifter and a white crewcut chopped tight to his skull in stark military fashion. His slate grey eyes are cold and cruel like a shark's, and a scar runs from his left eyebrow to the point of his cheekbone in a curved line. He is a master of close-quarter combat and still practises daily, despite now being in his sixties. His only directive is to shift the balance of power in the Alliance's favour, and he will go to any length to achieve that aim.

OTHER NOTABLE CHARACTERS

Alexander Bane: Owner of The Golden Palace nightclub. Bane is a reformed gangster now in his fifties and built with a layer of fat covering a hard body honed by years of learning the fighting arts under a master which helped him climb the ladder in the planet's largest gang. His face is scarred and he has a broken nose which he refuses to have repaired because he sees it as a testament to all the fights he'd fought to get where he was. His salt-and-pepper hair is combed straight back from a prominent forehead, below which deep brown eyes peer out at the world.

～

PLANETS

Earth: Home Planet of the Colonial Confederation. Col Sec Headquarters is located here, situated in New York City on the site of the old United Nations Building.

Mars: One of the first colonised planets in the Solar System the population live under domed cities as it was colonised before terraforming was made possible. It is also the head-quarters of the Offworld Special Intelligence (OSI), a new branch set up by President Takagi to investigate the mysteries found on Tartaran.

Io: The fourth moon of Jupiter and the most geologically active object in the Solar System.

Celeron: Terraformed into an Earth-class planet over three hundred years ago and is the home world to Kurt Stryder. Its two main cities were named after the first two leaders of the colonists who arrived with the first colony ship: Jamestown and Jacksonville. Haven is a popular resort town on the coast near Stryder's family home.

Toldax: Situated twenty four light years inside the Confederation and Alliance border in Alliance space, Toldax is an E Class planet, one of the few that hasn't needed terraforming before the colonisation programme had begun fully. It has a population of close to four million and the military base is located far away from them on the opposite side of the planet, on the second largest of the two largest land masses.

Dalos IV: Over a thousand light years from Earth, deep in Alliance space, it is an E Class planet that serves as the headquarters for General Solon, Head of Alliance Intelligence and all operations concerning the Black Knights.

Canto: An E Class planet located fifty seven light-years from Earth, three systems away. It is highly populated with five billion people, several continents, and hundreds of cities. One of the larger mountain ranges called the Quad was formed by four mountain peaks simply called Q1 to 4. At the base of the Quad is a forest that is popular with visitors who prefer the outdoor lifestyle.

Cordoba: An E Class planet located forty three light years from Earth in the Praxima system. New San Fransisco is the capital city, located on a bay.

Tartaran Battlefield: A debris field of broken and damaged starships that fought for the planet Tartaran. It is close to the border of Colonial and Alliance space where a massive battle was fought for control of the planet.

Tartaran: An E Class planet thought to be destroyed ecologically during the battle fought over it. It sits close to the border between Colonial and Alliance space. The initial landing party fifty years ago performed an autopsy on a surviving indigenous life-form. The research gained from that expedition is the basis of the programme Kurt Stryder volunteered for.

Tula Rhan: An E Class planet. Famously home to Prince Aswan. It is an unaligned world that has economic deals with both Colonial and Alliance trading partners.

Pallisto: An E Class planet renowned for its sandy beach resorts. Situated nine light-years from the solar system, it has long been considered the vacation planet of the Confederation.

RH426: A barren world populated by a series of cavernous regions where Omega Command is located. The 'RH' refers to Roger Humphries, the astronomer who discovered the planet in the early years of colonisation. It is a barren rock orbiting a star like Sol, our own sun, and although it was barren of organic or indigenous life, it does hold a variety of rare earth elements used in propulsion systems of starships. The Confederation strip mined it until it had nothing left.

Tarsus Prime: An E Class planet colonised for a century. It has twelve million people living in the two main cities, and several smaller communities dotted around on the outskirts.

Tarsus II: A small planetoid orbiting Tarsus Prime.

Paradisia: An E Class planet and Home Planet of Elysium Alliance.

Osiris: An E Class planet with heavier gravity than Earth. Its existence is shrouded in myth, as the colony is believed to be mysteriously abandoned.

Genotia: An E Class independent world located several sectors out of Confederation space.

Talipso: An E Class planet with a population of approximately 150 million in 6 cities, with others dotted around the world on other land masses. Talipso is dependant on trade with other worlds to be sustainable. Previously an Orion Cartel stronghold.

Qaobos: An E Class planet orbiting a star several times more massive than Sol. It is the fifth planet in the system and only populated planet in the entire sector. Not much is known about this world, due to its secluded location far from any other inhabited systems.

C4515: (Morphos): An E Class planet and an independent world in a system that has three other inhabited planets. Morphos is considered the vacation spot in this part of the galaxy.

Pentonville Outpost: A small yet important colony near the border of Confederation and Alliance space.

Andor: An E Class planet near the border of Confederation and Alliance space. Andor is still very much a frontier world, since the colony that has been located there for the last decade is still developing.

Binda: An E Class planet that supplies the needs of the largest ship yards of the Confederation. It is in high orbit around the planet, which also serves as an R-and-R facility for the shipyard workers.

Titanus IV: An E Class planet and the fourth planet orbiting around the star Titanus. It is an independent world and home to the New Order who want to take control of the galaxy and have their home world as the centre of it.

FOREWORD

By the mid-twenty-fifth century, after decades of war over the colonisation of planets between the Colonial Confederation and the Elysium Alliance – an alternative to the government of Earth – an uneasy peace was reached and a cold war prevailed.

The events of this story are set a few days after those depicted in *Ronin*. Things have started to settle down again between the Colonial Confederation and the Elysium Alliance, the status quo has returned.

CHAPTER 1

The entrance to the chamber was dark, shrouded by shadows. He'd dropped into the area by parachute and made his way to the chamber overland by foot until he arrived at his destination.

Reporting back to the drop-ship via a combat channel accessed by his Neural Interface he told them he was on station. His mission was to infiltrate the chamber that Intel had told them was the base of a terrorist cell planning on attacking a Col Sec base, then report back on the conditions there so that the squad of Recon Delta marines who were waiting on board the drop-ship could be deployed.

Wearing a jumpsuit incorporating the Rapier battle helmet with a full face visor attached to the jumpsuit's main breather unit in the backpack holding the retracted parachute, he blended in well with the shadows the night had brought. He had an Mk II Remm assault rifle that he held at high port ready to bring up to his shoulder to sight at any target that presented itself, and under his left armpit was the standard-issue Sig P996 pistol. On his left forearm was

13

strapped the Howell combat knife which completed his armament.

His NI had connected with the computer in the Rapier, which gave a HUD that showed all relevant data pertaining to his present mission, such as weather conditions, ground conditions and com. channels that were established before the drop.

The chamber was underground and the entrance before him was left unguarded which he thought strange. Did that mean they were too late and the terrorists had left, or that the Intel was false and they had the wrong location? Or maybe they were walking into a trap.

There was only one way to find out. He had to go on into the chamber to learn the answer.

"I'm going forward into the entrance. Will report back my findings as soon as possible," he said, sub-vocalising so that he couldn't be overheard by any concealed mic or anyone hidden from view.

Bringing up his Remm assault rifle to his shoulder and sighting down the barrel he stepped forward into the shadows of the entrance.

The entrance itself was an arch just over seven feet high so he didn't have to stoop down to get through. Aiming his Remm assault rifle ahead of him he proceeded down the dark tunnel, his Rapier battle helmet automatically switching to night vision so that the ambient light was ramped up and everything seemed to be bathed in a greenish glow.

As he got deeper into the chamber he began to hear what sounded like voices coming from further within.

He advanced cautiously; acutely conscious that he had no cover now that he was in the chamber heading for the main section. If anyone came out towards the entrance they were bound to see him.

Slowing to a crawl, he carefully continued forwards

aiming his Remm assault rifle ahead of him ready for any sign of a terrorist approach.

The chamber suddenly opened out before him into a cavernous area. He stopped in his tracks when he saw the reason behind the voices he'd heard.

Before him in the centre of the chamber was a small table set up with a monitor on top of a computer terminal. Around it was various pieces of equipment, which he couldn't quite make out because of the distance between them. They were being obscured by the two guards with assault rifles who were on a constant vigil over the man between them, who was talking to the face on the monitor screen.

The moment he saw the two guards he dropped to the floor on his stomach with his assault rifle stretched out before him as he sighted down the muzzle. He was confident that his presence had gone unnoticed by the guards. At that particular moment, he was more interested in discovering who the third man was.

Before setting out for this base he had viewed all the files pertaining to the terrorist cell he had been told operated from there, and so far he had not recognised the stranger.

Admittedly, at that point, he had only seen the back of the man's head and a partial glimpse of the side of his face, but from the files, he knew the size and shape of the main players and, although this man looked and acted like a main player, he wasn't on file as one.

Even though his Rapier helmet boosted the sound via a directional mic he could still only hear snatches of the conversation.

He had to get closer.

First, he had to report his findings and he had to do it without the guards' knowledge. Sub-vocalising to prevent them from hearing, he said, "I have visual on two armed guards and one man who appears to be in charge. He is in contact with another via a computer link. No others have been sighted at this time."

"What action is being taken?" asked the commander of the mission, Colonel De Boer. He stood six feet three inches tall with a strong, lean body honed through hard exercise during his many years in Recon Delta. Blond hair that was almost white and a strong jawline harked back to his Dutch ancestry, as did the steel-blue eyes that watched his men avidly from a rugged face that rarely smiled. He was a veteran of the Recon Delta marines and someone who through his career had gained the trust and respect of the men who served under him. Those above too, especially General Sinclair who was in command of all the Recon Delta marines' missions as well as being the head of the Intelligence Division of Col Sec. Sinclair personally picked De Boer to command this mission and he had also chosen the operative who was on the ground at the moment, at the sharp end as it were, Captain Matthew Hawk. It had been Hawk who had commanded the rescue mission that brought Kurt Stryder back from Alliance space a few days previously and since then he had been back on Earth, filing reports and being debriefed over that particular mission.

This was his first chance to get out of the office and see some action since then.

"None that I can see at this time. The other seems to be talking with someone through the computer link via a monitor. I can't make out what the conversation is about but it seems important," replied Hawk.

"Okay, keep me informed of any developments, stay on station while we decide what action to take," De Boer said and broke the connection.

"I don't seem to have much choice in the matter just now," Hawk said to himself sarcastically.

The guards must've been using a scanner set on infrared

because they suddenly seemed to become aware of his presence near the entrance to the chamber. One of them turned to speak to the man who was talking through the computer link and said something Hawk couldn't quite hear, but the meaning was explicit, they had found an intruder.

The third man, who was clearly in charge, beckoned for the guards to take care of the situation and they began to advance on Hawk's position.

"I may have a spot of bother here, I think they've found me," Hawk sub-vocalised through the com. link.

"Do not; I repeat *do not* engage or give away your position until we have secured the location. We have your back-up routed to your location and will be there in ten minutes, until then you are ordered to stand down. Is that clear?" replied De Boer.

"Perfectly sir," Hawk said, but De Boer perceived the lack of conviction in his words.

"Don't do anything rash and jeopardise the mission, Captain Hawk. I've heard of your reputation, so I know what you are capable of. Follow your orders," he said.

"Gotta go, got two guards bearing down on me," Hawk said. Quickly looking around for somewhere to conceal himself from the guards he realised there was nowhere, especially if they had located him with a scanner. Wherever he went they would find him and before the ten-minute deadline.

"Aw fuck this," he said and, standing up with his assault rifle held against his thigh, he said, "Hi guys, you looking for me?"

The two guards turned to look at him but before they could bring their weapons to bear on him Hawk had opened fire on them. He fired two rapid bursts of three shots, one for each stationary guard. The plasma bolts struck each man in the chest and travelled upwards as the recoil forced the muzzle in that direction so that the final shot struck each guard in the head virtually blowing it apart. Both guards were sent flying backwards in a mist of blood to land on the floor of the chamber, dead before they hit the ground.

"Freeze!" Hawk shouted as he aimed the Remm at the third and final man in the chamber.

The stranger slowly looked over his shoulder and Hawk saw utter contempt in the opaline green eyes. The face that had turned to him was striking in that it was completely average and symmetrical, there was nothing out of place and both sides looked identical, which made him appear odd somehow. The hair was dark and straight, cut in a military fashion, which was short but not too short. He was wearing a dark business suit that looked completely incongruous to the situation and surroundings.

After the short glance, the stranger returned his attention to the monitor as if the command was merely an annoyance.

Hawk strode up to the stranger, who continued his conversation via the computer link. Hawk slapped his left hand on the man's shoulder whilst keeping the assault rifle aimed at the back of his head. To facilitate this he had to turn sideways slightly to reach forward with his left arm.

"I'm talking to you," Hawk said and spun the man around to face him. The assuredness of the stranger was quite unnerving and Hawk began to wonder if there was something he'd missed. What made this man seem so confident that he was not in any danger, he wondered?

The stranger simply smiled at him then calmly placed a hand on the muzzle of the Remm and slowly moved it away from his face.

"You're not going to hurt me, you need to know what I know," the stranger said in a voice that was calm and measured and had a pleasant timbre to it. There it was, the answer to Hawk's unspoken question. That was why the stranger was so sure that he would not be harmed; Col Sec needed what was inside the man's head so they would do whatever was needed to keep him safe and alive.

"Situation secure. Have one captive, no other hostiles present. I shall transport said prisoner to your location for immediate transport to Col Sec for debrief," Hawk said so that the stranger could hear. The moment the words had left his mouth the stranger's mouth curved in a satisfied smile. Hawk began to wonder if what he was about to do was such a good idea after all.

CHAPTER 2

Hawk was met at the rendezvous point by the squad of Recon Delta marines who had just debarked from the drop-ship. They all went back on board and the drop-ship took off to return to the cruiser that was in geostationary orbit around the planet. Within a few short moments, the cruiser had made the jump to hyperspace en route back to Earth.

Colonel De Boer was not happy about Hawk disobeying a direct order but chose to do nothing about it considering he hadn't had any choice but to act. His decision was tempered by the fact that they seemed to have completed the mission with no casualties and had come away with a result that could be quite beneficial to their fight against interstellar terrorism.

Once the cruiser had completed its jump through hyperspace they were soon in orbit around Earth and the prisoner was being transported down to Col Sec HQ in New York on the site of the old United Nation's building from centuries before. Now it was the centre of the Colonial Confederation.

The stranger, who had refused to divulge any information about himself whilst on board the cruiser, seemed to perk up on their arrival. He appeared to be quietly confident at the prospect of being in the HQ of Col Sec with no prospect of escape. Colonel De Boer led the squad from the landing pad at the spaceport to the interior of Col Sec HQ. Hawk went with them, even though his part in the mission had ended, as he was intrigued to learn what could be gleaned from the man he had captured.

Once in the interrogation room in the basement of the huge building, the stranger was ordered to sit down in the chair provided. It was behind a simple desk that had one more chair on the opposite side. Hawk stood in one corner of the small room leaning his six feet six frame against the wall, his muscular arms folded across his broad chest and his ice-blue eyes intently watching the events unfold.

Two of the Col Sec security guards stood behind the stranger as they all waited to see who would take charge of the interrogation.

The door slid open and a man walked in; a man they all recognised.

"I'll be taking over this interrogation myself," said General Sinclair. He was still ramrod stiff in his mid-fifties, no doubt from his many years in Col Sec. His brown hair was receding from a high forehead into a widow's peak, below which his deep brown eyes were unfathomable. His habitual stoic expression gave nothing away as he looked at the man before him. "You were scanned the moment you entered the building and we found some amazing facts about you. We don't know who you are yet, but we do know that you are a clone of whom we have no idea but we will find out," he added.

The stranger sat back in the chair and his face split with a wide grin.

"Perhaps I can help you out, fill in the blanks as it were," the stranger said, his voice almost a contemptuous laugh.

"Have no doubt about it, you will tell us everything we want to know. This is just a chance we are giving you, the only chance, to divulge what we want to know before we force it out of you," Sinclair said, mistaking what the stranger said.

"It's quite amazing that you think you captured me, but I can assure you Omega planned this in every detail," said the stranger with amused contempt.

"Omega? What or who is Omega?" asked Sinclair.

Hawk pushed himself off the wall and went to stand by Sinclair. "Planned this? This Omega planned for you to be brought here, is that what you're saying?"

"You have no idea who we are, do you? We are everywhere, we know everything about you and yet you know nothing about us," the stranger said, looking straight at Sinclair. He then turned to look at the guard at his shoulder and said, "Isn't that right?"

The guard took out his sidearm, a Sig P996, and shot the clone in the head spraying blood and gore over Hawk and Sinclair standing opposite him. The clone fell forwards like a rag doll onto the table, stone dead. The guard then turned and shot the other guard next to him in the head also, the bolt pulping the man's head, throwing him sideways to hit the wall spraying blood on impact.

Hawk saw the guard adjust his weapon and pushed Sinclair to the floor as he drew his own Sig P996. Hawk landed on top of the General, shielding him as the guard fired his weapon. Hawk aimed at the guard but couldn't get a clear shot because the table was obstructing his view.

Pulsed plasma bolts struck the table blowing bits of it away as the guard tried to get a clear shot at the two of them lying on the floor.

"Sir, we have to make a move to get you out of here and fast," Hawk said urgently.

"What do you suggest Matt, he's got us pinned down pretty good?" Sinclair asked quite calmly. He knew he was in good hands with Hawk.

Seeing the guard's legs beneath the table, Hawk quickly took aim and fired a low power shot at his right leg. The plasma bolt struck him and, instead of blasting through the flesh down to the bone, it disrupted the nerve pathways effectively paralysing the leg.

The guard fell over as that leg could no longer support his weight. However, as he collapsed he saw his intended targets through the table legs and fired.

The plasma bolts narrowly missed Hawk and came close enough to Sinclair behind him that the General felt the heat from the blast as it singed the hair on his head.

Hawk shot the guard in the centre of his chest stunning him for a few seconds as he was forced backwards. Hawk was amazed when he saw the guard was still conscious and shaking his head to diminish the effects of the stun-blast.

"Stay where you are, sir, I'll handle this," said Hawk motioning for the General to stay down out of sight.

The guard struggled to his feet and, grabbing hold of the desk in his right hand, heaved it over to land on top of Hawk and the General. Seeing what was about to happen, Hawk threw himself over the General once again to shield him from harm, using his own body to protect his commanding officer.

The guard used the momentary respite to take out a hypospray and inject himself in the leg to counteract the effects of the stun-blast. The medication took effect almost immediately and the guard found he could walk properly again. Getting to his feet he made a dash for the exit.

Hawk threw off the desk just in time to see the guard try

and rush past him out of the room. Reaching out he grabbed the running guard's ankle, managing to grip it just hard enough to send him flying off balance and spinning to the floor once more.

Hawk was up in a flash, moving over to the guard who lashed out with both his feet striking the advancing Hawk in the chest, sending him staggering backwards. He flipped himself back onto his feet ready to continue the fight.

Forgetting he had a Sig P996 close at hand the guard lashed out at Hawk with a series of jabs and front kicks, which Hawk, himself adept at close quarter combat, easily dodged or blocked.

Suddenly remembering the pistol, the guard lunged for it on the floor but Hawk reached his first and fired at the Sig sending it skittering across the floor. Before Hawk could fire again the guard was up off the floor and running at him, head down for a tackle. The two of them collided and collapsed onto the floor again with the guard on top this time. He quickly went on the offensive, pummelling Hawk with a series of punches to the kidneys and stomach, then quickly changed his attack by reaching for the Howell combat knife and tearing it free from the sheath on Hawk's forearm.

As soon as Hawk realised what had happened he knew he was in trouble and that the chances of him capturing this man alive had just plummeted. This had turned into a real death struggle where the only victor was the one left alive.

The guard brought the knife round in an arc hoping to stab Hawk in the neck, but Hawk stopped the plunge by grabbing both his wrists. The point of the blade was mere inches from his neck and Hawk's arms quivered with the strain of holding it there.

It came down to a battle of who was the strongest, but the two of them quickly became aware that they were quite evenly matched and Hawk noticed a strange look in the guard's eyes. It was a look of surprise, almost as if he couldn't believe what was happening, like he expected to win this power struggle with no questions asked.

Hawk had always been unusually strong. When he was growing up his father had always made him exercise with weights, but he had been unaware of the fact that the gravity in his environment had been a little heavier than that of Earth so that when he came to enlist in Col Sec Military for the Recon Delta he aced all the physical tests. General Sinclair noted this in his reports and, after two years, seconded him to the Intelligence Division.

The guard began to get a little frustrated and started to growl in anger at not being able to force the point of the knife down into his victim. Hawk, on the other hand, remained as calm as he could, not allowing anger to invade his thoughts or his clear-headedness would evaporate and he would lose whatever advantage he had in the struggle.

Hawk brought up his right knee to strike the guard in the side, which threw him off balance just long enough for Hawk to gain the upper hand and roll the guard off him. As he rolled away and onto his knees the guard looked at Hawk with an expression that was purely feral in nature. With teeth bared, brow bunched and eyes that positively sparked with fury, he lunged at Hawk with the knife as he got to his feet.

Hawk had to step back to evade the point of the knife as the guard swept it from side to side, then suddenly changing tactics he lunged forward hoping to plunge the tip into Hawk's stomach. Seeing the attack, Hawk twisted sideways allowing the knife to travel past it's intended target. He grabbed the wrist with both hands preventing the guard from bringing the knife back to repeat the move.

Quickly assessing the new situation the guard punched Hawk in the ribs with his free hand. The blow made Hawk wince and he knew he had to stop that from happening again. He smashed the point of his right elbow into the unprotected face of the guard to intimidate him from any further punches.

The guard reached beneath Hawk's legs with his free hand and lifted him off the ground with ease. Hawk was surprised at the strength of the man and realised that he must have taken something to enhance his natural abilities.

Before he could do anything to counter the move Hawk found himself hurtling towards the ground. The guard had reversed his move and was in the act of slamming his attacker to the ground in a move popular with pro wrestlers called the sidewalk slam.

As his back struck the floor all the air was forced out of Hawk's lungs and for a second he couldn't get his breath. The guard took advantage of this and pulled his arm free. Still holding the knife he dived on top of Hawk this time hoping to plunge it into his chest.

Hawk had little time to counter the attack and thought he was going to die from knife wounds. All he could think to do was to bring up his knees to try and prevent the knife from reaching him. The guard landed on top of the knees, his face colliding with Hawk's kneecaps. It was a move born out of desperation but it seemed to have the desired effect, for when the guard's face collided with Hawk's knees his nose exploded on impact.

The sudden pain made the guard involuntarily fall away from Hawk and he rolled onto his side clutching at his damaged face giving Hawk the opportunity to regain his breath and get to his feet.

Hawk knew that the fight would end in the next few seconds with one of them lying dead on the ground, there was no quarter here and only one outcome was possible.

Looking at him through pain-filled eyes the guard

realised that this man before him was no ordinary man and that it might be best to escape rather than fight. Glancing towards the door the guard realised he must make his move now or suffer the consequences.

Hawk saw the glance and knew what his attacker was thinking. He thought that the guard must be mad to think he could escape from the HQ of Col Sec. With all the security lockdowns in place, the moment he stepped outside the confines of that room he would be surrounded by other guards.

Unless, of course, this OMEGA had infiltrated Col Sec deeper than anyone realised and the guards waiting would be there to help instead of capture. In that case, Hawk had but one option, to stop him from leaving the room.

The guard lunged at Hawk for he knew he had to kill him to escape from the room. The knifepoint narrowly missed gouging a deep rent in Hawk's stomach, but he managed to evade the lunge by moving backwards just at the last second. Grabbing the wrist holding the knife, Hawk twisted outwards so that the arm was bent against the joint.

The guard screamed from the pain that suddenly lanced up his arm and he let go of the knife, which Hawk immediately scooped up. The guard lashed out at Hawk with anything and everything he had, punches, kicks and even part of the table that had been smashed during the fight. Using part of a table leg he attempted to stab Hawk in the arm, but Hawk saw the move and blocked the guard's arm above the wrist plunging the knife he was holding into the same arm rendering it useless for further combat.

Blood sprayed out from the wound and the guard knew his freedom could be counted in seconds. He switched grips on the table leg from one hand to the other and came at Hawk again, more in desperation than with any realistic effort.

Hawk blocked the blow once more and this time struck with the knife, burying the blade deep into the man's neck. The guard screamed in pain as he realised he was about to die.

He dropped the table leg and placed his hand over the wound in his neck. Blood pumped from the wound and trickled through his fingers as his attempts to stem the flow failed miserably.

He sank to his knees then keeled over as his life's blood leaked out from him at an alarming rate. As weakness overcame him, he fell onto his side and lay there like a rag doll. Within a few seconds, he was dead from loss of blood.

"Did you have to kill him?" asked General Sinclair getting to his feet. He came to stand by Hawk's side as the latter looked down at the dead guard.

"There was no way he was going to allow us to take him alive, sir. We can learn what we need from his NI, hopefully," Hawk replied.

"A post mortem interrogation like the one we performed on the Alliance agent a few days ago," Sinclair said remembering the incident, but before Hawk could reply they heard a noise coming from where the dead guard lay. A strange popping sound came from the guard's head and his entire skull seemed to expand slightly as if something inside his head had blown up.

"What the fuck!!!" exclaimed Hawk and he stooped down to inspect the guard's head. The tissue had gone soft to the touch, almost like the bones of the skull had dissolved. Blood began to seep through the eye sockets, ears and down his nostrils.

"Whatever that was sir, it seems the post mortem interrogation will have to wait. I don't think we'll learn anything from him now," Hawk said and got to his feet.

"What's that sound?" Sinclair asked and Hawk tensed as

he heard it too. It was the unmistakable sound of a timer counting down. Hawk looked across to where the clone lay and saw a thin twist of smoke escaping from what remained of his head.

Acting swiftly, Hawk grabbed the General and pushed him through the door and as he dived through himself he activated the locking mechanism to seal the room. He had acted just in time, for the instant the door closed and sealed the room off an explosion erupted from inside the chamber.

The walls of the room seemed to pulse outwards with the released energy from the blast, but the seal held.

Sinclair looked at Hawk and said, "What just happened?"

"I'm not sure without having the Tec guys go over that room with a detailed scanner, but I'd say that somehow they smuggled a bomb into HQ inside that clone."

"Are you serious?" Sinclair asked, not sure if he'd heard right.

"Yes, sir. Somehow they found a way to shield the charge from our scanners and sensors."

"Well, if that's true then they planned this whole scene to kill me and whoever was with me at the time," Sinclair said as the realisation hit him.

"Yes, sir, this goes deeper than any of us ever thought possible," Hawk said.

"The implications of this are too huge to contemplate. I'll have to inform the President. We may have to take special and unusual measures to combat this threat. You find out what you can from what's left in there and report back to me personally when you have something," Sinclair said with a sense of urgency in his voice.

"What about you, sir, where will you be? You need to get yourself looked at by a medic," Hawk said.

"I'll do that later. I'm going to see the President right away, he needs to know about this," and with that Sinclair stormed off leaving Hawk alone outside the interrogation room.

"If anyone can do it, you can, sir," he said as he watched the commanding officer of the Intelligence Division disappear down the corridor.

As he pondered the task before him he wondered what, if anything, could be done to combat a threat about which you knew nothing, but which seemed to know everything about you. He just hoped that the General would come up with something.

CHAPTER 3

Hawk got to work on directing a crew to investigate the remains of the interrogation room almost immediately. As he stood around and watched the tecs set about the task with their various pieces of equipment, he realised that his skill sets were not suited to this job so he told them to inform him the moment they had anything and left them to it. He returned to his office to review the video data of the interrogation.

He was becoming increasingly frustrated at learning so little. What was the purpose of OMEGA and why had they set this whole thing up? If they were so clandestine why push themselves to the forefront now? What could they possibly gain from their recent actions? Was this, like Sinclair said, an elaborate scheme to take out the leader of Col Sec's Intelligence Division and so cripple that organisation? If so, apart from the obvious, what did they hope to gain and why at this particular moment? There was nothing of significance on the calendar that Hawk was aware of so the date of the incident seemed completely random unless there was something happening soon that he was not privy to. If that were the case then he needed to know all the facts if he was expected to combat this new threat.

He felt like he had just stepped into the boxing ring with both hands tied behind his back. Not a good feeling.

His NI tingled, alerting him to an incoming call.

"Hawk, my office, ten minutes," said Sinclair, his voice carrying through the channel as clear as if he was standing next to Hawk.

"On my way, sir," he replied and got to his feet and exited his office.

MAXWELL EISENHOWER WAS SEATED behind his rather large, ornate desk working diligently on several reports when he was alerted to the presence of someone outside his door. In his early sixties, he was a small man, standing only five feet seven tall. His greying hair was cut stylishly short, costing him more than the average worker in one of his many factories earned in a week. He was a mediocre man except for his opaline green eyes, the only remarkable feature about one of the richest men in the galaxy. The sensor that was fitted in the locking mechanism scanned everyone who approached the door and told the occupant of the room everything about them – what they were carrying and what they were wearing even down to the contents of their stomachs. The chances of anyone slipping anything dangerous past this sensor were remote in the extreme.

Eisenhower had built his business from the ground up and as he sat behind his desk working away he was content to be the CEO of the largest mega-corporation in at least ten sectors. His turnover was reputed to be in the trillions, his personal fortune was over one hundred and forty billion and growing.

All these facts were well known as he had business enterprises on several planets both in the Colonial Confederation and the Elysium Alliance, but what was not so widely known was that his fortune was also boosted by his criminal activities as the head of OMEGA.

Having grown bored with normal business practices he had gravitated to more unsavoury pursuits, which had turned out to be quite profitable. The best thing for him about his dual personality was that OMEGA was exceptionally clandestine. This secrecy ensured that no one had any idea that the mild-mannered CEO of a huge mega corp. was also the leader of a group that dealt with death and destruction on a huge scale. That was until now. Somehow, Col Sec had captured one of his Rovers, a name he coined for the clones he'd created to be the public face of the leadership of OMEGA. Using a bioengineering division of one of his businesses, he'd made a series of clones to act as the face of OMEGA, each one indistinguishable from the next with all of them sharing the same DNA and memories.

They were the leadership of OMEGA and only they dealt with the running of the clandestine operations OMEGA was concerned with. In that way, no one could ever tie them in with him or his legitimate business operations.

That was until now.

Someone had taken it upon themselves to go up against Col Sec and bring OMEGA out from the shadows and into the light of day, not something he had ever wanted. But now it had happened he had to find out who and why and then stop them before they ruined everything.

The person outside his door was the man tasked with finding out what he could about the recent Rover incident, his chief aide and confidante, Jonas Wilde.

Wilde had been with Eisenhower for over ten years, working his way up the business ladder until, eight years ago, his efforts had come to the attention of the CEO. Wilde had been appointed his chief aide and allowed into his confidence about OMEGA and he had been in that privileged position ever since.

Eisenhower operated the door lock remotely allowing Wilde to come into his office.

"What have you learned?" Eisenhower asked without preamble.

Wilde entered the spacious office and walked up to the desk. Around five feet eleven inches tall he was of average build yet trim and fit. He had nondescript features making him almost invisible in a crowd. Dark hair and dark eyes went unnoticed by most, along with an almost expressionless face. His expression today told Eisenhower what he needed to know without him even opening his mouth to speak.

"Nothing, sir. So far my enquiries have drawn a blank. I've had to be careful not to arouse the suspicions of the authorities investigating the incident. Should they get wind of my enquiries then it could lead them straight back to this office and that's the last thing I want, sir," Wilde said apologetically.

"Well, before they do that, I think it best we close off any avenue they might be chasing down by sending a team to where the Rover was apprehended to destroy any signs that it was there. Once their investigation hits a dead end we can find out who sent it there and why, but our priority at the moment has to be stopping Col Sec from finding anything that could lead them to us here," Eisenhower said. He looked up at Wilde, his opaline green eyes almost sparking with a rage so intense Wilde could almost feel it. "We cannot allow Col Sec to tie the Rover to us. Tell the team to do whatever is necessary to prevent any data falling into Col Sec's hands, is that clear, anything?"

"Perfectly clear, sir," Wilde said, his reed-thin body

ramrod straight as he stood before the table, pinned there by the glare from those eyes.

"Handle this personally Jonas, I can trust no one else with this you understand!"

"Consider it done, sir. You have my word." Wilde said, then turned and left the room leaving Eisenhower to return to his work.

The moment Wilde left the room he contacted the team leader who would clean up this mess. Tanis Rygar was a contract soldier who until five years ago had been in the Black Knights, the Elysium Alliance's Special Forces. Said to be the equivalent of Col Sec's Recon Delta marines, the Black Knights were elite in the extreme and had faced off against Col Sec on many occasions.

Rygar was a large man with a block-like head set on broad shoulders and a well-muscled torso. His strength and ruthlessness were renowned amongst the Black Knights. He had a bald head, a black goatee and a scar on the edge of his left eye that made it appear puckered. He had worked for OMEGA as a team leader for the past five years, since Eisenhower had poached him from the Black Knights, and had proved a valuable acquisition.

For the past year though, Wilde had become close to him, using him more and more, gaining his trust with promises that one day he would be a man of power within an organisation that would be THE power in the galaxy.

It had been Wilde who had sent the clone to the chamber, it had been Wilde who had leaked the data about a terrorist strike against a Col Sec base, upon which the latter had no option but to act. So far his plan was going smoothly.

"Rygar, take your team back to the chamber and destroy any evidence you may find there pertaining to the Rover," Wilde said after the call had been connected via his NI. All MaxCorp higher echelon employees were fitted with top-grade Neural Interfaces almost to military-grade and so the call was made easily enough.

"It's about time, I've been sitting on my butt for the past twelve hours waiting for your call," Rygar answered sullenly.

"Just remember who signs your pay cheque, Rygar, and show some respect or I'll have you on garbage duty for the next twelve months," replied Wilde sternly. He was not a man to cross. What Eisenhower didn't know was that Wilde had a military background and had served in Col Sec Intelligence Division for several years before being kicked out for an op that went bad and in which several marines lost their lives through his tainted Intel. He was ruthless and determined with sociopathic tendencies and his plan was to rip control of OMEGA from Eisenhower's fingers. If it was from his dying fingers he didn't care, as long as he got control.

"Yes, sir, I'm on my way, will report back as soon as we arrive on station," Rygar replied showing the correct amount of respect and not overdoing it with a tinge of sarcasm, for he knew better than to anger Wilde. He had once seen him chastise a team member in front of the rest of the team. The member returned a sarcastic comment after being reprimanded and Wilde took out a Sig P996 and calmly shot him between the eyes, witnessed by the whole group. After that, no one was ever sarcastic to him in any situation.

"Good, I'll look forward to your call," Wilde said, then broke the connection. As he continued walking down the brightly lit corridor his thoughts were on the chamber and what Rygar would find there. Once his orders had been carried out and all incriminating evidence erased, it would be time to move on to the next phase of his plan.

Now he must make preparations so that when the time arrived he would be ready to make his move.

Col Sec would soon learn the true power that OMEGA wielded and that there was nothing they could do to stop them. His revenge on them for his humiliation would soon be complete.

～

HAWK WAS SOON ENTERING General Sinclair's office eager to see what he wanted to tell him.

"I came straight away, sir," he said when he saw the General check the time. He had got there in just over five minutes.

"No need to apologise, Matt," Sinclair said.

"I wasn't, sir," replied Hawk who stood to attention in front of the large, ornate desk.

"At ease Captain, relax before you strain something," Sinclair said in a more friendly tone. "What have you learned from the interrogation room?"

"Still waiting for the preliminary reports, sir, but if I may suggest something?" Hawk replied.

"What is it, Captain?"

"I don't think we'll learn much from the room, sir, not as much as we could from the chamber where I captured the clone. They picked that particular place for us to go and capture the clone and I think we need to know why," explained Hawk.

"Okay then take a squad of marines with you and go and do your thing. I'll inform Colonel De Boer that you'll need his services once more."

"Thank you, sir, I'll leave right away."

"Before you go I have something you need to know. My recent talk with the President went rather well. I put to him the situation about OMEGA and my recommendations on how to combat it. He agreed and gave me carte blanche to do as I see fit. To that end, I intend to set up a new special unit to combat such threats, a unit of agents who will be the elite from Recon Delta and I want you to join them. In fact, I want you to be the first of my recruits. For the time being, I want you to carry on with your present investigation until I've finalised the details of this new unit. As soon as I have anything I'll let you know."

"I'm flattered, sir. What's this new unit going to be called?"

"That hasn't been decided yet."

"If you want any nominations for recruits then I have a few: Captain Storm and his team. They helped with the rescue of Kurt Stryder and they are already a team who work well together. I must say that they are the best soldiers I've ever had the privilege of working with."

"I'll take that under advisement Captain and we'll talk about it soon, but for now you have work to do. Contact me on a secure channel the moment you have anything."

"I will sir."

"Dismissed," Sinclair said and with that Hawk turned on his heel and left the office.

CHAPTER 4

Hawk went straight to the spaceport where he found Colonel De Boer waiting for him with a squad of five men.

"I understand you want to go back into the chamber to see if you missed anything the first time around, is that it?" De Boer asked as Hawk approached.

"Yep, it seems we drew a blank with the captive and the only lead left to us is what we might find back in that chamber," replied Hawk. He paused slightly while he thought out what he was going to say next. Just how much did the Colonel know? Had Sinclair confided in him the true nature of the situation or was he as much in the dark as before and should he tell him about OMEGA? All these questions rattled around inside his head as he chose his next words carefully.

"Might find? Are you trying to tell me this is a goose chase of the wild variety?" De Boer asked, clearly not impressed with his new mission.

"Look Colonel, I know you're not impressed with me or my methods, or the fact that a mere Captain is in charge of this mission, calling the shots with the authority to issue you

41

with orders. I know all that, you make it abundantly clear, but I tell you what, I don't give a shit. You will carry out my orders when I give them and you will show some professional etiquette. I can't expect you to show respect when you clearly have none but I do expect you to act like a Recon Delta marine Colonel."

De Boer took a step back to look at Hawk, this time with a little more respect. The man had actually stood up to him and in fact had torn a strip off him, which he knew he deserved.

"Of that, you can be assured, Captain," he said.

"Matt, call me Matt. I'm an officer of the Intelligence Division and I prefer not to stand on ceremony except when it's warranted, I just want to get this job done. I'm afraid I cannot tell you too much of what's going on, but what I can say is that this is of the utmost importance. I don't say this just to get you motivated; I say it because it's a fact. There is a danger to Col Sec here and I have to find out as much about it as I possibly can. Now we may have no trouble back at the chamber, but protocol demands that I return there escorted by a squad of marines. The faster we get there, the faster I can learn what is behind this menace," Hawk said.

"In that case, Matt, I suggest we get on board," De Boer said with a smile.

"What, no more questions?" asked Hawk.

De Boer looked at him and said, "I'm sure you'll inform me of what I need to know when I need to know it."

"Right," Hawk said and they all boarded the shuttle, which promptly took off and headed straight towards the cruiser, Valkyrie, which was parked in orbit.

The Valkyrie was a military transport placed at Hawk's disposal for the duration of the mission and was crewed by some of Col Sec's finest. Colonel De Boer had only brought five men along with him for this trip and not having had the benefit of all the mission details, he had been unable to do a proper risk assessment of the task ahead. Assured that this was just an escort job he believed a five-man squad would suffice. He would be proven wrong.

Captain Jefferson, a twelve-year veteran of the Col Sec Space Navy, took the Valkyrie into a full thrust away from orbit so they could safely make the jump through hyperspace to their destination. Canto was only fifty-seven light-years from Earth, three systems away, so they could reach it in one jump.

Canto was a highly populated planet with several continents and hundreds of cities where most of her five billion inhabitants lived.

There were several less populated areas on the planet also; deserts not unlike those of Earth and, as Canto was an E class planet (Earth-type), there were mountainous regions too.

The chamber was in one of these, at the base of one of the largest mountain ranges called the Quad. There were four huge mountains in the range simply called Q1 through to Q4. The chamber was hidden at the base of Q3 the third largest mountain.

The Valkyrie arrived at Canto and immediately went into a parking orbit.

"Well, gentlemen, I got you here safely," Jefferson said to both Hawk and De Boer who stood at his side on the bridge. Jefferson was seated in the captain's chair, one hand on the control panel in the armrest and the other up to his face, his elbow resting on the opposite armrest. He had a smile on his chiselled features that seemed a permanent fixture, almost as if he couldn't take life seriously, but anyone who knew him well knew that to be untrue. Jefferson was one of the most qualified and experienced captains in Col Sec Space Navy. "The rest, as they say, is up to you," he added.

"Is the ATV loaded onto the shuttle?" asked Hawk.

"Everything is ready for you, sirs, just be careful with it, please. If you break it I don't want Col Sec taking it out of my next paycheque," Jefferson replied, the smile still in place.

Turning to leave, Hawk said, "Okay Dad, I'm taking the car out for a spin, I promise to be back before nightfall, and I promise not to scratch her." He and De Boer were gone leaving Jefferson holding back a laugh.

"Kids!" he said, then returned to watching the forward view- screen.

This time Hawk had chosen not to wear the combat suit he had worn the last time he was there, even though the marines were. Instead, he chose to wear something more casual; cargo pants and a shirt, over which he wore a soft leather jacket. On his feet, he wore walking shoes rather than combat boots. He preferred the walking shoes as they were more flexible, lighter and allowed his feet to breathe even though they still retained extensive durability and were waterproof. Not expecting trouble he left most of his armament on board the Valkyrie and chose to take the Sig P996 only. He kept it in a soft leather holster beneath his left armpit, hidden by the jacket.

The shuttle was piloted by Lieutenant Hall, an expert pilot of five years, the last three of which he'd served aboard the Valkyrie under the command of Captain Jefferson. He dropped the small craft out of the shuttle bay of the Valkyrie and aimed her straight at the planet below. Before long they were entering the atmosphere and gliding down the controlled descent towards the Quad in the northern hemisphere.

Hall said, "There is no way I can put this baby down any closer than the base of the Quad, you'll have to take the ATV as far as you can from there. I'll remain on standby 'til I hear you're on your way back and then I'll get the shuttle prepped for immediate take-off. That's the best I can do, sirs."

"Don't worry about it Lieutenant, we'll be fine. A nice drive in the country will be most relaxing, just what the doctor ordered," Hawk said smiling.

"You seem quite upbeat about this mission. What's changed?" asked De Boer, a little concerned about Hawk's altered mood.

"Nothing has changed Colonel, I just have a good feeling about this mission that's all. I think we'll find something of value down there that will help us to fight this terrorist threat," Hawk replied, allowing the smile to slip as a sudden thought struck him, one that he chose to keep to himself. What if they found more than they bargained for down there?

Yes, that was definitely a thought to keep to himself. He got behind the wheel of the ATV and drove it out of the rear exit of the shuttle. Colonel De Boer sat next to him whilst the marines were seated behind.

The road ahead was nothing more than a dirt track that ran around the base of the mountains and up to the summit. The chamber was at the base of Q3 but to get to it they had to drive part way up the path before they could even see it.

There was shrubbery dotted here and there, sprouting out of the hard ground and between the boulders that were strewn around and up the mountainsides.

Hawk steered the rugged vehicle towards the path leading up the mountain.

"Here we go," he said and boosted the power just enough to send the ATV along at a steady pace. There was no need to rush, especially along these treacherous paths.

45

AFTER THEIR JUMP THROUGH HYPERSPACE, Rygar and his team re-entered normal space on their way to Canto. They were in a modified freighter and with a crew of twelve and his team of ten mercenaries the small ship felt a little cramped.

"Scan the area for any signs that the chamber has been tampered with since the last time it was used," Rygar said as he came onto the bridge to marshal his men before going down to the planet's surface.

"Sir, there is a vehicle approaching the chamber by road. It looks like a Col Sec All Terrain Vehicle," said the crewman operating the sensor array.

Like a bird of prey swooping in Rygar came to stand by the man's shoulder as he said, "What!"

"See for yourself, sir," the crewman said, indicating the sensor screen.

After viewing the screen Rygar said, "Get us down there as fast as you can." By the tone of his voice, the Captain of the freighter knew not to argue or throw up any obstacles. "Aye sir," was all he said and he urged the pilot to comply.

"Right men, tool up, I want us to be ready to move the second we touch down. Whoever is down there we can't let them leave with anything from that chamber, even if it means killing them all. No one leaves that chamber alive, is that clear?" to which his men all answered in the affirmative.

"HERE WE ARE, just where we left it," joked Hawk as they arrived at the entrance to the chamber. "I suggest you leave one of your men at the ATV just as a precaution and the rest can follow me. The quicker we complete this search the quicker we're on our way home," he added.

"Can't argue with that," De Boer said.

Hawk stopped the powerful vehicle at the entrance to the

chamber and secured it. The doors opened and he left the craft followed by De Boer and four of his men.

"Wilson, you stay with the ATV, we'll keep in touch with regular updates via battle com. We're not expecting trouble, but just in case be ready, okay?" De Boer said to the last man exiting the vehicle.

Wilson shouldered his Mk II Remm assault rifle and stood by the front of the ATV.

$\sim$

"Sir, a freighter has just dropped out of hyperspace and is heading for the planet's surface," said the ops officer on board the Valkyrie.

"What's so special about that?" asked Jefferson, already guessing the answer.

"Sir, they're heading straight for our boys," replied the officer.

"Scan it, I want to know who's on board and what their intentions are and whether it is armed," Jefferson ordered.

"I'm reading more life signs than should be on board, sir, and there are an awful lot of weapons for a simple freighter," the ops officer replied, having started scanning the moment his suspicions were aroused.

"Hawk, we have a freighter heading your way. It has more than the usual compliment of crew on board so we have to assume they're coming after you," Jefferson said through the battle com.

"Thanks, Captain, we'll keep an eye out for them," replied Hawk and turning to De Boer he asked, "Did you get that too?"

"Yes," said the Colonel with a concerned expression. He turned to the men following him and signalled that they keep alert.

"Lieutenant Hall, we may be having visitors quite soon. If they make advances in your direction take off and return to the Valkyrie, I don't want our only method of transport off this planet compromised, is that understood?" said Hawk through the battle com.

"Understood sir," Hall replied.

"If you have to leave us here we'll keep you apprised of our status so we can reschedule the pickup," Hawk said as he continued walking towards the chamber.

"Also understood, sir."

"Wilson we may have hostiles coming your way real soon, I want you to secure the ATV. Under no circumstances must that vehicle fall into their hands is that clear?" said De Boer.

"Absolutely, sir," Wilson replied.

"If your position is compromised relocate the ATV but, if that is impossible and only as a last resort, destroy the ATV, get yourself to safety and rendezvous with us later, understood?" added De Boer.

"Understood, sir."

"Everyone, stay frosty, we may be outnumbered but we are Recon Delta," De Boer said to all his men. That was all he needed to say really because they all knew they were the best that Col Sec had and they would perform the job they had been ordered to do.

"Right Hawk, let's get this done before we have company," De Boer said to the man leading them.

"I'm on it, Colonel," Hawk said as they arrived at the chamber entrance.

THE FREIGHTER CAME through the atmosphere and slowed down using its thrusters, but even so, the speed of their arrival was greater than any normal freighter. The pilot said to Rygar, "I won't be able to put her down on the ground where you want to go, you'll have to rappel down as I try to keep her steady."

"Do it," Rygar replied turning to his team, "Get ready, we're going in hot and fast. Kill anything that moves." He fastened his rappelling line to the interior bulkhead adjacent to the nearest hatch and then connected it to his webbing belt. His team followed suit and soon they were all ready for the drop-down to the planet's surface.

THE CHAMBER WAS JUST how Hawk remembered it, a tall archway over two and a half metres high with solid granite walls. It was just a tunnel entrance to a larger chamber that opened out as they reached the end. This was as far as he'd gone initially. Having secured the clone here he had left not really seeing the need to explore any further.

Now though, with the possibility of others coming to prevent them from seeing what was here, he found it imperative to go further and find out just what was so important to OMEGA and to Col Sec.

THE FREIGHTER CAME IN HOT, swooping in, firing her thrusters at the very last moment to bring her to a deliberate hover over the ATV.

Ropes were thrown out of the side hatch of the vehicle and within seconds Rygar and his men began to rappel down towards Wilson. Rygar had a Remm Mk II assault rifle in his right hand as he descended and he fired a quick three-shot burst at the ATV.

From inside the ATV, Private Wilson had his Remm Mk II assault rifle primed and ready to fire.

"Colonel, I have several bogeys rappelling towards my position. They are hostile and I am taking fire. At the soonest opportunity, I will relocate but before that, I must defend this vehicle," he said through the battle com.

Colonel De Boer continued walking as the call came through to him. "You have your orders soldier, we're relying on you to carry them out. Keep me informed of your status, carry on."

Hawk also heard the call and he turned to look at the Colonel. "Looks like this is going to get real interesting, real fast," he said and his eyes showed he was concerned even if his voice didn't.

"Let's just hope this little trip turns out to be worth all the trouble that someone is taking to prevent it," De Boer said as he walked on behind Hawk.

Hawk said nothing as he had exactly the same thought.

INSIDE THE ATV Wilson watched as the ten mercenaries rappelled down towards his position, all of them armed with Remm assault rifles, a few of them already firing at him. He was safe from small arms' fire inside the ATV as it was a Col Sec vehicle and therefore shielded from anything up to plasma pulse cannon fire, but stationed there he was of little use to the men inside the chamber. He decided on the only course of action open to him and that was to move.

The engine of the ATV came to life at his touch and he steered it away from the mouth of the chamber as quickly as he could. Plasma bolts from the Remm assault rifles followed him as he made his way along the twisting pathway with little hindrance to his retreat.

～

RYGAR PUMPED a round into the chamber of the grenade launcher attached beneath the barrel of his assault rifle and fired at the retreating vehicle. The MX4 grenade left the barrel of the launcher with a soft 'whoosh' and soon closed the distance between Rygar and the ATV. It struck the rear of the vehicle and exploded with a force that destroyed the rear doors to the ATV and actually lifted the rear axle off the ground by half a metre, slamming back down onto the uneven ground making it slew across the track. Rygar quickly followed up with two more grenades, which exploded close together destroying what was left of the damaged ATV in a huge fireball.

Wilson died instantly before he could call the others to warn them of the vicious attack.

Rygar landed on the ground and released the rappelling rope, as did the other men in his team.

"You two stay here and guard the entrance. No one gets in and no one gets out apart from us, is that clear?" he said as he pointed to two of the men in his team. They saluted affirmation of their orders and took up positions on either side of the entrance.

Rygar turned to the rest of his team and said, "The rest of you, with me," and he headed into the chamber entrance after the Col Sec men.

CHAPTER 5

Hawk was searching the chamber frantically looking for something, anything that could be considered important, but was continually coming up short.

Colonel De Boer stood in the centre of the room watching what was happening and keeping an eye on the narrow entrance waiting for the moment when the mercenaries would come charging down it to invade the chamber.

"How long before you've completed your search Hawk?" he asked.

"Hard to tell Colonel, I'll know when I find whatever it is that's so damn important that a bunch of mercs want to stop us finding it. But I tell you this, from what I've seen so far I can't see anything that would warrant the attention."

"Sir!" shouted Johansen, one of the three remaining marines facing the mouth of the chamber, as three loud explosions rocked the walls from the outside.

De Boer turned to his men and said, "I know." They all knew that the explosions meant they had lost a comrade and that the situation had just become serious.

"This is getting beyond interesting Matt, just what the hell is going on here?" the Colonel demanded.

"This place is linked to the prisoner we captured here and he belongs to a terrorist group we've yet to learn anything about. I was ordered here to find out what the captive was doing here. That's as much as I can say. I'm sorry, but this is classified and the fact that they've sent someone to prevent us from learning the importance of this place indicates that there is something vital to learn here, but I'm damned if I know what it is," Hawk replied, the frustration evident in his voice.

"Well, keep looking. My men and I will try and hold them off as long as we can; you make sure that you find something. I'd suggest you also try and find us an alternative exit 'cause it looks like we may be blocked in here and I don't think we have the hardware to enable us to fight our way clear of this place. By the sound of what happened outside, it seems they've brought more to this party than we did," De Boer said as he divided his attention between what Hawk was telling him and what was happening at the mouth of the chamber.

"Sir, I think we're about to have company," Johansen said without taking his eyes from the tunnel entrance.

"Kill anything that comes in here," De Boer said with grit in his voice. He'd lost a man and he would make whoever was responsible pay tenfold. They wanted to get serious; he excelled at serious.

"Time to rock and roll," Johansen said as he stole a glance at his two teammates. They all knew what had happened and what was about to happen next, they were about to get bloody. It was what they signed on for and they would not shirk their duty, they were Recon Delta.

Hawk renewed his efforts with increased intensity. There must be a reason for the clone being here, something of value to OMEGA, something vital, vital enough for them to want it destroyed; he just had to find it.

Then a thought struck him, if whatever was here was so vital, why didn't the clone try to destroy it? Why did he come so easily with them? It was almost as if he had wanted to be captured, but why? What had they gained from that action apart from gaining access to Col Sec HQ?

Their attempt to destroy part of it was thwarted by Hawk, the explosive device they had hidden inside the clone wasn't powerful enough to do any serious damage to the building and General Sinclair was spirited to safety just in time. What if that was the purpose of the capture all along, just to kill Sinclair?

If that was the case then perhaps there was no significance to this chamber, but then why send a team of mercs to stop them? Had they been ordered to prevent Hawk from finding out that there was nothing of value here? If so how did OMEGA know he would be returning here? Or were they sent to destroy this place on the assumption that if Col Sec found out it had been destroyed they would think there was something of value here and would then waste precious time trying to find out what, which would divert their attention from what was really going on? Perhaps Hawk and the team being here was an unexpected aspect of this riddle. Perhaps they weren't expected to be here, or at least not until the mercs had done their job.

If this was a diversionary tactic, what was the real objective of OMEGA and what was it they were so desperate to hide from Col Sec? Whatever it was, Hawk was certain that it wouldn't be found in this chamber, but to find it he had to get out of there with his skin intact. With that in mind, he switched his attention to locating a possible exit other than the obvious one. They had to get out of there and getting past the mercs was probably not going to happen because, as

De Boer had said, they had brought more to this party than his team.

"We have to get out of here," Hawk said to De Boer who was surprised by the sudden turnaround.

"You found what we came for?" asked the Colonel.

"No, and I don't think I will either. I'm not even sure there's anything to find. I hate to admit this Colonel but I think you were right in your assumption that this is a wild goose chase."

"Then what are these guys doing here, and why did they kill Wilson?" De Boer wanted to know.

"I haven't pieced it all together yet, but I don't think the answers to your questions will be found in here," Hawk replied.

"Where then?"

Hawk shook his head. "I don't know, but I swear to you that I'll find out and when I do someone will pay."

De Boer saw the intensity in Hawk's eyes and realised that he wouldn't like to be the person responsible for this and to have to face Hawk and his retribution. Ignoring the sudden chill speeding through his blood De Boer said, "In that case, we'd better get the hell out of here."

"Sir, here they come," said Patterson from slightly ahead. From the marines' position, they had a good panoramic view of the entire lay of the land before them and could see the advance of the mercs as they entered the chamber's entrance.

"Get ready men, pick your shots and make 'em count," De Boer said in encouragement to his team.

"Hold them off for as long as you can while I try and find us a way out of here," Hawk said as he went deeper into the chamber. Most cave systems had multiple entrances and exits but the trick was finding one that hadn't caved in or one that was wide enough for a grown man to crawl through. Hawk said a silent prayer that

OMEGA hadn't collapsed all the other exits when they made this chamber in an effort to make it more secure. The only thing preventing him from believing this was the fact that now he was sure this place was merely a decoy and therefore there would be no need to secure it. Hoping that would turn out to be true, he kept on looking for that elusive exit.

The three Recon Delta marines waited until the advancing mercs were clearly visible before opening fire with their Remm Mk II assault rifles. With short measured bursts of pulsed plasma fire, they struck each man in the centre of their chest sending them hurtling backwards in a haze of blood. Clearly, their body armour was not as good at absorbing the blasts as that worn by the Recon Delta marines as they were dead before they hit the ground and before the others knew what was happening. The other mercs made a hasty retreat out of harm's way until they could gauge the level of opposition.

"We're holding them off, for now, Colonel, but I can't say how long that'll last," Johansen said through the combat channel, sub-vocalising so that the mercs couldn't pick up any chatter between them.

Before De Boer could say anything, Hawk replied, "Still working on it."

RYGAR WAS LYING flat on his stomach just outside the chamber entrance along with his men. Baring his teeth in a predatory smile he said, "Blow the shit out of that chamber. If they want what's in there, then let's make sure they get to keep it for a long, long time."

"You got it, sir," said the merc next to him and signalled to the rest of them who, like Rygar, had grenade launchers fitted to their assault rifles. They pumped grenades into the launchers and fired.

The grenades arched towards the entrance and landed just inside rolling in the direction of the three Recon Delta marines.

Johansen saw the first one land, followed by another then another and then he lost count as his eyes widened with the realisation of what was about to happen.

"Incoming!" he shouted as he and his teammates got to their feet and hurled themselves towards the inside of the chamber just as the first explosion rocked the walls around them.

CHAPTER 6

Wilde was sitting at his desk waiting for confirmation from Rygar that the chamber had been destroyed. He was getting anxious for evidence that the mission would be a success. He had so much riding on it that he could not afford the slightest failure in any aspect of his plan.

He had all the information he needed to start the next phase of his operation against Col Sec and he couldn't wait to get it underway.

The megacorp that Eisenhower owned held a huge amount of contracts for the military on both sides of the divide. Wilde had often thought that if the CEO had wanted to make a success of OMEGA, he had all the hardware available at his fingertips to provide the firepower needed for any action he chose to take against any government on any planet. It had irked him to the nth degree that Eisenhower had chosen to remain hidden and act behind the scenes rather than take a stand against Col Sec. That was something that he hoped to rectify in a very few hours. He planned to use some of the hardware that they had been holding back in the development stage for Col Sec and the Alliance; new weapons that Wilde was sure they would have no defence against, weapons that he was sure would bring the much-vaunted Col Sec to its knees.

Using his NI he made a call to one of the Rovers. "Rover 5, it's time," he said once the call was securely connected. He didn't need to wait for confirmation that it had been heard, the NI did that automatically when the call was placed via the satellite, scrambling it immediately so that it couldn't be overheard. Again this was technology that he had held back from his customers, the military, for his own personal use without the knowledge of Eisenhower.

Rover 5 was one of several strains of clones that Wilde had manufactured without Eisenhower's knowledge. He had instigated a programme whereby the clones were engineered with specific abilities. Eisenhower wanted the Rovers just to be the public face of OMEGA, the identity that would deal with the clandestine operations that the group ran, but Wilde saw the opportunity to form a unit of clones who could be the face and also other facets of the group such as the teeth. Rover 5's were the teeth; they were the warriors. He planned on them being the new breed of team leaders, loyal to him alone, able to be manufactured swiftly and replaced instantly from an almost endless supply, stockpiled in secret, each as lethal as the one bred before.

He was nearly ready to put the final phase of his operation into play, but first, he had to get rid of the one obstacle in his path to ultimate power. Rover 5 would be the instrument by which he would do that.

He sat back pleased with himself at how things were progressing when the sensor in the door told him that his daughter was about to enter.

As the door opened and she walked into the room, not

bothering to announce her presence, as was her usual style, he was again struck by the resemblance to his dead wife.

"I thought we were going to lunch?" she said, with just a hint of the petulance she was prone to. Having grown up in a wealthy family she was used to having things her own way most of the time.

"I'm sorry, my dear, but I'm a bit tied up at the moment, we'll have to postpone today. Perhaps tomorrow?" he replied. He may have been a stern master to those beneath him, but with his daughter, he was the same as most doting fathers, putty in her hands.

She came forward to stand in front of his desk, her arms folded across her firm breasts and the expression on her face was that of a spoiled child, pouting almost to the point of looking miserable.

"But you promised," she said tapping her right foot.

"I'm sorry, Tanya, I'll make it up to you in a few days. I'm swamped at the moment but in a day or two my schedule will be cleared and we can go and do something together, okay?" he replied trying to smooth out her ruffled feathers.

"I've heard that before Dad. Don't do this, please! You always cancel when we've made plans, even for the simplest of things like taking a few hours out for lunch. If you're not careful I'll begin to think you don't want to spend time with me," she said and paused before smiling her dazzling smile, indicating he was out of the woods and would not be subject to one of her furies, something she had inherited from her dead mother.

"Okay, this time I'll let you off, but in a couple of days we're going to Callistos. We'll spend some time in the sun, swimming in the clear waters of the ocean, snorkelling, lazing about on the perfect white sands of the beach. It'll do you good. Promise me. If you make me a promise I know you'll keep it," she added smiling hopefully.

"You sound like an advert for the tourist board," he joked.

"Promise me," she demanded.

"Okay, okay, I promise, now go on and leave me in peace or I won't finish in time for our trip, and you don't want me to have to break my promise now, do you?" he said, smiling for the first time.

"Okay, I'm out of here. I'm off to lunch. If you can't make it I'll just have to make do with what's-his-name from Security."

"Who, Taylor?"

"Is he the cute one on the front desk?"

"I don't know about 'cute' but he does work on the front desk."

"Yea that's him then."

"He can't, he's on duty."

"You want me to be safe, don't you? And besides, it's so boring having lunch on my own, you don't know who may come up and want to chat with me."

"Okay, go and tell him I gave him new orders to escort you to lunch and not to let you out of his sight at all."

"Don't worry Dad, I'm sure he won't," she said with a cheeky wink that left her father wondering if anything was going on between the two of them.

Tanya Wilde twirled around and left the office far happier than when she had arrived. Wilde called Taylor through his NI.

"My daughter is on her way down, you are to escort her to lunch. You are not to allow her out of your sight for the briefest of moments, is that clear? This is not important, it is so far past important that it's beyond your comprehension. Is that perfectly clear to you?"

"Perfectly sir, I won't let her out of my sight," Taylor replied nervously.

"Yes, she said you'd say that, just make sure you don't," Wilde said then broke the connection.

Using his NI to connect via subspace to Rygar, he said, "Give me a sit. rep."

"The chamber is destroyed, sir. We've blocked the entrance but the interior has been destroyed along with those inside," Rygar replied.

"Those inside? Explain," Wilde said his voice rising slightly.

"When we arrived there was a group of Col Sec marines entering the chamber. We destroyed the vehicle they arrived in then blew up the chamber blocking the entrance. You'd need heavy excavation gear to clear away the entrance to get inside now, so whoever's in there, if the grenades didn't kill them, won't be getting out."

"And you're sure of that because…"

Rygar paused before answering, "They have to be dead, there's no way they could've survived."

"Confirm that report and check all possible alternative exits before you vacate the area. No one and I repeat *no one* must escape from that chamber alive. You make sure they are all dead before you return here. I don't care how you do it but you don't come back here without proof that they are dead. Do I make myself clear?"

"Perfectly, sir."

"Then carry on soldier," Wilde said, breaking the connection. Rygar was probably right in his assumption but he had to be sure. There could be no slip-ups, not this close to the end, not when he was so close to ultimate success.

OUTSIDE THE DOOR to his office, Tanya Wilde stood, having returned to tell her father that she loved him. She overheard the conversation, all of it.

She was in shock. At first, she thought she had misheard him but as the conversation progressed she was left in no doubt.

When she arrived at the door to his office she had heard her father speaking, so rather than interrupt him she had decided to wait until he had finished his call. Then she overheard him order the deaths of those men and she was aghast.

Her father couldn't have said those words, not her father. She wanted it to be a mistake, but clearly, that wasn't the case. She had heard correctly. Her father had said those words, the words that had destroyed her long-cherished image of him.

Not knowing what to do or say she turned and quietly left the room heading for the elevator to go back downstairs. She walked as if in a trance, knowing that she couldn't remain there any longer.

WILDE FINISHED the call and noticed that his daughter was leaving the outer office again.

How long had she been there and had she heard anything?

If she had, what would he do?

She was his daughter; surely he couldn't order her death too?

Could he?

Before he came to any decision over this new and very disturbing development he had to learn just what she had overheard, perhaps then he could make a more informed decision.

As much as he loved her, and he loved her more than life itself, he knew he could not allow her to jeopardise the success of everything he had worked so hard for over the past decade. He had endured too much at the feet of Maxwell Eisenhower. He would have to prevent her from spilling the beans to anyone. He must speak with her and hope that she would see sense over this. If not then he would have to take drastic measures. As much as it would pain him to, he could not allow anyone to get in his way, no matter who it was.

CHAPTER 7

Hawk heard the warning shout from Johansen then the first explosion and knew they were in deep trouble. Inside the confines of the cavernous chamber, the sound of the explosions was amplified enormously. The walls shook from the concussive blasts and large chunks began to fall around them.

"We have to move NOW!" screamed Hawk, hoping his voice would carry above the deafening explosions. He needn't have worried though as it was a thought that had occurred to them all and they moved to the rear of the chamber hoping to escape, or at the very least, find refuge from the falling rocks and blasts.

De Boer was at Hawk's side as was Johansen, but Patterson and Gates were lying on the floor closer to the entrance. Patterson had his back ripped open by shrapnel from the explosions and Gates was lying to his side crushed beneath a huge chunk of rock that had been blasted free from the wall.

"I swear to God those bastards will pay for this," said De Boer as he saw the bodies of his men.

"Get in line, Colonel," Hawk replied with barely contained fury emanating from his ice-blue eyes.

They found a tunnel at the back of the chamber and managed to squeeze through as the explosions ripped apart the main chamber. It was narrow but they could feel a slight gust of air as they went deeper.

"We may have found a way out that they overlooked," Hawk said as he led them down the tunnel. They had to stoop as they travelled further along the narrowing passage, but they began to feel fresher air stirring around them as they squeezed their bodies down it. Soon they were on their knees in a half crawl but their hopes were high that they would get out of their predicament.

The light was fading as they entered the tunnel, intensified by all the dust thrown up by the explosions, but as they crawled down the tunnel that seemed to fade away and light from ahead began to force itself through the haze so they could see where they were going.

Hawk led the small group followed by De Boer then Johansen. They had managed to keep hold of their weapons, which they planned to use at the first opportunity against their attackers.

Finally, after what seemed like an eternity, they reached the end of the passage, but then their hopes faded when they saw there was nothing more than a mere slit in the rock wall facing them.

"Shit!" exclaimed Hawk when he saw the narrow aperture.

De Boer looked over Hawk's shoulder to see what had caused the exclamation and said, "Great, a fucking dead end."

Hawk looked behind him at the Colonel and said, "Is that the attitude they teach in Recon Delta now? We're not dead yet, we'll get out of here I'm sure."

"Oh this I've got to hear, just how do you intend getting

out of here then? Do you plan on squeezing through that slit?"

"Sort of," Hawk replied with a grin.

"Excuse me?" De Boer said, a little confused.

"Pass me your Remm."

Passing the assault rifle to him, De Boer backed down the tunnel as he realised what Hawk planned to do. He hoped his actions wouldn't make their plight any worse than it already was.

Hawk ramped the assault rifle up to full power and ensured it had a full battery pack inserted then fired a continuous burst at the slit.

The pulsed plasma bolts struck the slit and blasted through the rock blowing a wide rent in the wall.

The walls started to shake from the energy being blasted into them and chunks of rock began to fall around them.

"Out now, move fast," Hawk said as he scrambled free from their confines quickly followed by the two remaining members of the team.

As the wall collapsed after them, closing up the exit, they all breathed a sigh of relief as they watched from a few feet away and safety.

"Well, Colonel, we did it," Hawk said.

"Yes, now it's payback time," De Boer replied. Hawk realised he was glad he wasn't the one to face the wrath of this man.

RYGAR and his men heard the blast from the assault rifle and knew what it meant.

"Over there, the bastards found a way out, unbelievable," he said. "Make sure their escape is short-lived," and they headed straight over to where the Recon Delta men had escaped their tomb.

～

"COLONEL, do you think it's wise to engage an enemy who has superior forces and superior fire-power in a frontal assault?" Hawk asked, hoping to give the Colonel time to think before he rushed off to fight in anger.

"Captain, I'm not about to allow these bastards to get away with attacking us and killing three of my men," De Boer replied, clearly angry at both the mercs and Hawk for not wanting him to exact revenge on said mercs for the losses his team had endured.

"Fools rush in but a wise man runs away to fight another day," countered Hawk.

De Boer rounded on him, his eyes blazing with fury.

"Are you telling me to run away?" he snarled, his teeth clenched tightly together as an animalistic bloodlust threatened to engulf him.

"Run away? Never! But if we leave on our own terms we can engage them at a future date when we're better prepared. There's no telling how many of them there are, but we're down to three and who knows what other weapons they may have. I'm still in command of this mission, and as much as I want to rip into those bastards who attacked us, I'd rather find out who's responsible for sending them here so we can get to the bottom of all this."

"Does any of that make sense to you, Colonel?"

"Unfortunately, yes. Okay, I'm in agreement so let's get back to the shuttle and get off this planet so we can alert Col Sec," De Boer said.

"This way then," Hawk said, starting to climb up the side of the mountain. The wall before them was full of crags and rents suitable for hand and footholds. They soon made it up the side, high above where they had exited only moments earlier.

Sub vocalising through a battle com. channel Hawk said, "Lieutenant Hall, we're working our way around to you. We'll be coming in hot so get the shuttle ready for take off the moment we arrive."

"Will be ready on your arrival, sir," Hall replied through the same medium.

∿

RYGAR LED his team towards the sound of blaster fire.

"Where are they?" he said when they arrived at the place where they thought their targets should be.

"Here's where they escaped, sir," said one of his team, indicating the rent in the wall caused by the blaster fire.

"They can't be far. Find them and kill them," ordered Rygar.

∿

THE TRIO CLIMBED AS QUICKLY and quietly as they could, scaling the mountain known as Q3. There was a large overhang they had to navigate around before they were out of danger from being spotted by Rygar and his team of mercs at the base. They climbed until they reached the overhang and then began the arduous route that would take them around and over this section of the mountain. Without any climbing gear their task was that much harder, made even worse by the fact that they were carrying weapons.

Just as they reached the overhang and had started to climb around it their luck finally ran out. One of Rygar's team happened to glance up and saw them.

71

"There they are," he shouted and the rest of the mercs looked up to where he indicated and raised their weapons to aim at the trio, easy targets.

"Shit!" Hawk said as he heard the shouts from below. He glanced down and saw all the weapons being aimed their way. Quickly he reached for his Sig P996 and fired down at the group.

"Move, I'll try and hold them off until you clear the overhang then you can cover me," he added. His pulsed plasma bolts struck the first targets he aimed at, killing two of the mercs with headshots. Blood and gore splashed their teammates as they stood in shock, their easy targets proving to have teeth.

Hawk fired his Sig until the battery clip was empty but by that time De Boer and Johansen had reached the top of the overhang and were under cover.

Hawk holstered his Sig and began to climb after the other two who had taken positions up ahead and were aiming their assault rifles down at the mercs who had fled to cover.

"Hurry, we won't be able to hold them off for too long," De Boer sub-vocalised through a battle com. channel so that only Hawk could hear him.

There was no need for any answer; his actions were the only reply the Colonel needed. Hawk climbed the overhang as fast as his tiring arms and legs would carry him and he was soon alongside his comrades.

"Where to now? They have us pinned down. They'll be able to work their way around and attack us from the rear," De Boer said, a little angry at the way things had turned out for them.

"We'll just have to prevent them from doing that or get out of here before they can get the drop on us," Hawk said as he quickly formulated several options in his mind.

Using his NI he called Lieutenant Hall. "We're not going

to be able to make it to you, we're pinned down on the mountainside. Use your scanners to locate us via our tracking chips, then come and pick us up." Turning to De Boer he said, "Our ride home will be here shortly, we've just got to be ready and try and keep those bastards busy while Hall picks us up."

"Good move, it'll be tricky but we should just make it, if we're lucky that is," replied the Colonel.

"Lucky's my middle name," Hawk joked.

"Thought it was 'Trouble'," said the Colonel with a half-smile.

Hawk took out his Sig P996 and ejected the battery clip from the butt, selected another from his belt and rammed it into the butt, pulled back on the slide to prime it which meant he was then ready to rock and roll. The spent battery clip was replaced into the slot in his belt where the minute charger would recharge it ready for use again. In that way soldiers and operatives in the field could have an endless supply of ammunition, solving a problem that had arisen when the space fleet's supply lines were spread out across light-years of space.

Soon they heard the sound of the shuttle's engines as the small craft approached them from above.

Rygar also heard the approach of the craft and he looked up and caught sight of the shuttle coming towards them through the clouds.

"Shoot that shuttle out of the sky, don't let it get near them," he ordered his team. The mercs brought their assault rifles to bear on the approaching shuttle in an attempt to bring her down.

"Sir, they're firing on the shuttle," Johansen said as he saw what they were doing.

"Let's persuade them otherwise," Hawk said and he fired down at the mercs with his Sig. His first shot killed one of the mercs standing furthest away from the mountain wall, the plasma bolt blowing his head apart.

De Boer and Johansen joined in killing two more before the mercs found cover behind some rocks and continued firing from their hidden position at the approaching shuttle.

Hall steered the shuttle towards the mountain known as Q3, where the remainder of the team was positioned precariously on the mountain wall.

Before taking off he had secured ropes next to the lateral hatch and as he approached Hawk and the two soldiers he released them through the open hatch so they dangled down towards the trio.

"Get up there, I'll hold them off same as before," Hawk said as the ropes came close to them from above. "You'll have to hurry, he won't be able to hold that position for very long," he added.

De Boer and Johansen grabbed hold of the ropes and began to climb as fast as they could whilst Hawk laid down covering fire with his Sig P996. As soon as they reached the hatch they climbed aboard. Hanging out of the hatch and holding a Remm assault rifle aimed at the mountain wall below Hawk's position, De Boer shouted, "Okay Matt get your ass up here NOW."

Holstering his Sig, Hawk reached for the one remaining rope and started to climb up.

De Boer and Johansen fired down at the mercs giving them something else to think about other than killing the climber.

Disregarding the fatigue that was creeping up on him Hawk climbed the rope as fast as his aching arms would allow. Climbing aboard the shuttle he breathed a sigh of relief for a moment. "We're not out of the woods yet guys, they could still come after us with their own craft. Let's get back to the Valkyrie as quick as we can."

"Hall, get us outta here and back to the Valkyrie as fast as you can," De Boer said and the pilot acknowledged by steering the shuttle away from the mountain.

RYGAR CALLED the pilot of the freighter they came in on to come and pick them up too. He was not about to lose them now, he would give chase until he ran them down and killed them like the irritants they were.

The freighter came swooping in low and dropped the rappelling lines out of the lateral hatch for Rygar and his men to climb up. Rygar was the first to reach the lines and was soon climbing up to the hatch. Once inside he went straight to the forward pilot's cabin and said, "Get after that shuttle, if it escapes I'll kill you myself. Bring the weapons systems online, I'll man the targeting scanners."

"Weapons systems online, sir, targeting at your discretion," replied the pilot who kept the freighter in a low hover while watching the hatch for the rest of the mercs to climb back on board, not an easy task when Rygar was barking orders at the same time. The fact that he remained calm under pressure showed the high calibre of pilot the young man was.

Once the team were all on board the freighter, the lateral hatch was secured after the rappelling ropes had been dragged back inside and, with Rygar seated beside him in the co-pilot's chair, the pilot gave the freighter full thrust which took the craft up into the air once more as they gave chase to the shuttle.

"It looks like we may not get away so easily, Colonel," Lieutenant Hall said as his scanners indicated the freighter was lifting off from its hover to come after them.

"Can we outrun them?" De Boer asked.

"I'm not sure, sir, but I'm gonna try anyway," Hall replied.

"What's the shielding like onboard this thing?" Hawk asked, as he had an idea.

"We have just the standard reinforced hull plating, it's a shuttle for general use, not a battle craft, sir, why?" Hall replied.

"I've got a feeling that these guys came better prepared than we did for this op and they just may have weapons on that freighter," Hawk replied, a little concerned.

"Well, in that case, if they get within weapons range of us we're screwed," Hall said, fatalistically.

"Well son, you're among the best of the best so make sure they don't come within weapons range," De Boer said.

"I'll do my best, sir," Hall replied proudly.

"We'll soon know if my suspicions are correct because if they get within range they'll go immediately to weapons lock," said Hawk. The three of them were crowded around Lieutenant Hall as he piloted the shuttle with expert touches on the controls.

"Get us as close as you can," Rygar told the pilot as he manned the weapons' controls. The pulse cannons mounted below the front pilot's cabin were controlled by a console that had a joystick, and the targeting scanners were shown on a heads up display on the forward viewport. Rygar had primed the cannons and was targeting the shuttle awaiting weapons lock tone to signify that he would hit what he was aiming at.

The freighter was being flown on full thrust as they tried to close the gap between the two ships. The freighter just about had the edge being the larger craft. The engines were more powerful and could put out more thrust and they soon found the gap between the two ships was closing as they bore down on the shuttle.

"We're within weapons range, sir," the pilot said and Rygar aimed carefully as the weapons lock tone sounded.

"I've got you now," Rygar said as he fired the pulse cannons.

INSIDE THE SHUTTLE, the weapons lock tone sounded and they all knew what that meant. Hawk looked at De Boer not needing to say that his suspicions were correct, they all knew they were in deep trouble.

Hall threw the shuttle into a series of severe twists and turns to throw off the aim of the gunner ready to kill all of them.

When the plasma bolts came, the first things hit were the engine thrusters, but luckily it was just a glancing blow and caused hardly any damage to the engines. Hall banked away from the next salvo hoping to evade being destroyed.

"We're going to have to take her down towards the ground and try and lose that bastard another way," Hall said as he steered the shuttle frantically in a series of twists and turns that it wasn't really designed for.

"You'd better strap yourselves in, this could get a little scary," he added.

CHAPTER 8

On board, the Valkyrie Captain Jefferson had kept an eye on the proceedings between the shuttle and the freighter.

"Is there nothing we can do to help them?" he asked the bridge crew. "Come on people give me some options here, I'm not about to let our guys down there get killed while we sit up here with our thumbs up our asses," he added, getting more and more frustrated as they watched the action develop close to the planet's surface.

"Sir, we could enter the planet's atmosphere and fire a QX missile at the freighter," suggested the weapon's officer.

"By the time we got close enough to fire it would be all over," added the pilot.

"What about firing from orbit?" asked the Ops officer. "If we tie in the targeting from the missile console to the scanners we just might get a more accurate long-range weapons lock," he added.

Jefferson thought about it for a second before replying, "We have no other choice, we have to try it. Make it happen people."

The Ops officer went immediately to work in matching the weapons lock sensors to the long-range scanners and within a few short moments that seemed to stretch out into eternity, he had done it. With an exuberant smile, he turned to the weapon's officer and said, "She's all yours."

"Limit the yield on the missile, I just want to damage that craft enough to allow our people to escape. The last thing I want to do is destroy a freighter over that terrain, the debris would scatter over too large an area and would just bring unwanted attention to us being here," Jefferson said as a last-minute thought.

"Limiting the yield now, sir, and scanning," replied the weapons officer. "We have weapons lock sir," he added.

"Fire!" Jefferson commanded.

$\sim$

"Fuck! Someone has a weapons lock on us," said the pilot of the freighter when his console lit up warning him of the incoming missile.

"What?" Rygar said incredulously. "They must have a support craft in orbit, that's how they got here. Of course, I didn't make the connection that a shuttle must have had a lift here and not made it on its own power," he added, feeling rather foolish as he realised his mistake.

"The shielding on this ship can withstand a lot more than any normal freighter," said the captain, whose presence Rygar had forgotten as he was so wrapped up in the action.

"Explain!" Rygar commanded without looking in his direction, all his concentration being centred on targeting the pulse cannons.

"This ship has been fitted out with extra deflectors and has a double hull feature only present on ships of the fleet," replied the captain smugly. It pleased him that he had some information that this merc leader didn't, it restored some of the power taken from him by Rygar.

"You'd better be right about this or we'll all pay," Rygar said angrily, for he knew this design of freighter could not evade a missile even fired from a distance. They would just have to take the hit and hope it wasn't a nuke.

~

JEFFERSON CONTACTED Hawk through the battle com. via his NI. "We have fired a QX missile at the freighter on your six, a low yield just to disable it somewhat to give you enough time to evade it and reach us in orbit. Can't have the locals pick up on us destroying a ship in their atmosphere, wouldn't be good for publicity," he added.

"Thanks for the assist Cap, and in that case, we'll be with you shortly," Hawk replied, then explained to the rest of the team just what was about to happen.

The QX missile locked on to the target once its initial targeting link to the Valkyrie's sensors had uploaded all the relevant data. Once fired its internal sensors locked onto and homed in on the target, latching onto a series of stimuli, electronic emissions, heat signatures and electromagnetic pulses. Once locked on, the missile's own power supply would propel it along until it struck its target. Once fired the QX missile rarely missed its target.

~

THE CAPTAIN aboard the freighter behind the shuttle carrying Hawk and his team said, "Brace for impact," just before the QX missile struck the engine thruster outlet.

The explosion ruptured the freighter's outlet and the force of the blast sent the craft spinning laterally, giving those on the shuttle the time they needed to make their run for the upper atmosphere.

~

HAWK SAW the blast as the QX missile struck the rear section of the freighter behind them and as it started to spin he shouted, "Now, get us out of here." Lieutenant Hall complied by giving the shuttle full power and steered her up towards the upper atmosphere and the waiting Valkyrie.

~

THE PILOT of the freighter soon regained control but by the time he had her straightened out the shuttle was out of weapons range.

Rygar was incensed; he slammed a fist into the weapons control console in fury and screamed at the pilot, "Get after them."

~

JEFFERSON SAW the missile strike the freighter and said, "Right, that should give them time to make their escape so let's make it easier for them and get into position to meet them as they exit the planet's atmosphere."

Hall took the shuttle up into the upper atmosphere with one eye on the sensors that were tuned to the following freighter. Their speed was just enough to keep the distance between them constant and he finally took in a deep breath as he saw the welcome sight of the Valkyrie fast approaching them.

~

THE CAPTAIN of the freighter ordered the pilot to give chase once more and the freighter's powerful engines gave out the thrust needed to propel them after their quarry.

"We might not make it, sir, they have too much of a lead on us," the pilot said, as he calculated quickly in his head their speed and the distance between them.

"Just get me within weapons range and I'll do the rest," Rygar snarled viciously.

~

"SIR THAT FREIGHTER is giving chase again, doesn't seem like we did much damage with that missile," observed the Ops officer on the Bridge of the Valkyrie.

"I'm hoping the sight of us will discourage them from further action against the shuttle," Jefferson replied confidently.

"They're gaining on us again. What have they got in that thing?" Hall said as he steered the shuttle towards the Valkyrie.

Hawk had been watching closely since the freighter had come after them and was asking himself the very same question.

Through the battle com. via his NI Hawk contacted the Valkyrie. "You may have to discourage our hunters a little more forcefully Cap. They don't seem to want to give up on us just yet."

~

"COMING UP ON WEAPONS RANGE," the pilot of the freighter said.

"Hold her steady on this line," Rygar replied, as he aimed the pulse cannons waiting for the weapons lock tone.

≈

"CHRIST, they're acquiring weapons lock on us again," Hall said as the sensors told him what was happening behind their shuttle.

"Valkyrie it's time to discourage them further," Hawk said through the battle com.

Jefferson turned to his weapons officer and said, "You heard the man, discourage them."

The weapons officer fired another QX missile at the freighter, being careful to target the right vehicle so that the shuttle wouldn't be hit by mistake. Once the missile left the forward missile tube it acquired the correct target, skirted around the shuttle in front of the freighter and headed straight for its intended target.

≈

"INCOMING!" shouted the pilot of the freighter as he saw the missile homing in on them and realised there was nowhere for them to go to evade it. Within a few seconds, the missile impacted their craft just below the flight deck where the bridge was situated, exploding on contact in a fireball that lit up the darkening sky as the two fleeing craft exited the atmosphere of Canto.

≈

"THAT SHOULD DO IT, SIR," the weapons officer on the Valkyrie said as they all watched the fireball engulf the freighter's forward section. What they were unprepared for was seeing the freighter fly through the fireball unharmed, scorched a little but unharmed.

"Holy crap! What the hell have they got there, it's more

like a military gunship than a standard freighter," Jefferson said in shock.

"Hit them again, but this time make it count," he said.

"What did I tell you about them being more prepared for this op than us?" Hawk said to De Boer.

"They're almost within range, if the Valkyrie doesn't stop them soon we'll be blown out of the sky," Hall said as he attempted to get the last dregs of power out of the shuttle's engines.

"They're firing again," De Boer said as he saw another missile leave the Valkyrie.

"Let's hope they have better luck with that one then," Hall said with trepidation.

They all watched the QX missile swerve around them and head straight for the freighter behind them once more. The missile struck the freighter almost directly over the same spot as the first missile strike and the ensuing explosion was almost double the intensity. A huge fireball engulfed the entire ship and the shockwave raced the Valkyrie through the atmosphere as the energy released was close to a full-power blast.

The freighter was thrown off course by the blast and sent spinning off vector. The pilot lost control of the craft momentarily as it headed back down to the ground pulled by the gravity of Canto. Explosions broke out inside the bridge as a series of systems overloaded and they had to wait for the backup systems to come online to regain full control.

Hall saw the outcome of the blast and used the time wisely, getting to the Valkyrie before the pilot regained control of the craft chasing them.

As Hall took the shuttle into the docking bay in the belly of the Valkyrie Hawk said, "Take us to hyperspace now." Jefferson, still leaning forward in his command chair, gave the command to jump. Only when they entered hyperspace did he sit back and start to relax.

~

RYGAR PULLED himself back to an upright position as the pilot regained control of the freighter and looked through the forward viewport just as the Valkyrie made the jump to hyperspace.

Getting to his feet, the reality of what had happened washed over him. They had failed. *He* had failed and he had the unenviable job of relaying that little detail to Wilde. Knowing what Wilde's reaction would be sent a chill through his blood and for the first time in ages he knew real fear.

~

"WE DID IT," Hall said, the relief evident in his voice.

"But at what cost!" said De Boer and he looked at Hawk with recrimination in his intense eyes.

Hawk returned the glare with a steady gaze of his own. Straightening to his full height he squared up to the Colonel, "Go on say it."

"We lost good men down there, all because you wouldn't divulge relevant data about the op," De Boer said angrily, standing almost nose-to-nose with the operative.

"That's total bullshit and you know it. You know how these things go, it's a need to know basis and you just weren't in the loop. No one at HQ was aware of just how this would go down. We didn't expect any action and certainly not of the intensity they brought along, so no one could have foreseen the losses. I'm sorry we lost those guys and you have my word that their deaths won't go unpunished," Hawk said with equal anger. He was angry at not getting it right, at not having the foresight to predict what would happen and so avoid the loss of life, but at least now he had a better understanding of how OMEGA worked. Not much of one, but an idea anyway.

"The next time you go after them, whoever you take, make sure you're better prepared because those guys play for keeps," De Boer said calming down slightly.

"You can count on that," replied Hawk.

"What's your next move then?" asked the Colonel.

"Report back to HQ and inform them of my findings, and then start to look for the real objective behind this mystery group. If it's any consolation I'll try and get you included in anything else we do so that your involvement today will mean something. It seems a pity to waste your abilities and your knowledge of what's gone on so far, why waste time bringing another team up to speed?"

"I don't know if I should thank you or not, considering how this little jaunt turned out," De Boer said, then smiled as he relaxed a little, the adrenalin easing out of his system as the danger had passed. He liked this man, he had integrity and wasn't afraid of standing up to a superior officer if he thought he was in the right. "When you go after them again you had better include me, I have a serious score to settle with whoever's behind all this," he added.

"I will Colonel, don't worry on that score," Hawk said, adding, "I'd better go to my quarters and start preparing my report," and he left the shuttle.

The Colonel and Lieutenant Hall disembarked from the shuttle too after securing it and went to the recreation area to relax before the short flight home. They reflected on what they had been through and the friends they had lost. Preparing for the debrief when they arrived back could wait till later. Col Sec HQ would handle the details of the burial ceremony; even without the bodies the ceremonies would proceed.

Hawk went to his quarters to ponder what had happened, what the consequences were and what action should be taken next. All he could do at this juncture was submit his report, tender his suggestions for future action and see what decision was made.

What were OMEGA's real intentions? What did they intend to do and why had they started now when, according to the captured clone, they had been around for ages, unseen and unknown? What was significant about them wanting to be known now and what would they gain from this action? There must be something hugely significant about the time frame for them to take overt action now after working behind the scenes for so long. Whatever it was, Hawk swore a silent oath that he would learn all he could before stamping on the neck of this beast, choking out its very life.

CHAPTER 9

Tanya Wilde and Gavin Taylor, the security guard, were having lunch at The Peaches, a Chinese restaurant that was famous for its authentic meals.

They were seated at a table near the window overlooking the bay of New San Francisco on Cordoba, a planet in the Praxima system forty-three lights years from Earth.

Cordoba was the HQ of the Eisenhower Mega Corp. and it was home to Tanya Wilde. Their meal was over and they were drinking coffee.

"I should be getting back soon, Miss," Taylor said as he placed his cup back in the saucer in front of him. He was in his late twenties, six feet one tall with a good physique maintained by a daily ritual of hard exercise. His black hair was cut short as part of his job requirement to appear neat and tidy at all times, and he was clean-shaven. His deep brown eyes had never wavered from his lunch companion the whole time they had been together and although he was considered good looking he was certain Tanya Wilde didn't know he existed.

"Excuse me?" Tanya said, lost in her own thoughts and

unaware of what her lunch companion had said. "Are you okay Miss, you seemed distracted throughout the entire lunch," Taylor elaborated.

"I'm sorry I've not been much company today. You must think I'm awful," she said.

"Not at all, Miss, I could never think that," Taylor said, then immediately regretted it. He began to feel uncomfortable as the hot flush flooded his cheeks. She glanced up from her coffee cup and saw his expression and the colour in his cheeks and couldn't help but smile, just a little, to herself.

"I do apologise, I've been thinking about something and it's made me neglect my charming companion. I will make it up to you I promise," she said, her voice low, soft and full of promise. She was teasing him, something she liked to do and she smiled as she saw Taylor's colour deepen.

"It's okay, Miss, there's no need for you to do that," Taylor replied.

"Just give me one moment and I'll be with you and we can leave," she said rising from her seat. Taylor stumbled to his feet, forever the gentleman, as she walked away from the table. He put a finger down the collar of his shirt to let some of the steam out. He blew out his cheeks in relief, as he was beginning to feel rather uncomfortable with her flirting. She was the boss's daughter and as much as he would love to get to know her better he knew that it was out of the question. Jonas Wilde would send him to the most remote location he could possibly think of if he even suspected anything had happened between Taylor and his daughter.

He couldn't help but like her though, more than like in fact, he had had a crush on her since the very first time he'd seen her walk into the building.

The tingle in his NI told Taylor that a call was coming in.

"I hope you have my daughter with you, Taylor," said Jonas Wilde.

"She's not been out of my sight the whole time, sir," Taylor lied.

"She's there with you now then I presume."

Taylor hesitated before answering, "Erm... she's just gone to the powder room, sir. I couldn't possibly go in there with her, sir," he stammered.

"What part of 'don't let her out of your sight for even a second' are you having trouble with?" Wilde said, the rebuke evident in his voice.

"I'll go find her straight away, sir," Taylor said getting to his feet immediately, hoping to reduce the level of punishment he knew was coming his way as soon as they got back to the office.

He was halfway to the powder room when he met Tanya on her way back to the table.

"Miss me that much 'eh?" she said with a smile, yet she half expected that she knew the real reason, which was confirmed with Taylor's next words.

"Your father said not to let you out of my sight, Miss."

"Not even to go to the bathroom?" she said, already suspecting the answer.

"You know your father better than most, Miss, if he says not for a second it includes going to the bathroom," Taylor replied a little sheepishly.

"Yes, you'd think so wouldn't you," Tanya said thoughtfully.

"Excuse me, Miss?"

"You'd think I'd know my father, though I'm not so sure."

"You've lost me, shall we return to the table?" Taylor said, a little confused. Then, as he glanced around at the rest of the restaurant's diners and realising they were garnering some attention, urged her to sit down. His boss and her father would not relish any unwanted publicity, for if the media got even one hint of a sniff of anything they considered newsworthy then they would be all over them like a school of piranhas over a fresh carcass.

Once they were seated he picked up on what she had said, "Why are you unsure about your father, Miss?" he asked. He immediately regretted it, not wanting to pry into personal affairs.

Never expecting a reply other than a rebuke he was surprised when she said, "I overheard something that I'd never thought possible from my father just before we came here."

"What did you hear?" he asked, wanting to help her. He was drawn to her; she had turned out to be someone he had not expected, warm, charming and friendly, not at all like the spoiled brat he had been warned about by some of the other security men.

She looked at him appraising the man before her. Could she take him into her confidence? Possibly not, after all, he worked for her father, it was he who signed his paycheques so his affiliations would be clear. But what if she had got it wrong and there was some plausible reason, some excuse for those words she'd heard, perhaps this man could explain, he might even know the truth. As sad as it was to admit, she realised she did not know her father as well as she would like and perhaps this man did know him better than her and therefore would know if her suspicions were well-founded or if she had simply misheard the conversation. Taking all that into consideration she decided to take a chance and confide in him.

"I overheard my father issue orders for someone's death," she said. There it was, she'd said it, no taking it back now.

Taylor didn't know what to say, he suddenly realised that he was in a position that could get him in some serious trouble. He sat back in his chair and looked down at his plate while considering his next words very carefully.

"You think I'm kidding or I misheard don't you?" Tanya said when she saw his hesitation.

"Did you?" Taylor asked carefully.

"No, I didn't. I wish I had but I know what I heard and I'm not prone to telling lies to get what I want either, before you even go there, besides what would I get out of this? What could I possibly gain from an accusation like this?" she replied calmly.

"The attention of a father who possibly gives his daughter everything she wants other than what she really needs, his attention," he suggested.

"Oh thank you! So now I'm a spoiled brat who, just to get her father's attention, accuses him of plotting the deaths of some people. I'm so glad you have such a high opinion of me," Tanya replied and got to her feet. "You'd better take me home then," she added.

"You've got it wrong, I just meant that some people could think that," Taylor said, gesturing to her to sit back down.

"What do *you* think then?" she asked putting him on the spot to find out where he stood on her statement. She wanted to know whether he would back her up and help her get to the bottom of it or just take her father's side without question.

"Okay, let's look at this logically," he said as she sat back down. "Who was your father talking to and who was he talking about? Is there any possibility that you misheard any of it?" he added.

"I only heard his half of the conversation but he talked about people being inside a chamber, about someone checking that whoever was trapped inside the chamber was dead, and that he was to make sure they were dead and not to return until he had proof they were dead. That to me was pretty conclusive, how's it sound to you?" she replied with more than a trace of sarcasm.

Taylor felt his blood run cold. What was he supposed to do with this? Who would believe this story if they could find anyone to listen? If this was true and she had heard correctly, then if they even tried to take this any further their lives could be forfeit. If her father were responsible for ordering the deaths of those people, who's to say that he would stop there. If Taylor got in Wilde's way then surely he wouldn't think twice about dealing with one security guard in the same way. Who could he call anyway, who would listen?

"Oh shit," Taylor said, not knowing what else to say.

"Is that it? Is that all you're gonna say?" asked Tanya getting a little uncomfortable. She started to think she had made the wrong decision in telling him.

"What would you want me to do, without proof there's not a soul on this planet who would believe your story," he said finally once his thought processes began to return to normal after the shock of hearing her story.

"Proof, you want proof?" she said as an idea formed in her head.

"What you gonna do?" Taylor asked as he saw the look of determination in her eyes.

"I've always been able to hack into my father's files so if I can do that now and find anything pertaining to this chamber he mentioned, would that help convince you?" she asked.

"You can do that from here?" Taylor asked. He knew all personnel in the Mega Corp. were fitted with better than average NIs but to be able to access a computer from this distance required the equivalent of a military-grade one. He knew that the Corp. had many contracts with the military and were suppliers to Col Sec and the Alliance, but as far as he knew the top quality tec. was saved for the military.

There were safeguards in place that prohibited manufacturers supplying the military-grade tec. to civilian corporations, institutes or persons. This was to prevent criminal organisations or terrorists from becoming a real threat to the military. If Tanya could access her father's file from their present location, it meant that she had a military-grade NI and that Wilde had total disregard for the law, which also gave credence to Tanya's story.

Taylor was suddenly afraid.

"Of course," was all she said, "hold on." Her eyes took on the thousand-yard stare that Taylor was familiar with when anyone used their NIs to access a link to a computer.

"I'm in," she said and then added, "I've accessed his call log."

Taylor glanced around to see if anyone was paying them any attention and when he was certain that no one was even remotely interested he returned his gaze to the woman before him.

"Do you know anyone named Tanis Rygar?" she asked, then said, "Hang on, I've got the call I overheard, I'll link it over to you, get ready."

Before Taylor could say anything his NI had linked with hers. He was now in receipt of the call logs and he knew he was dead.

"Oh shit!" he said as he replayed the call in the receiver in his brain. He looked across at Tanya and saw her expression change.

"What?" he asked.

"An alarm has just gone off. I don't know why, it's never gone off before. Dad knows I've taken his file," she said and her face was a mixture of confusion and fear.

"It was when you transferred the file to my NI, it triggered the alarm. Your NI must be authorised whereas once the data was transferred to me it was logged as an unauthorised transfer and set off an alarm. If what you say is true, and now I have no reason to doubt you as I have the proof, then they'll come after us to prevent us passing it on to a third party," he explained.

"What do you mean?"

"What do you think? Your father authorised the death of some Col Sec marines. Do you honestly think he'll take the risk that we'll talk to anyone about this? He'll send someone after us," Taylor said his face ashen as he knew his life was over.

"We have only one choice then," Tanya said.

"And that is what?" he asked.

"We have to get to someone in Col Sec. My father can't get away with this," she said, more determined than ever.

Taylor looked at her and his training kicked in. Before working for Jonas Wilde he had been a Col Sec marine. He only took this job because the pay was better and his rotation was at an end. Now, at that moment, his old training took hold of him again and his mind raced with alternate scenarios for his situation. He had to get away and keep this data safe from the enemy; he also had to protect the young woman who had got him involved in all this.

"Come on, we have to move," he said and offered her his hand. He now knew what he had to do.

CHAPTER 10

Tanis Rygar was in his quarters in the freighter on the way back to Cordoba. He'd delayed the call as long as he possibly could but he knew he had to make it and take the consequences. He took a deep breath and called Jonas Wilde via a secure subspace channel through his NI.

"What is your status?" demanded Wilde when the call was received.

"Sir, I have to report that the chamber was destroyed," Rygar said, hesitantly.

"And the Col Sec marines, are they dead?" Wilde had detected some reluctance to give a full report in his man's voice.

"I'm afraid that some escaped, sir," Rygar said.

"What!" Wilde was furious and Rygar could feel the venom in his simple exclamation.

"We were unable to prevent three of the marines escaping despite our best efforts," Rygar said. "I take full responsibility, sir."

"Damn right you take full responsibility...." his angry

retort was cut short when the alarm sounded, set off by Tanya's unauthorised incursion to her father's files.

"What the fuck?" he said as he searched for the cause of the alarm. When he realised what had triggered the alarm he was dumbfounded. How could his own daughter do this to him? What did she hope to gain from this and who else would she tell. She'd already involved the security man Taylor and, because of his involvement, caused his death. He would have to get her back and try to contain this. He knew his daughter, if he got her back he would make her see sense, he would just have to close off all loose ends en route to her. If, when he got her back, she refused to see sense he would just have to take the necessary steps to ensure what she knew went no further and if that meant ending her life, so be it. He would not be stopped in this by anyone and that included his own daughter.

"Get back here as quickly as you can I want a full debrief ASAP," he said to Rygar before closing the call. He had to take the necessary steps right away to contain this situation. Rygar had outlived his usefulness and Taylor had to be silenced. For this mission, he would use one of the new Rover 5s. It was time for them to become the new team leaders and take their place in the hierarchy of the new OMEGA – *his* OMEGA. It was time to usurp Maxwell Eisenhower and take full control of the organisation that would propel him forward so he could fulfil his destiny as one of the most powerful men in the galaxy and, in time, *the* most powerful man in the galaxy.

With that in mind, he made the call.

～

HAWK and the Valkyrie arrived on Earth and the pilot took the disguised freighter into a docking approach with

Research Station One, which was the planet's first orbiting platform. It was a huge city-sized station that was positioned in geostationary high orbit around the planet and had been in use since the mid-twenty-first century. It was the stopping off point for most missions and had a permanent crew of five hundred personnel on a six-month rotation. The base also handled large numbers of visitors from a few hundred to almost a thousand. Col Sec kept a permanent office there for debriefs and other consultations, but for this debrief Hawk would have to go to Col Sec HQ, Intelligence Division, where General Sinclair would handle it personally.

Once they had docked at Research Station One, Hawk got into a shuttle and piloted it straight down to Col Sec HQ leaving Colonel De Boer and the rest of the team to go their own separate ways, to their own debriefs.

On the journey through hyperspace Hawk had taken the time to formulate his debrief, going over and over in his mind just what had happened in the chamber, trying to make some sense of it all.

Why had OMEGA wanted the chamber destroyed if there was nothing of value inside? Was it merely to waste time for Col Sec so that they wouldn't learn what their real objective was? What was their real objective? He had so many questions and not enough answers. He wasn't sure he would get the answers he needed any time soon either.

Going over his report with Sinclair was his only solution. He hoped a new pair of eyes and ears would identify something that he'd missed.

They had no time to lose; they had to get to the bottom of this riddle before OMEGA unleashed whatever fiendish plot they had planned. With that in mind, he increased his pace through the corridors of Col Sec HQ towards Sinclair's office.

~

TAYLOR AND TANYA left the restaurant, got into the nearest sky-cab and left the area as quickly as they could.

"Where are we going?" asked Tanya, looking out of the windows as the sky-cab soared into the flight lanes.

"We just need to get away from that area because your father will look there first. As soon as we are away from there, I'll contact someone I know in Col Sec and see if they can send an operative to help us. It's imperative we keep on the move until they can reach us otherwise your father could track us through your NI and from what you've told me, we don't want that to happen," replied Taylor. The screen between the passenger compartment and the pilot of the sky-cab was down and locked. They could communicate via an intercom panel in the screen, which could be locked from the passenger side to ensure they had privacy during their journey.

"We're in real trouble aren't we?" said Tanya, which was more of a statement than a question. "I'm so sorry to have dragged you into this," she added sincerely.

"I can think of better, much easier and safer ways of getting to know someone without endangering their lives," replied Taylor concentrating on his next move. Then he glanced across at his travelling companion and smiled to let her know he was okay with it all. "But I wouldn't miss this for anything," he added and reached across to hold her hand, squeezing it gently to reassure her that they would be okay.

"Do you think that Col Sec will believe us and send someone to help?" she asked a little nervously. This was an awful lot to take in. She'd lived what she had always considered was a normal life; normal if your father was the right-hand man to a multi-billionaire, possibly one of the ten wealthiest men in the galaxy. In her few moments of normality, she realised that she had lived a rather sheltered life compared to others, but she also realised that what she had got herself and Taylor into was not normal either and that others of her generation would probably handle this no better.

"Let's see shall we," he said, accessing a subspace com. channel via his NI and contacted the person he knew in Col Sec. He just hoped he was in HQ on Earth. "Matt, I don't have a lot of time but I need your help," he said.

Matt Hawk was in Sinclair's office when the call came through deep in his debrief. "Gavin? I've not heard from you in ages man, but look I'm in the middle of something here I'm going to have to call you back," he replied and was about to close the call when Taylor said, "Listen, Matt, it's about the deaths of some marines recently in a chamber somewhere."

That immediately got Hawk's attention. Linking the call with Sinclair he said, "Tell me." Taylor told him everything he knew including all the files that were passed over to him by Tanya to corroborate what he was saying. When he'd finished he said, "So Matt, what do you think, are we screwed?"

"Oh boy are you ever, but don't you worry, I'm gonna do everything in my power to help you. I want you to get yourself immersed in the most populated area you can find, they're less likely to try and get to you if there are people around you. I've logged your signal into my NI so I'll be able to track you and find you wherever you go, okay. Don't worry I'll get to you and get you to safety; in fact, I'm leaving now. I'll contact you when I reach Cordoba," Hawk ended the call and looked at General Sinclair.

"Sir, this is the break we were hoping for. I've got to get to them before Jonas Wilde sends someone to shut them up," he said getting to his feet.

"Jonas Wilde, I can't believe this. He works for Maxwell

Eisenhower, why would someone so powerful want to get involved with a criminal cartel? Why would he need to, it just doesn't make sense?" said the General bewildered by this new and disturbing development.

"It does make some sort of sense in the way that our attackers had better weapons than ours. They had technology that was just a step ahead of what we have and who supplies most of our tec. and weaponry, sir, the Eisenhower Mega Corp," Hawk replied.

"This has just got a whole lot worse than we ever dreamed possible, Matt. If they can supply troops with weaponry more advanced than ours how are we supposed to defeat them? You have to get to those two; we need that proof so that we can deal with Wilde if he is, as they propose, behind all of this. Take Colonel De Boer and as many men as you think you need and bring them back safely."

"I will, sir. I'll take point and inform the Colonel to follow on my six. I need to leave now. Tell De Boer I'll contact him when I find Gavin and Wilde's daughter and he can coordinate our extraction," Hawk said as he walked towards the door.

"You got it Matt and good luck," Sinclair said as Hawk left the office.

It seemed that they had been given an opportunity to combat this new threat but he wasn't sure if things had just got better or worse. Only time, as they say, will tell.

"WE NEED to find somewhere like Matt said, with a lot of people," Taylor said, after his call with Hawk had ended.

"I know somewhere, the mall; it's in the centre of the city. There's everything there and at this time of day, it'll be jammed with shoppers. Once the shops close there's plenty of other things such as cinemas, restaurants and gaming halls which will have enough people for us to get lost in," Tanya said.

Taylor looked at her, smiled and said, "Good girl, we'll get through this okay." Operating the com. panel in the screen he said, "Take us to the mall please."

CHAPTER 11

Hawk made his way to the spaceport as quickly as he could. The shuttle that had brought him to Earth not so long ago was still where he had left it, so he simply boarded it once more and prepared for take-off. General Sinclair had already logged his flight plan to Research Station One with flight control so all that was required was for him to start the engines and take off which he did with alacrity.

He was soon at the station and heading for the Valkyrie. As he boarded he went to the bridge where Captain Jefferson was waiting for him.

"Welcome aboard Matt, your flight plan has already been logged by General Sinclair. Where to this time, sir?" Jefferson asked as he rotated in the command chair to greet Hawk as he entered.

"Thank you Cap, we're going to Cordoba," said Hawk as he came to stand by Jefferson.

"I'm not going to ask what this is about. No doubt it's another black op or you wouldn't be here, just do me the courtesy of informing me if we're heading into harm's way please so that I can take the necessary precautions."

"No guarantees Cap, sorry, you know as well as I do how these things go but I'll do what I can, will that do?"

"I suppose it'll have to," Jefferson said, turning to his helmsman, "Let's get this show on the road. Inform the dock commander we'll be leaving immediately, I assume there's some haste to your mission," this last was directed at Hawk who nodded his agreement.

Leaning in close to Captain Hawk said, "Do I detect some reticence in you Cap, about this mission?"

"I was hoping for some downtime before we went off on another mission. My crew have not had any shore leave for months, except for a few days after the Stryder mission. We've been hard at it getting the Valkyrie ready for her new duties."

"I know what you mean, it's been the same for me too but this is important and when we get back I'll do what I can to get you some R&R, is that acceptable?"

Jefferson smiled as he sat back in the chair. "There's no need Matt, I knew what I was agreeing to when I signed on, we're just tired that's all. We'll do what is required of us, you don't have to worry."

"Oh, I'm not worried, but I need you at your optimum and for that, you all need to be well-rested, but for now we'll just have to suck it up and get the job done. I know you won't let me down on that score," Hawk replied.

"You're not taking any back up this time?" asked Jefferson. "Colonel De Boer is to follow me and wait for instruction to coordinate our extraction from the planet," explained Hawk.

"Extraction, so this is a rescue op then? How many are you going to pick up?"

"Two people, they carry proof that is vital to our fight

against a group of terrorists who could do untold harm to the Confederation. My job is to go to Cordoba, rendezvous with them and bring them back safely so that we can assess the aforementioned proof and take the necessary steps to bring the terrorists to justice. There you see, I could tell you after all."

"Are you expecting any opposition?"

"Of course, the bad guys aren't gonna want us to get our hands on this proof so they'll send someone to stop me, who or how many is an unknown factor but I'm sure they'll present themselves when the time is right."

"Back into the fire then I see."

"I'm afraid so, yes. It comes with the job."

"Okay, then you'd better hang on, we're about to make the jump," Jefferson said and the pilot, who had already taken the Valkyrie away from the station, entered the coordinates into the nav-comp then took the craft into hyperspace.

It was just a short jump and the Valkyrie was soon in the Praxima system. They re-entered normal space close to Cordoba so that they could go into orbit as soon as possible.

"Here we are Matt, go do your stuff, I'll have you tracked from your NI. As soon as the Colonel arrives I'll keep him informed of your status so that you can coordinate your efforts," Jefferson said.

Hawk said, "Wish me luck," and left the bridge heading for the docking bay where he'd left the shuttle. As he took the shuttle out of the docking bay towards the planet Cordoba he accessed a battle com. channel to call Taylor. "Gavin, are you and Miss Wilde still together and safe?" he asked.

"Matt, glad to hear your voice again, Cap. We are together and at the mall just strolling around the shopping area. It's getting near closing time for most of them so we were going to head into one of the gaming halls," replied Taylor with a trace of relief in his voice.

"I'm en route to your location, I'll be there as soon as I can, just hang tight okay?"

"Will do Cap, how many guys you got with you?"

"Just me, but don't worry I'll get you out no problem," Hawk said with conviction.

"Just you, sir, oh that's just great," Taylor said.

"Have faith," Hawk said then broke the call off to concentrate on piloting the shuttle.

Taylor turned to Tanya and said, "You know when he said earlier that we were screwed, well, he wasn't kidding."

THE ROVER 5 was walking through the mall looking for Tanya Wilde and the security guard Gavin Taylor. He was tall, at least six feet six tall, with a muscular physique that was hidden beneath a well-tailored suit. In appearance, he was exactly the same as the other Rovers except for a more masculine appearance, if that was possible. He had perfect balance and coordination with increased strength, speed and agility and he followed orders implicitly with no trace of a conscience, the perfect killing machine.

For this job he had gone alone, for a simple pick up like this he did not require any backup. Wilde was confident that the Rover 5 could handle this job alone. The Rover had been supplied with Tanya Wilde's tracking code implanted within her NI much like those supplied to Col Sec personnel, so there was no way he could not find his quarry. Jonas Wilde was also confident that the Rover could handle one ex-marine security guard. Wilde fully expected the Rover to reach his quarry long before the authorities could be alerted. Once the security guard had been neutralised there was no doubt in his mind the Rover would secure his daughter and bring her back to him.

Up ahead he could see his targets; they were slowly strolling through the crowd of shoppers seemingly oblivious to anyone who could be following them. This would be easier than he thought.

~

"Just keep walking and don't look around," Taylor said *sotto voce*.

Tanya was immediately alerted to the fact that something was wrong but she did as she was told and carried on as if nothing had happened.

"Good girl," he added as they carried on through the crowds. Accessing the battle com. through his NI, Taylor spoke to Hawk. "I think we've picked up a tail, can't be sure, he's good, damn good but I don't want to take the chance. How soon before you get here?"

Hawk had landed the shuttle and commandeered a sky-cab to the mall. The moment he received the call from Taylor he had just entered the main thoroughfare and was closing in on them.

"I'll be with you asap, I'm in the mall not far from your location, just keep an eye out for me and keep close to Miss Wilde and as many people as you can. I'm banking on them not being foolish and trying to capture you in front of so many witnesses, they'll want to separate you from the crowd first," Hawk replied.

"Will do, Cap," Taylor replied.

Although Hawk had told him that the danger was minimal it didn't stop the sudden feeling of dread that almost overwhelmed him, forcing him to increase his pace. He felt underneath his armpit for the Sig P996 he knew was there and felt only slightly reassured.

~

THE ROVER CLOSED the gap between himself and his targets. They were only a few metres away from his grasp but there were still too many bystanders around for his liking. His orders were to terminate the guard and bring back the daughter, but they didn't say how. He was programmed for independent thought and that included the ability to improvise, but there was the problem of trying not to bring attention to himself or what he was about to do. His life was forfeit but OMEGA had to remain behind the scenes until Wilde was ready to bring them out into the light. He wasn't privy to when that was to happen but he did know it would be soon and he wasn't to be the catalyst.

The walkway they were on was three floors up from the ground and there were still plenty of people around even though some of the shops were beginning to close after a full day of trading. Malls such as this one were still popular even though the population could get anything they needed through the GalaxyNet. These malls gave something that the GalaxyNet couldn't, which was social interaction on a personal level. People could get out and interact with each other and that was still so important in these days of the ever-widening expansion of the galaxy. People still needed to have relationships, not just online but in the real world.

If he could get them close to one of the shops in the process of closing then perhaps he could isolate them inside it, get rid of the guard, then walk out with the daughter.

To the left of them was a clothes shop that was beginning to close up for the night, switching off the advertising lights that illuminated the exterior of the shop front. Quickening his pace the Rover closed in on his targets, he wanted to reach them just as they got level with the shop he had selected.

HAWK HAD ZEROED in on Taylor's NI tracking signal, Col Sec had reinitialised his original tracker and relayed it to Hawk's NI. The third floor beckoned as he left the escalator and he looked for the two people who were depending upon him for help. The crowd was beginning to thin as some of the shops began to close but he could not see them at first. What he did see though was a tall man making his way forward, his head quite clear above most of the people on this floor. Not unusual as there were many people who topped six feet six, but this particular man was focused on something ahead of him and had increased his pace almost forcing his way through the people who were just there to enjoy themselves. This worried Hawk and he began to rush forwards.

"Taylor, I'm on this floor and just behind you, there seems to be someone closing on you so keep moving. I'll be with you in a few seconds," Hawk said through the battle com.

Drawing his Sig, Hawk pulled back on the slide to prime the weapon, holding it down by his leg so that no one would see it and be alerted to the danger and possibly cause panic. He continued towards Taylor and Tanya hoping he would reach them before the large man did.

Less than a couple of feet to go and the Rover would be within range of his targets. His timing had been impeccable; in a few short steps, they would all be where the Rover had planned them to be. Being totally focused on his targets, the Rover was unaware of anything other than them.

BEHIND HIM, closing the gap to within six feet, Hawk was watching the tall, well-groomed man intently.

TAYLOR WAS TRYING DESPERATELY NOT to look behind him, hoping that his one-time friend and captain would not let him down. Tanya, on the other hand, was getting more and more nervous and as they reached the shop front she turned to glance behind and saw a huge, muscular man right behind them.

Taylor saw her glance over her shoulder and the colour drain from her face and immediately knew they were in trouble.

Rover saw the girl turn and look right at him and then the guard. The game had changed, his advantage of surprise negated somewhat, but it was nothing he couldn't handle. He was confident he could handle anything they threw at him.

TAYLOR SAW the huge man react when he looked at him and knew he had to act fast if he was going to gain any sort of advantage.

Reacting as quickly as he could he aimed a punch towards the huge man's face. Rover saw it coming and caught the fist in his left hand then back-handed Taylor across his face with his right hand contemptuously, sending him staggering back away from the girl who started to scream, a scream that reverberated through the mall as people nearby picked up on what had just happened. They started screamed along with her until total chaos broke out.

"Oh shit!" Hawk said as he saw what was happening and knew time had run out. He saw Taylor go flying and the huge man turn towards the girl who he knew must be Tanya Wilde. Knowing what was to come he launched himself across the remaining space between them at the huge man.

Hawk landed on the Rover's shoulders sending the two of them crashing to the floor. Hawk rolled off the Rover and was first to recover his feet. "Get behind me," he said to Tanya without taking his eyes from the Rover who looked up at him, smiling so savagely it chilled his blood, then got to his feet.

"Are you their protector from Col Sec?" the Rover asked, as he looked Hawk in the eyes still smiling with a look that said 'you fool, don't you realise what you've stumbled into?'

Taylor got to his feet and shook his head to regain his senses then grabbed Tanya by the hand and pulled her towards him away from the fight.

"Glad to see you, Cap," he said.

Hawk looked the Rover up and down and realised that he wasn't as big as he'd thought. Hawk stood at six feet six and the man before him was no more than an inch taller and probably no more muscular than him either, so he returned the smile then added a wink.

"Yep," he said, "so bring it on."

"Oh, you will so wish you hadn't said that," the Rover said just before he launched himself at Hawk.

Hawk sidestepped the onrushing giant and smashed his right fist into the man's ribs as he went past him. The Rover stopped on an instant, turned and struck Hawk across the face with his right fist.

Hawk staggered slightly caught unawares at the speed and ferocity of the counter-attack and didn't see the giant move past him to go for Taylor and the girl.

Taylor stood in front of Tanya hoping to prevent the attacker from reaching her. The Rover struck Taylor a straight right to the face, which snapped his head backwards viciously, causing the ex-marine to stagger to the point of almost losing his balance. The Rover then grabbed the front of Taylor's shirt and heaved him over the balcony into the abyss to fall towards the floor three stories below.

Before he knew what was happening Taylor was in the air over the balcony falling to the ground. The knowledge that he was about to die wasn't as bad as knowing he would never see Tanya again. He hit the floor without uttering a sound and died instantly.

Hawk saw his friend thrown to his certain death as casually as someone would toss away a soiled tissue and knew that he had a real fight on his hands, not only with someone who was incredibly strong and fast but completely ruthless and devoid of any moral compass. Having lost his weapon when he'd launched himself at the giant, he realised that he'd possibly lost his advantage and until he regained the Sig, he would have to handle this the old fashioned way.

The Rover turned to Tanya and gave her a smile, "You're coming with me or you die here too," he said.

Unable to move through sheer terror, all Tanya could do was stare up at the giant killer standing before her with an evil grin on his face.

Rover reached for her, his hand appearing impossibly huge to her and she stepped back away from him until she was backed up against the balcony railing.

Hawk lashed out with his right leg in a *mawashi geri*, a roundhouse kick to Rover's ribs, which felt like kicking a slab of plascrete.

Rover just turned to look at Hawk and said, "That was a mistake," then backhanded Hawk across the face sending him staggering away a few paces.

"I can see I'm going to have to deal with you first," Rover said and turned to face Hawk.

"Bring it," Hawk said not showing the trepidation he felt

at the upcoming battle. He had to find a way to hurt this guy and so far nothing he'd done seemed to have any effect on him.

"You'll live to regret saying that, but don't worry, it won't be for long," Rover said coldly as he advanced on Hawk.

"Say, haven't I seen you before?" Hawk said, as the realisation dawned on him that the man before him was almost the twin of the clone he'd captured at the chamber.

Rover stopped momentarily, the thought that he'd be recognised never occurred to him but now that he had he knew that he would have to deal with all leads, and quickly.

"You saw my brother, but I will be the last thing you see," Rover said with menace.

"Wow, that was really bad, did you mean it to come out like that, you know, like it was from a comic book?" joked Hawk as he prepared for what was going to happen. If he could rattle the giant then perhaps he could find a weakness.

Rover snarled at the insult and swung a tremendous right hook at Hawk's face. Hawk ducked beneath the punch at the very last second, actually feeling the wind go through his hair above him, and then delivered two very fast punches to Rover's midriff. Hawk moved out of range before Rover could react. The punches would have doubled a normal man in half but the giant simply grunted and shrugged off the effects coming after Hawk once more.

Rover swung another punch at Hawk as his fury built up inside and again Hawk ducked beneath and smashed another salvo of punches into the giant's stomach and ribs. Rover bellowed his rage as this time he felt the blows.

"I'm going to crush you," Rover snarled and came at him again. This time though he threw a punch at Hawk's head then an uppercut, hoping to catch him as he went low to avoid the first attack.

Hawk's reflexes were on an almost hyper level by this

time. He saw the first punch, then almost as if he knew what the giant had planned, stepped back out of range then back in to jab Rover full in the face with a left that smashed his nose. When Rover tried an uppercut, Hawk hit him with a tremendous right cross, rocking his head so viciously sideways that he almost went down.

"So he can be hurt," thought Hawk, then went in for the attack again. Rover tried to hit him again and again but Hawk was too fast for him.

Hawk started to get too confident though and as he punched Rover repeatedly in the face opening up cuts with every blow, Rover began to accustom himself to the pattern of attack and he blocked the last blow and countered with a punch of his own that rocked Hawk back on his heels. As he staggered back he looked at the clone and knew then that somehow the clone would fight until he died without allowing whatever pain he felt to encumber him or slow him down. Hawk would have to end this fight quickly and decisively if he wanted to come out of it alive and intact.

Rover smiled at Hawk. He'd taken everything the man could throw at him and he was still standing. He knew how that would intimidate most men and, thinking Hawk was like most men, he came forward once more.

Punch after punch he threw at Hawk who blocked or ducked every one without showing any signs that he was troubled by the attack.

A slashing right cross opened up a cut on Hawk's left cheek, the only blow to connect, but he didn't allow it to slow him down or affect his response.

Rover knew it was just a matter of time before his attacks got through and did some real damage so he continued his onslaught.

They were still close to the balcony railing that led to the floor and certain death should either of them fall over, the same fate to which Rover had assigned Taylor. Rover was trying to force Hawk closer to the railing in the hope he could throw him over as well. Rushing at Hawk he tackled him around the waist and slammed him into the railing with such a bone-crunching impact that Hawk felt it right down to his toes. He cried out in pain as his back was slammed into the railing and his breath was forced out of his lungs.

For once Rover had the advantage and this time he would not squander it.

Slamming his forehead into Hawk's face to further weaken his resistance he then rammed a slab-like fist into Hawk's stomach to expel any air that was left in his lungs.

Hawk felt his strength leaving him as the punch forced him into paroxysms of coughing; he was already seeing stars before his eyes from the head butt. His legs threatened to no longer support him; he felt them begin to give way as he began to think that he would lose this fight after all. Doubt filled his mind and he was thinking that perhaps it would be better to just give in and let the clone throw him to his death. The only thought that kept him going was that he would be letting down thousands, maybe millions of fellow humans. He knew that should OMEGA win this then it would leave many lives at risk and Hawk realised that no matter what he couldn't let that happen. He couldn't give in.

Allowing his legs to sag he bent at the waist slightly, taking the weight fully onto his legs.

Rover smiled a confident smile thinking he had won and that the girl would be his to do with as he wished, to return to her father or to kill if he thought fit.

Reaching back with his right hand in readiness to strike the final stunning blow before hurling the intruder to his death, Rover was caught unawares by what happened next.

Hawk grabbed the clone by the legs, slammed his shoulder into his midriff causing him to double over, then picked him up and tossed him over his shoulder into the air past the railing and to the floor. As with Taylor, there was no way he could survive that fall.

In fact, Rover never uttered a single sound as he flew to his death, the only sound being the sickening thud when his body hit the floor below, killing him instantly.

Hawk looked over the railing to see the outcome of his action. When he saw the blood pooling around Rover's head he knew he was dead and that, for the moment, the girl was safe.

"Phew!" he said as he wiped blood away from his cheek with his left hand. Looking around there were only a few people who had remained behind to watch the struggle, not realising just how deadly the conflict was, and of course, Tanya Wilde. She had been rooted to the spot by sheer terror at what was happening. Never in all her short life had she been witness to such brutality and she found it terribly fascinating in some perverse way.

"Is he dead?" she asked hesitatingly.

"Yes, quite dead, which means that you are safe," replied Hawk. Offering her his hand he said, "Come on, let's get out of here and back to Earth."

CHAPTER 12

Tanis Rygar and his team had returned to Cordoba fully expecting to be debriefed then tasked again to go after the marines who had escaped the chamber on Canto, wherever they may be, to tie up all loose ends. He had no idea what Wilde had in store for him and, if he had, he probably would have run for the nearest starship, jumped to hyperspace and kept going as far away as his engines would take him.

As it was, his demise was postponed by the recent actions of the man he'd been sent to kill, an irony he would never see.

As Wilde waited for the return of his daughter he monitored the progress of the Rover 5 he had sent to bring her back. When the signal was terminated with the death of the Rover he was furious. A delay to his plans was something he just would not tolerate. Using his NI he called another Rover 5. He would have to clean up what had happened and rectify what had gone wrong, and perhaps use this to his advantage by implicating Eisenhower and getting rid of Rygar at the same time. He had planned to do that anyway but this way he could utilise what was already at hand and adapt the present situation to his demands, rather than create a new situation.

"WHAT ABOUT THE LOCAL CONSTABULARY, won't they want to investigate what happened here?" asked Tanya as Hawk beckoned her to follow him out of the mall.

"They will but I've got a feeling that we'd be safer leaving before they get here," replied Hawk.

"Where're we going?" she asked again, a little of the shock of witnessing the brutal fight and the two deaths beginning to settle on her.

"Back to Earth, I've got friends who'll assist us in getting there and I can assure you it's where you'll be safest," Hawk said grabbing her hand and gently urging her on. "But we have to leave right now, okay?"

"My father's responsible for this you know, my own father. How could he send someone to kill me, his own daughter?" she said and Hawk could see the shock beginning to take effect. She was unravelling before his eyes and if he didn't act soon to try and bring her around, to snap out of it, she would be a gibbering wreck.

"Look, Tanya, we have to move now. I've got some people who will meet us and help us get away to Earth where you'll be safe and then we can work out what all this means, okay, but we have to move now," he said and he added a slight pull on her arm to get her moving.

She responded slowly and as she began to walk with him he called Colonel De Boer through a subspace battle com. channel via his NI. "Colonel, can you give me your status please, am in need of immediate evac."

The Colonel's voice came through loud and clear to his ears alone, it being a battle com. channel. One marine had likened it to telepathy after using it for the first time. "We are in orbit awaiting your coordinates, latching onto your tracker code now. We have your location and are on our way to pick you up," he said.

"Have encountered a hostile who is no longer a threat but the local Constabulary will be en route so we must try to avoid all contact with them. We don't know just yet how deep any infiltration has gone so best to stay away from them," Hawk warned.

"Understood. Will contact when we're in the vicinity," De Boer said then broke the contact.

They increased their pace as they went down the escalator to the ground floor and the exit. Hawk was pulling Tanya with him to some extent as they pushed their way through the thinning crowd. The entrance loomed before them and as they burst through into the cool night air he searched for an available sky-cab. There were always some parked outside the mall entrance ready for their next fare and he was banking on getting into the nearest one to escape from the scene as quickly as he could, taking Tanya with him.

Hailing one, he dragged Tanya inside with him after it had pulled up by the curb. Once inside he told the driver to take them to the Imperial Hotel. It was as good a place as any and it was purely random and away from the mall so it couldn't be anticipated by OMEGA.

As the sky-cab left the curb and headed out into the flight lanes designated for sky-cab traffic they saw three Constabulary ground cars pull up outside the mall entrance, their sirens blaring to herald their arrival.

"Something funny going on there, did you guys see anything?" asked the cabbie in a friendly tone.

"No, there was some trouble inside, a fight I think but we didn't see anything, did we honey," replied Hawk smiling at the cabbie. Tanya looked at him and simply shook her head in agreement.

"There's always something happening in this town," the cabbie added. Hawk closed the screen between the two cabins and sealed it so they would have total privacy in the rear compartment. Accessing a secure subspace com. channel via his NI he called General Sinclair. "Sir, just reporting that I've got Miss Wilde with me despite an attempt on her life," he said once the call was connected.

"How on Earth did anyone get to her so quickly?" asked Sinclair.

"Presumably her father knew where she had gone and he sent the clone to find her using that as a starting point."

"Clone? Are you saying he sent another of those after her?" asked the General, a little surprised.

"Yes, sir, but this one was different in the respect that he looked bred for battle," explained Hawk.

"How so?" wondered Sinclair.

"He was built with more muscle than the first one we encountered and his pain threshold was almost through the roof. It was like he almost didn't feel pain at all; at least he never let it bother him. He was one tough mutha, sir, I'd hate to think of having to face an army of them," said Hawk.

"That thought had occurred to me after our first encounter here in HQ but it seems more of a threat now that you've discovered there are some bred for battle," said Sinclair.

"I think we ought to move pretty quickly on Jonas Wilde, sir, before he has time to take precautions. No doubt he'll have an army of legal representatives to defend him if we try and take him to court. We may have to try another route," said Hawk.

"We'll discuss that when you arrive back at HQ. Keep me posted on your progress, Matt," Sinclair replied before closing the connection.

"What are you planning to do to my father?" asked Tanya seeming to come out of her shocked state.

"I won't lie to you. If he's responsible for what I think, he'll be brought to justice, one way or another," Hawk replied simply.

"What exactly do you mean by that?" she wanted to know.

Hawk looked at her, saw a beautiful young woman who had found herself in the worst position of her life and felt sympathy for her, but he had to put that out of his mind. He had to steel himself for what was inevitable. "It means if he's guilty, he'll pay," and he left it at that, turning to look away from her out of the side window so she couldn't see the turmoil evident in his ice-blue eyes.

Using her NI Tanya accessed a local com. channel and called her father. "Dad, what's going on, what are you caught up in? Why did you send that man after me?" she said once the call was answered.

Hawk spun around in his seat when he heard her talking to her father, "What the fuck are you doing?" he said angrily.

"Who's that with you sugar?" said Jonas Wilde not answering her question.

"Dad, do you realise they'll come after you now? Tell me it wasn't you, tell me it's all a huge mistake," she pleaded.

Jonas Wilde was silent as he thought about the implications of this call. She was still his daughter, he remembered all the little things about her childhood, but as they ran through his conscious mind he realised that he didn't remember too many of them simply because his career in Col Sec had kept him away from his wife and daughter for so many years. The bond that he would have had – should have had – simply wasn't there. Yes she was his daughter and on some level, he was certain he loved her but she may as well have been just another faceless employee as far as he was concerned and that saddened him. It was one more reason why he hated the Confederation.

"I don't suppose for one moment that you are alone there my sweet and I do regret what you've just gone through and what is to come, but it is inevitable I'm afraid," Jonas Wilde said, then broke the connection.

"No!" Tanya screamed as the call ended. It was like a door slamming on a portion of her life that she had thought so secure. Now, suddenly it had all changed and she had no future, with one simple call her life was over.

"From your reply then I take it that it could've gone better," Hawk said, his anger receding. He saw her world, her reason for living crumble before his very eyes and his heart went out to her, even though he'd tried to keep himself at a distance.

"What am I going to do?" she said in a scared, little girl voice.

"You stay with me and we'll work this out together," he said after a pause, which seemed to comfort her a little.

JONAS WILDE SAT BACK in his chair thinking about what he was going to do next. His plans seemed to be changing faster than he could adapt to them. Things were at a stage now where he was swiftly running out of options so the only thing he could think to do was to go on the offensive. He would have to implement Phase Two of his plan and bring events to a head a bit earlier; the result would be the same though, regardless of the timeline. He contacted Maxwell Eisenhower through the internal intercom accessed through his NI.

"Sir, could you come to my office please, there's something here I think you should see," he said, injecting just enough urgency into his voice to get his boss's attention.

"Okay Jonas, I'm on my way," replied the owner and CEO of MaxCorp, one of the ten largest megacorps in the known galaxy.

Using his NI again Wilde contacted a Rover via a secure channel similar to the battle com. that Recon Delta used; a Rover who had been in the building for a while just waiting for the right moment to make his presence known. The right moment, which was to be heralded by a call from his boss. "Get ready, he's on his way, we're doing this a bit early but we're doing it," Wilde said to the Rover.

No answer was needed, Wilde knew the Rover was ready; he'd been ready for days just waiting for this call.

Eisenhower was soon at Wilde's office and let himself in walking straight up to the large, ornate wooden desk where Wilde was waiting.

"What's the matter Jonas, what's so urgent? Has it to do with your investigation into the chamber incident?" asked Eisenhower as he stood in front of his right-hand man.

"There's someone here I think you should meet Max," Wilde said and pressed a button on his desk which operated a hidden door in the wall to his right. Eisenhower glanced to his left as the panel slid open to reveal a room beyond. A figure came forward to stand in the doorway. It was shrouded in shadow and Eisenhower couldn't make out the features clearly.

"I don't understand Jonas, what's going on and who is this?" said Eisenhower beginning to wonder just what was happening and frankly, a little worried by it all.

"Max, meet Max," Wilde said and the figure emerged from the gloom of the secret chamber into the light of the office where Maxwell Eisenhower could see him, an exact replica of himself, another clone.

"I don't understand… what's going on here Jonas, who is this?" Eisenhower said, indicating the clone standing at the shoulder of his second in command.

"I thought it should be obvious, he's you," Wilde answered calmly and then from a drawer in his desk he withdrew a Sig P996 and aimed it straight at Eisenhower's face.

"What's the meaning of this?" Eisenhower exploded in anger.

"I thought that was obvious too, Max, we're replacing you," Wilde said with a half-smile.

"But, for that, I'd have to be dead," Eisenhower said.

"You are so right," said Wilde and shot him full in the face. The maximum power plasma bolt struck him right between the eyes and blew his head apart, spraying blood and brain matter across the floor behind him.

"You can come in now," Wilde said and two men came through from the hidden room. "Dispose of that, I want nothing to remain, and I do mean *nothing*, vaporise it so there's no trace left. Do you understand?" he added to which both men nodded their assent.

The Rover replica of Eisenhower looked at Wilde and said, "I'd better get to work," and left the office.

PHASE TWO WAS COMPLETE, adaptability was indeed the name of the game and the game had changed once more. Now he would implicate himself instead of Eisenhower. He would go straight to the underground base where they'd never find him, which he had secretly built using funds siphoned off from certain mega corp. accounts. He would be safe there and he could organise the attack against Col Sec with impunity. With his clone in place, all the wealth and power Maxwell Eisenhower had amassed building up his mega corp. would be at his disposal and he would have an organisation in OMEGA to rival that of the mighty Col Sec itself, now all that remained for him to do was ready the forces.

CHAPTER 13

The sky-cab dropped Hawk and Tanya Wilde off at the Imperial Hotel as instructed and they entered the foyer as casually as they could. Tanya was still in a state of shock over the incidents that had happened during the past few minutes of her young life, so Hawk covered for her the best way he knew how and that was to keep her away from as many prying eyes as he could.

The foyer was busy as one would expect in the premier hotel in the city and the carpet was lush beneath their feet as they slowly walked towards the bar.

"You need a stiff drink to calm your nerves," Hawk said as he guided her with a gentle hand on her elbow towards the mahogany bar at the end of the long room.

"Good afternoon and welcome to the Imperial Bar, what can I get you?" said the tall barman as they reached the bar. He had a ready smile and an eager to please attitude. Hawk guided Tanya onto a tall barstool, looked at the barman and said, "Two scotch on the rocks, please. Let's keep it simple shall we dear?" This last comment was said to Tanya who, realising they were in company, returned Hawk's smile albeit weakly.

"Two scotch on the rocks coming up, sir," replied the bartender jovially and he turned to prepare the drinks.

Accessing a battle com. channel Hawk called De Boer. "We're in the bar at the Imperial Hotel, we'll meet you here," he said as quietly as he could, not wanting to draw any attention to the call. The bartender returned just then with their drinks in tall tumblers, the amber liquid glistening under the lights of the room, the ice clinking musically as he placed them down on coasters before them.

"Can I get you anything else?" he asked, smiling.

"Not just yet thanks," Hawk answered returning the smile cordially.

He paid for the drinks by linking his NI to the hotel's account. Once they were alone and out of earshot of the bartender he turned to Tanya, "Our help will be here soon so we can relax for a few minutes. Why don't you enjoy your drink, we'll be moving as soon as they get here and I don't know when we'll get the chance again," he said quietly, leaning in close to appear like they were a loving couple, an image he was hoping to cultivate for anyone passing by and watching them.

She picked up her drink with trembling fingers so that the ice clunked in the glass and she had to steady it by holding it with both hands. Slowly she brought the glass up to her lips and took a sip letting the amber liquid slowly trickle down her throat warming her as it travelled down into her stomach.

"God I needed that," she said, acknowledging the stress she was feeling.

"Don't worry, we're almost home free here. Once we get picked up I'll get you safely to Earth and then you can truly relax," Hawk said with a reassuring smile. He took his drink and poured it down in one swallow savouring the warmth it brought to his insides. "Hmm, that was quite good," he commented.

Suddenly a commotion at the entrance of the hotel grabbed their attention and Hawk turned to see three marines stride into the bar wearing full battle gear and bearing arms.

"Is this your idea of low profile Colonel?" Hawk asked when De Boer was in front of him.

"Didn't have the chance to change into civvies. I thought we should come straight away considering the bind you found yourselves in," replied De Boer with a deadpan expression.

"Perhaps we should leave now before someone complains to the hotel manager about the sudden influx of undesirables who seemed to have invaded his hotel," Hawk added in the same deadpan way.

Grabbing Tanya's hand, Hawk led her away from the bar in the company of the three marines. They walked straight for the foyer and out of the front entrance where a shuttle was parked. It was a small, sleek craft built for speed with the capability of holding only a few passengers, whilst its dimensions enabled it to land almost anywhere making it ideal for the task Colonel De Boer intended.

Once inside the shuttle Hawk and Tanya sat in the middle two seats of a row of six down the centre of the craft. De Boer took the front seat with the two other marines positioning themselves in the seats behind their charges. Straps from hidden recesses inside the seats snaked out and wrapped around those sitting in them to secure them for take-off. Within a few seconds of them boarding the shuttle it was airborne, streaking towards the upper atmosphere and the waiting Valkyrie.

≈

TANIS RYGAR and what was left of his team were at the space-port on Cordoba wondering just what to do next when a call came through via his NI.

"Change of plans Rygar. The agent you failed to kill has once more escaped and this time he has my daughter with him. You will be joined by one of my Rovers and he will instruct you on how to proceed. You will follow his orders implicitly is that understood?" said Jonas Wilde through a secure com. channel.

"Perfectly, sir," Rygar replied.

"Do not fail this time or you will face the consequences," Wilde said and there was a sense of finality in his voice making the hairs stand up on the back of Rygar's head.

"You can count on us, sir," he replied. As soon as he'd said it he knew he shouldn't have for he knew that Wilde would not stand for any futile excuses if they failed this time. There was only one thing to do and that was hope and pray that what this Rover expected of them was within the realms of human possibility and they could carry it out otherwise he would have no choice but to run and hope that he wouldn't be found. That in itself was a lesson in futility, for the resources at Wilde's disposal made it virtually impossible to hide from him. Rygar felt an overwhelming sense of doom and despair wash over him when the call was terminated. He felt like he'd just signed his own death warrant. This wasn't far from the truth as Wilde had no further use for him and planned on using him and his team as cannon fodder in the upcoming battle against the Confederation.

≈

ACCESSING a subspace com. channel via his NI, Hawk called General Sinclair. "Sir, I think we need to move on Jonas Wilde immediately and with your permission I, Colonel De Boer and some of his team can be at his office within the hour to make the arrest," he said with some urgency.

"What about his daughter?" queried Sinclair.

"We have two ships here in orbit, sir, the Valkyrie and the ship the Colonel arrived on. We can either send her to Earth on one now and bring her father back in the other, or leave her in orbit in case we need the support of both ships. We have no idea of the strength of resistance Wilde will put up but we do know, from what we've seen so far, that he has resources and he's not afraid to call upon them, so my guess is he won't come willingly."

"Okay then Matt, this mission is at your discretion. I'm patching this call through to Colonel De Boer and the captains of both ships. This mission is under your control and you are to make use of the ships and personnel at your discretion. Ensure the safety of Miss Wilde at all costs, capture and arrest her father and bring him to Earth for questioning," Sinclair replied. During the call, De Boer turned in his seat to look at Hawk.

"Thank you, sir, I'll keep you posted," Hawk said then broke the connection.

"Colonel, I want you to assign a few of your best men to guard Miss Wilde on the Valkyrie while you and the rest of your team accompany me to arrest her father. This time I think it best if you dress in civvies to lessen our impact on the population, plus we'll blend in with them better should the need arise," he added when he saw De Boer looking at him.

"If we want to blend in we'll have to limit what we take with us, that means no body armour, no pulse rifles..." De Boer started but Hawk cut him off by saying, "We're not going into battle here Colonel, I don't expect us to have a fire fight, so I think we can make do with just small arms. A Sig each with a few extra battery clips should suffice don't you think?"

"You're probably right, I don't think Wilde is crazy enough to risk a running gun battle in his office or the streets," agreed De Boer.

"If you're going after my father then I'm coming with you," Tanya said adamantly.

"No chance," retorted Hawk. "My boss would have me thrown out of an airlock in deep space without an environment suit if I allowed that."

"I don't care; you're not leaving me here alone."

"You won't be alone, there will be some of the Colonel's men with you at all times. You'll be quite safe."

"But you might need me down there, to get into my father's offices, I can help you. Without me, you won't get near my father, but with me, you'll get right to him. I'm known on sight so it'll be easy to get past security," Tanya said, trying a different tack.

"She may have a point there. If we just show up at his door there's no guarantee we'll even be allowed inside without a warrant or the physical presence of someone from the local Constabulary," agreed De Boer.

Hawk looked at the Colonel as he mulled over what had been said. His ice-blue eyes seemed to spark as if the firing of the neurons in his brain lit a fire behind them as they worked on the problem ahead.

"Okay," Hawk said finally, coming to a decision. "You come with us, you get us into your father's building and up to his floor but then you step back and stay behind these men. Colonel, I want you to assign two of your best men to remain by her side at all times and at the first sign of trouble get her to safety, is that understood?"

"You have my word," De Boer replied solemnly.

"Let's do this then. Colonel, I hope you have a change of clothes with you because I want to head straight back down there now, before I change my mind about Miss Wilde coming with us."

"We always carry spare clothes with us, you never know when you might need to blend in with the indigenous population, you should know that Matt from your time with Recon Delta or has it been so long that you've forgotten your training?" asked De Boer with a friendly smirk.

Returning the smile Hawk said, "Once Recon Delta, always Recon Delta, you know that, sir," reciting the motto of the corp.

Tanya Wilde listened to the banter between the two men and she found herself wondering what it was she had fallen into. It was a dangerous situation for sure, she had already seen two men killed before her eyes and, judging by how things were progressing and from what these men were hinting at, she didn't suppose the death toll would remain at that number. Knowing all these things and realising the danger she was about to face, she still felt safe as long as she was close to that man with the ice-blue eyes, those fathomless eyes that hinted at disdain for everything they viewed yet showed such warmth when he looked at her.

She began to hope that once this was all over she would get the opportunity to see him again. There was more to him than just the obvious alpha male exterior and she thought it would be interesting to peel away the layers of his protective veneer, very interesting indeed.

JONAS WILDE HAD RETURNED to his office to gather the last of the belongings that he'd need to take with him. Accessing the

135

building's computer network with his NI he asked for the location of his daughter using the tracking chip in her NI. What he learned surprised him somewhat. She had been heading away from Cordoba on her way to Earth and Col Sec HQ no doubt, but now she was on her way back towards the planet's surface.

Perhaps all was not lost, she was handing herself to him and he would not allow this opportunity to go to waste. He had his team ready; all that remained was for him to give the order.

He would give her one last chance to join him, after all, she was his daughter and he owed her that much at least, but if she refused then she would meet the same fate as all the others who stood against him, she would die.

CHAPTER 14

Before he and his team left their seats, Colonel De Boer contacted his transport and Captain Jefferson on the Valkyrie to issue orders for them to stand by in orbit and at full readiness to proceed. They bypassed safety protocols so the straps would release them to go into the rear cargo area to change clothes and stow their gear.

Tanya used the opportunity to speak to Hawk while they were alone. Leaning towards him so that she wouldn't have to raise her voice she said, "I've never thanked you for what you did back there. You saved my life. Wow! How many people actually get to say that? I mean you read about it and see it in movies but this was real and ... listen to me, I'm babbling."

Hawk placed a reassuring hand on top of hers, looked her in the eye and said, "It's okay, I understand, you're scared and still in shock, so am I."

Suddenly she felt herself begin to relax a little and she knew then that as long as this man was by her side she'd be safe. He didn't have to say the words she just knew he would die before he allowed any harm to come to her. Even though they were heading back into what could be the most dangerous situation she'd ever faced in her young, sheltered, spoilt life, she felt safe, truly safe, possibly for the first time in years.

"You're scared?" she asked incredulously when she finally found her voice.

"I'd be a complete idiot if I wasn't and Momma Hawk didn't raise any fools," joked Hawk, hoping to lighten her mood.

"You need to put something on that," she said gesturing towards his cheek, which had been cut during the fight in the mall with the muscle-bound clone.

Touching where she had indicated he noticed a trace of blood on his fingertips. "Ah yes, thanks, I will. Can't have a scar spoiling these good looks," he joked then added, "even though the opposite sex are supposed to find them interesting."

"Personally I've never found facial disfigurement appealing," she replied.

"Disfigurement? That bad, eh?" he said, consciously placing a hand over the scratch.

"No, no not at all," she recanted swiftly reaching up to pull his hand away in an attempt to reassure him. When she saw the mischievous glint in his eye she realised she'd fallen for the joke and was suddenly embarrassed, dropping her eyes from his momentarily. When she looked up again she saw him smiling playfully. "Sorry couldn't resist," he explained.

She took her hand off his and punched him in the shoulder, "You brute," she chided in the same playful vein and turned her head away from him in mock anger.

"Aw don't be like that," he pleaded and placed his hand on hers again and this time she allowed it to remain and they sat there in companionable silence for a few moments.

When the marines returned led by De Boer he spotted the hands and said, "Getting on well I see."

Nervously she pulled her hand away, instantly regretting the action and missing the closeness the contact brought.

The Colonel and his men were all dressed in casual clothes – cargo pants and open-necked shirts over which they each wore a short leather jacket. Similar shoes to those worn by Hawk adorned their feet while the ubiquitous Sig P996 was hidden away in a soft leather holster beneath the jacket of each soldier.

As De Boer regained his seat he turned to Hawk and said, "ETA at our destination, ten minutes, then things get interesting."

Tanya looked at Hawk with a worried expression and asked, "Interesting how?"

"Don't worry, you'll be fine, trust me," Hawk replied avoiding the question, and she glanced at De Boer who winked at her as he turned to face the front of the shuttle once more. Although his comment was made to unnerve her, to make her rethink her decision about coming along, to make her realise she was putting herself in harm's way, it was unnecessary because she already understood that. She wasn't some dumb kid hell-bent on a thrill ride or some spoiled brat determined to get back at Daddy for stopping her allowance. Okay, she was spoiled but that was not the point. Her father was responsible for the deaths of more people than she liked to think of and she had no reason to think he wouldn't continue if he wasn't stopped. These men were going to try and stop him and they had a better chance at success if she helped them. Yes, it was dangerous, she understood that but she had to do it; it was the right thing to do, it was that simple. She was comforted by the fact that she knew, without a shadow of a doubt, that the man seated beside her would protect her no matter what.

Having gone through the recent situation in the mall she wondered what the Colonel's definition of interesting could possibly be and knew that in less than ten minutes she would find out.

～

JONAS WILDE SAT in his office thinking. Having delayed his departure until he'd learned what his daughter was about to do, he'd made certain contingency arrangements. The master plan, which he was determined to stick to, would go ahead no matter what, but for that to happen certain other things had to take place first. It was a fluid situation and he had to adapt to the constantly changing scenarios.

He would have preferred to have kept his daughter out of it but it appeared she was as determined to involve herself as he was to see it through. Honestly speaking he hadn't considered her in his master plan, it was almost as if he had no daughter, which saddened him. The bond that should have been present between father and daughter was just missing; it had been prevented from forming by his involvement in Col Sec, which he blamed for everything. Col Sec was the focus of his hatred, he had devoted his life to it, forsaken everything else for it and they had kicked him out because of a failed psyche evaluation, or so he thought.

What his mind wouldn't accept, wouldn't allow him to see, were his own psychotic tendencies. He considered himself above everyone else, his own needs were always put first. When he thought he was devoting his life to Col Sec it was for his own selfish personal gratification and not for the betterment of the Confederation. The bond between himself and Tanya, which he blamed Col Sec for destroying by not allowing it to develop, had not been there from the start. He simply did not love her; he was incapable of loving her. She loved him though, and despite his long periods of absence, her love was unconditional for he was her father. During the times they had spent together when he had gone home on leave, she had bonded with him. Those were instances that his psychotic mind chose to forget.

Now she was involved in his plan, there was no denying it. What he needed now was to see exactly what she wanted, what she expected of him.

No doubt she would bring along that meddling agent who had escaped death too many times, but why, to what purpose? What did they hope to gain?

They had his files and call records which logged his involvement at the chamber and the subsequent attack on Hawk and his team there, but what did they intend to do? Were they planning on coming to arrest him? Were they that stupid?

The computer continued to trace his daughter's progress. It extrapolated her route and showed that she would be at the MaxCorp building in around five minutes or less.

If she was coming there to see him then he must make sure he made the proper arrangements, he thought with a sly grin.

⁓

"I've had the pilot invoke Col Sec authority to allocate us a landing area in front of the building so we can go in through the front door," De Boer said over his shoulder to Hawk and Tanya. "ETA thirty seconds, get ready," he added.

"We're ready, Colonel," Hawk replied and he turned to Tanya with a reassuring smile to ask, "You okay?"

She nodded her head and returned his smile and then they all felt the landing thrusters fire as they came in to land.

As the shuttle settled onto its landing struts and the

engines powered down the straps automatically retracted into the seats, freeing the passengers.

The doors slid open and Hawk and the rest were on their feet moving out from the confines of the sleek shuttle back into the warmth of the Cordoban air.

Before them was the huge building that stretched up towards the azure sky. The sun had almost set below the horizon but there was still quite a lot of light left as they headed up the steps towards the huge entrance.

As they walked through the huge doors the foyer opened out before them. The reception desk was in the centre of the floor; a circular desk at which sat two young women who greeted visitors, answered any questions and announced new arrivals. They presented a very human face that many businesses had rejected in favour of automation.

A huge staircase ran up the centre of the building with balconies on each floor as it snaked its way up the middle of the huge tower block.

A group of men came towards Hawk and the team from the staircase where they had obviously been awaiting their arrival. One man led them, a man Hawk and De Boer recognised instantly as the clone they had captured in the chamber and transported to Earth, or at least, another like him. Behind him were eight burly men all dressed in business suits, all with the same hard expressions worn by security men all over the galaxy.

"Good afternoon Miss Wilde, we've been expecting you," the Rover said as he walked up to the group at the entrance. The guards all fanned out just behind him forming a barrier.

"I don't know you but I'm here to see my father," Tanya said casually, she was on home ground here and felt more confident.

"Your father is extremely busy Miss and not to be

disturbed," Rover replied smiling, his expression remaining calm and pleasant throughout.

"I'm sure he's not too busy to see his own daughter," Tanya insisted.

"I've been instructed to allow you through Miss if the situation is extremely urgent, but I'm afraid these gentlemen will have to remain here in the lobby," Rover said.

"But they're with me and are here to see my father also."

"I'm Matthew Hawk from Col Sec Intelligence Division and we're here to see Jonas Wilde and ask him some questions regarding a grave security matter," Hawk said by way of introduction as he stood by Tanya's side.

"Do you have a warrant?"

"No."

"A representative from the Local Constabulary?"

"No."

"Then I must ask you to leave, and these gentlemen here with me are to ensure that you do. You have no jurisdiction here Mister Hawk and any attempt to gain access to this building now would be deemed as trespass and we would be within our rights to evict you, forcibly if need be, and then bring charges against you. Is that what you want?"

"Haven't we already met?" Hawk said suddenly changing tack.

"No, sir, we haven't. I'm sure I'd remember if we had," replied Rover calmly.

"How long has Mister Eisenhower employed clones, you are a clone aren't you? Identical in every way to the clone I captured and took to Earth and who then committed suicide by activating a bomb he'd somehow hidden inside his body. Do you have a similar device hidden inside you? Is it something you're all equipped with or was he specially designed for that purpose?" Hawk continued as he watched the expressions not only of the clone but also the guards with him, to gauge just how much they knew of their employer and the business he ran. None of them showed any signs that they were disturbed in the slightest by his words or that they'd even heard them. They were there to do a job and their attitude was truly professional. The clone on the other hand, with a knowing smile slowly spreading across his face emphasising his air of supreme self-confidence, said in a calm and pleasant voice, "Again, sir, I must ask you to leave."

"And if we refuse?" asked De Boer, stepping forward to stand next to Hawk.

"And you are?" asked the clone.

"I think you know, so let's drop all the charades shall we," De Boer said bluntly.

"Ah, the voice of the military no doubt," Rover said in way of recognition, then gesturing for them to look at the guards added, "Gentlemen it seems the numbers favour the house as it were, and as any gambler knows, it's unwise to bet against odds as the house invariably wins. In laymen's terms, for our military friend here, we will use force if required to prevent you from getting any further."

De Boer smiled at the sarcastic jibe but kept his cool preferring to ask, "Would you risk a gun battle here if we decided to force our way in?"

"Would you?" Rover replied calmly.

De Boer looked at Hawk and they both knew the answer to that question. Although they were both soldiers and accustomed to battle conditions, their priorities had always been the protection of the Confederation and its people and they would never needlessly endanger innocent lives in the pursuit of their goal.

"Thank you for your time, sir," Hawk said as he turned to go, then as the group were about to leave he added, "Tell Mister Wilde we'll catch him later." Within seconds they were through the entrance and out of the building.

Softly, more to himself really, Rover said, "I'll pass that message along personally, sir."

Outside the building, De Boer said, "Well that went well."

"At least now we know how deeply ingrained this goes," replied Hawk thoughtfully.

"How so?"

"Well, look, who or rather what was the representative who spearheaded our welcoming committee, a clone. I now think this goes right to the top although it is conceivable that Wilde could have run a programme of cloning through a business as big as this one with so many offshoots and subdivisions without Eisenhower knowing, but somehow I doubt it. He didn't get to run one of the largest megacorps in the galaxy without at least some idea of what's going on throughout the entire business structure, otherwise, he could be ousted by an internal coup. No, I think Eisenhower is also involved here which makes our job just that much harder I'm afraid."

"What do we do now then?" Tanya asked, voicing the concerns they were all feeling.

"I think our best bet is to return to the Valkyrie for now. I'll contact General Sinclair with an update and take it from there. He may be able to get a warrant issued so we can come back and do this legally through the proper channels or he may want us to take other action. We'll know better when I've given him my report," Hawk suggested, leading them back inside the shuttle.

"Other action? I don't like the sound of that," muttered Tanya as she followed Hawk inside the shuttle.

JONAS WILDE HAD WATCHED the exchange through the Rover's eyes, the Rover's NI having been linked to the building's computer so that the visual images seen by the clone were transformed into electrical impulses that the brain recognised. These impulses were transmitted to the computer via the NI and transferred to the monitor on Wilde's desk, something the megacorp. was trying out for the military to eradicate the need for helmet cams. One day soon he hoped to make it possible to link the images NI to NI and therefore enable soldiers on the ground to see what each other saw. It would take some getting used to but he was confident it could be done and his Rovers would be the testing ground.

After hearing the exchange and watching his daughter leave he called the Rover 5, who by that time had arrived at where Tanis Rygar and his team were waiting.

Linking the call also to Rygar, he said, "They are heading back to their ship in orbit, make sure they don't reach it. I want them all dead."

Rover 5 looked at Rygar coldly and said, "Let's go."

CHAPTER 15

As the shuttle lifted off from the parking area allotted them in front of the MaxCorp building, Hawk was in contact with General Sinclair via a secure subspace channel. "It seemed like they knew we were coming, sir, and had time to prepare," he added after he'd recounted what had happened.

"Damn, I hate all this red tape and jurisdictional crap," Sinclair replied, giving vent to his frustration.

"Do you want us to go back and bring him with us, sir? We could do it as a black op, monitor his whereabouts and go in after dark around three am in the morning," asked Hawk.

"The direct method may turn out to be our best option, but not yet, Matt. As much as I want to give you the green light I must try other alternatives. I don't like the implication that Maxwell Eisenhower may be involved. I agree that it seems improbable that Jonas Wilde has done an end run around him and that he's unaware of the situation, which only makes it that much harder to make a case against them. The legal power they can bring to bear against us is phenomenal. For Christ's sake,

147

they supply the Confederation with seventy-five per cent of our weapons technology and eighty-seven per cent of the rest of our software so we have to be very careful here. I dread to think what would happen if they could raise any military force against us. They'd be a formidable threat," Sinclair commented.

"I don't want to be a doomsayer, sir, but what if that is their plan? I mean why else would they have a cloning programme? I've seen two of the normals and one military-grade, who's to say there aren't any more? We need to close them down and soon, sir," Hawk suggested.

"I take your point, Matt, and will take it under advisement. This is another reason why we have to bring an airtight case against them before the courts so we can stop all their activities," Sinclair agreed.

"You mentioned that they supply seventy-five per cent of our weapons technology?"

"That's right."

"What's to say that they haven't kept a few new developments for themselves plus, if they know what they've supplied us, then they know how to get around our security protocols, defence shield configurations and all the rest. If they could gain access to our computer network they could shut our entire military operation down, they could even cripple civilian operations too. What would the Alliance give to own that technology or what does OMEGA plan to do with it? Are they capable of implementing it themselves? Sir, I feel this threat is very real and we have to move fast."

"I agree, Matt, and believe me we're moving as fast as we can on this. Sit tight on the Valkyrie and I'll get back to you shortly with new orders," Sinclair said before closing the com. channel.

"You paint a pretty bleak picture," De Boer commented after Hawk had finished speaking. He'd noticed the expression on his face and knew how worried he was about what could happen.

"I just hope I'm wrong. So far in everything we've done, they seem to either be one step ahead of us or at the very least, one step behind and able to catch up and keep pace with us. It's almost like they're listening to our every word and watching our every move," Hawk replied.

Before De Boer could comment the pilot said, "We've got company," and the shuttle was buffeted by plasma cannon fire.

"What the fuck?" exclaimed De Boer as they were tossed around in their seats. Had it not been for the safety harnesses holding them in place they would have been thrown around the interior of the shuttle like rag dolls.

"Get the shields up," ordered Hawk, then to no one in particular, asked, "How did they find us so fast?" As soon as that thought was aired he looked at Tanya. A thought was clawing at his mind trying to break free but another salvo of plasma cannon fire rocked the shuttle sending it back into the recesses of his subconscious to languish there until the time it could safely surface once more.

"Get us back to the Valkyrie and fast," Hawk shouted to the pilot.

"I'm trying, sir," replied the pilot.

Inside the shuttle, situated on the back of the headrests of each seat, were monitors that could be used for external views and Hawk had the one facing him tuned to a rearview so he could see who was firing at them.

"Isn't that the same damn craft that attacked us before?" Hawk asked when he had a clear visual. The pilot of the shuttle was taking evasive action, throwing the sleek shuttle through a series of aerial manoeuvres he hoped would help him lose the attacking craft.

"It looks like it is," replied De Boer, once he had his monitor tuned to the same view.

"Then we're in serious trouble, if I remember right that thing had superior shielding, enough to withstand several missile strikes that should've destroyed a craft of that class."

"Yea, military class defence capability," agreed De Boer.

"This is a military shuttle too, sir. We have a few tricks up our sleeve also," the pilot added confidently from his seat as he threw the shuttle through a tight looping turn to starboard throwing his passengers against their seat harnesses once more.

"Do we have any weapons on board? I'd love to give those bastards a bloody nose," asked De Boer.

"We have plasma cannons fore and aft and a compliment of Sabre missiles," replied the pilot, "but I could sure use an extra pair of hands up here on the weapons console though."

"I'm on it," said the marine seated next to De Boer. He overrode the safety protocols on his seat so that he could release his harness, then he was up and running towards the forward section.

"Right then, one bloody nose coming up," he said as he strapped himself into the co-pilot's seat and began to familiarise himself with the weapon's console controls.

"Pilot, take us down low, as tight as you can against the rooftops. I'm hoping it'll confuse their targeting scanners with all the electronic interference from the buildings long enough for us to gain some distance," Hawk shouted as he ran different strategies through his mind hoping to come up with something they could use.

"Aye, sir," agreed the pilot and he put the shuttle through a tight looping dive back towards the city once more.

Plasma fire from the chasing attack craft narrowly missed them as they suddenly changed direction, but it wasn't long before the pursuit was on again with them firing regardless of their close proximity to the buildings and their occupants. As the shuttle flew in low across several flight lanes used by civilian craft such as sky-cabs, between buildings, above streets, the pursuit craft followed firing her plasma cannons in rapid bursts.

Plasma bolts struck buildings, destroying huge portions of the structures; explosions erupted along their flight path as they fired at them indiscriminately. In one instance a plasma bolt struck an escaping sky-cab sending it hurtling into the side of a building in a huge fireball. The building exploded where the sky-cab impacted with it and burst into flames that were soon spreading throughout the wreckage. Only the building's fire prevention protocols prevented the fire spreading onto those adjacent to it initially, but soon the flames were so intense that they overwhelmed even those and the Fire Department had to be called. Many people would die in that building alone before the fire was brought under control, a fact that Hawk could not allow to affect his decision-making processes.

Seeing the destruction their altered flight path had caused, Hawk said, "Take us back up and return fire as soon as you get a lock. I want those bastards stopped."

De Boer saw the expression on his face and knew that the decision to fly into the city for cover was a calculated risk that hadn't worked as hoped and the consequences would lie heavy on Hawk's mind for a long time to come.

Without a word, the pilot took the shuttle straight up out of the cityscape and into the air. The marine manning the weapons console was taking care to get as tight a lock on the attacking craft as possible to minimise the chance of missing and thus adding to the damage and loss of life already caused by their flight through the city.

"I have a lock," he shouted.

"Fire!" Hawk ordered and from the rear pods that had

elongated out from the sides of the shuttle two Sabre missiles ignited their fuel pods and, having locked onto the designated target, went streaking towards their pursuers.

Within seconds the forward momentum of the targeted craft and the speed of the missiles had closed the gap between them. The ensuing explosion when the two met sent a fireball followed by a shockwave outwards that almost reached the rooftops below. The escaping shuttle though had enough velocity to outrun them both. Sitting watching the monitor intently, Hawk waited to see the outcome of the retaliatory missile strike and was disheartened when he saw the craft come hurtling through the fireball trailing fiery tendrils in her wake.

"Still in pursuit," observed the marine at the weapons console and he opened fire with the aft plasma pulse cannons.

"We need more speed or higher yield to the missiles," suggested Hawk to the two marines hard at work in the two pilots' chairs upfront.

"That may be a problem, sir," replied the weapons officer calmly.

Almost afraid to ask, Hawk said, "Why?"

"Because they've just got a weapon's lock on us in preparation for firing a missile," came the reply.

Looking at Hawk, Tanya asked, "Can this thing survive something like that?"

Hawk glanced at De Boer for confirmation but all he received was a blank, non-committal expression, which meant either he didn't know or they were about to die. Always wanting to keep a positive attitude, he chose to believe the former and hoped that the boys who built the shuttle knew what they were doing. However, balancing that against not wanting to lie to her he said, "We're about to find out," then smiled in a reassuring way.

Tanya glanced away so that Hawk couldn't see the fear in her eyes. Then he saw De Boer look at him and he knew they were in trouble.

~

ON BOARD the attack craft Tanis Rygar was the pilot whilst the Rover was manning the weapons.

"Get closer," the clone ordered once more. It was the one order he'd kept on repeating since they'd locked onto the girl's tracking chip signal.

"If I get any closer we'll be on board with 'em," Rygar replied sardonically.

"I've got a missile lock on them," Rover said coldly.

"At this range, we'll be killed too, I'd better pull back," Rygar replied, not daring to take his eyes off the shuttle they were chasing for fear of either losing it or crashing into it.

"You do and I'll kill you myself," Rover replied coldly.

"But…"

"But nothing, our shields will protect us against the blast, now hold her steady," explained Rover coldly and calmly, so coldly in fact he reminded Rygar of a cobra about to strike.

"Missile away," Rover said with a press of a touchpad on the weapons console, then with a trace of satisfaction added, "I've got you now!"

~

"INCOMING," shouted the weapons officer.

"Shields to full power," ordered Hawk.

"Already done, sir," replied the marine.

Within seconds the missile had closed the gap between them as its onboard computer locked onto the signal from the shuttle's electronic equipment and homed in on its target. Whatever the outcome one thing was certain, it would not miss.

Captain Jefferson on the Valkyrie had been monitoring the action with intensity. Frustration fuelled him as he paced the bridge listening to the audio feed from down below.

"Is there nothing we can do?" he asked as he stopped at the ops station.

"I've got an active lock on them, sir, but at this range, I'm not certain it would do any good."

Making a decision, he contacted the other transport also in orbit and said, "Captain, you maintain position here and monitor this frequency. I've seen that craft before and our boys are going to need help so I'm taking the Valkyrie down. As soon as I have them we'll make the jump and head for Earth as ordered."

"Aye Captain, we'll keep scanners tightly on you and all our weapons charged just in case," came the reply.

Jefferson turned to his pilot and said, "Take us down there on an intercept course."

"Sir, we may be too late," warned the ops officer.

"What!" exclaimed Jefferson.

"They've just fired a Sabre missile at them, sir."

THE MISSILE IMPACTED against the aft shields of the shuttle and exploded in a fireball that threatened to engulf the sleek craft as it consumed the oxygen in close proximity as fuel. The force of the blast threw the shuttle forward and into a tight tailspin that the pilot struggled to control. The aft shields protected the shuttle from serious damage by absorbing the energy released by the explosion and deflecting the remainder away from it.

End over end the shuttle spun out of control for many

seconds during which her passengers were powerless to do anything to help until the pilot had her once more under his control. As he brought her out of the spin and on an even keel he said, "We can't take another hit like that, the shields barely held that time, so if you guys have any suggestions back there, I'm all ears."

"Soon as you get a lock on her, let her have everything we have. Let's see how they hold up against a full brace of Sabre missiles set to full yield. That should stop them cold and if it doesn't at least we'll have the time to make a run for the Valkyrie," Hawk replied quickly.

"I'm on it," replied the marine, manning the weapons console confidently.

"Sirs, the Valkyrie is approaching fast on an intercept course," the pilot said, informing the rest of the crew.

"She's coming to lend a hand, keep evasive manoeuvres going until you release the missiles then match her course. Our chances of getting out of this have just doubled," observed Hawk, with a smile aimed at Tanya.

RYGAR FLEW the attack craft through the fireball, momentarily losing sight of the shuttle. As they emerged, trailing fiery tendrils behind them, he saw the shuttle off to the side having been pushed off course by the blast.

"There they are," he muttered to himself.

"They must have improved their shield capability," observed Rover when he saw no discernible damage to the shuttle.

Rygar attempted to bring the craft around and get behind the shuttle once more, but the shuttle pilot had anticipated the manoeuvre and had looped his craft over to starboard whilst firing both forward and aft plasma pulse cannons laterally at her attacker. The plasma bolts had no effect on the attack craft shields other than to push her away slightly, but it was just enough for the shuttle to complete the turn and put more distance between them.

"They're getting away you fool," shouted Rover angrily.

Rygar brought the attack craft around again in an attempt to match the shuttle's course.

"They won't escape again," Rover said through clenched teeth as he released a salvo of Sabre missiles.

"Sir, the attack craft has just fired three more Sabre missiles at the shuttle, detonation in less than thirty seconds," the ops officer reported.

"Target those missiles with our pulse cannons and open fire," ordered Jefferson. "Get us closer, be ready to fire our own Sabres at that attack craft," he added urgently.

THE MARINE MANNING the weapons on the shuttle saw the trio of Sabres fired from the attack craft and immediately targeted them with the shuttle's aft pulse cannons. The joined effort of pulse cannon fire from both the Valkyrie and the shuttle blasted the three Sabre missiles out of the sky in a multiple explosion that lit up the darkening sky with its intensity.

"Sirs, the Valkyrie is closing on us, we also have three other craft approaching, they're from the local Constabulary," said the pilot, who had also kept an eye on the scanners.

A voice came through the com. channel saying, "This is Commander Iverson of the Cordoban Constabulary. I order you to disarm your weapons, drop your shields and follow us to the nearest spaceport. You are under arrest."

"I'm sorry Commander but we can't do that," replied Hawk, adding to his men, "Open fire on that attack craft."

"Then you leave me no choice but to force you to the ground," Commander Iverson said with finality in his voice. He'd obviously been given his orders to bring down both of these crafts that were tearing apart his city and he would obey those orders.

The weapons officer on the shuttle urgently said, "They have weapons lock on us, they intend to fire."

"Now this is getting really interesting," De Boer said.

THE ATTACK CRAFT had received the same communiqué as the shuttle.

Rygar said, "I'm getting a bad feeling about this."

Rover fired a Sabre missile at the lead Constabulary craft that had taken point whilst the other two had remained slightly behind, one to port and the other to starboard.

The Sabre missile struck its target and exploded destroying the craft in a huge fireball. Before the explosion had time to expand much past its initial ignition, Rover had targeted the other two Constabulary craft with the pulse cannons and fired before they had time to raise their shields.

The plasma bolts struck the port craft in the pilots' area smashing through, killing the crew of three, and sending the craft hurtling to the ground below. The starboard craft was struck on her port wing, which was shredded by the plasma bolts effectively destroying the stability of the craft without which she could not remain in the air. The smaller craft was sent spinning to the ground in a breathtaking tailspin.

"They are a threat no longer," Rover stated without emotion.

Rygar glanced at the clone seated next to him and felt a chill run through him. When he looked back towards the shuttle he realised he was too late.

～

SABRE MISSILES from both the Valkyrie and the shuttle streaked towards the attack craft and within seconds they had exploded in a huge fireball of cataclysmic proportions that engulfed the craft. The shuttle quickly boarded the larger Valkyrie who then reversed her course and headed into the upper atmosphere.

"Make the jump to hyperspace, let's get back to Earth," Hawk said through the com. channel via his NI.

As soon as the Valkyrie had reached the edge of Cordoba's atmosphere where the other starship was waiting, they activated the stardrive and both ships made the jump to hyperspace.

Rygar regained control of the attack craft after the explosion caused by the Sabre missiles.

"Damn, they escaped," exclaimed Rover furiously.

"Well, we'd better get away from here ourselves. After you shot down those three Constabulary ships they're bound to send more, probably larger with better weapons," Rygar replied.

Rover contacted Jonas Wilde via a secure com. channel using his NI. "They escaped us, sir, they're probably on their way to Earth by now," he said.

"Good, just as I'd hoped," Wilde said, sounding pleased with himself.

"But you said you wanted them to die," Rover said, perplexed by the contrariness of Wilde's statement.

"And if I'd told you that, then your attack would've illustrated that, but now they've gone exactly where I wanted them to go."

"So what do you want us to do now, sir?"

"Rendezvous with Nemesis right away, she will be leaving

for Earth very soon where the final phase will take place. I'll meet you onboard," Wilde said then broke the connection.

As Rover and Rygar contemplated the complexity of Wilde's revelations, the man in question was smiling as he sat at his desk. His plan had changed along with events in an almost organic way.

He was smiling because, despite all the changes along the way, the outcome was going to be the same, just as he'd planned all along.

He got up and left the room. It would all be over soon.

CHAPTER 16

The Valkyrie and her escort arrived back at Earth and were soon in orbit around the planet that was the centre of the Colonial Confederation and home to nine billion people.

"Here we are, Captain, and don't worry I haven't forgotten my promise to get shore leave for you and your crew. As soon as I've transported Miss Wilde here to Col Sec HQ and reported to General Sinclair I'll mention it to him, I give you my word," Hawk said as he was about to board the shuttle. Captain Jefferson was standing next to him along with Tanya Wilde, Colonel De Boer and his two marines.

"I'm sure you will, Matt, but I have a bad feeling that this isn't over just yet so my men and I will remain on board and at battle readiness just to be on the safe side," Jefferson answered with a dour expression.

"I agree with the captain, this isn't over yet," said De Boer.

"I hate to admit it but I think you're both right. Seeing the lengths Wilde is prepared to go to I can't see him giving up that easily," Hawk agreed.

"Whatever happens now will depend on the results of my

report to General Sinclair so I'd better get on with it," Hawk added, then entered the shuttle followed by the rest of the small party.

They were soon leaving the hold of the Valkyrie and heading towards the planet below. Col Sec HQ was a sprawling complex situated on the site of the ancient United Nations. The Intelligence Division was located in the bowels of the complex several hundred feet below the surface.

The Headquarters had its own spaceport close by which was where the shuttle was headed. Alongside the main complex were the barracks for the security contingent stationed there. Recon Delta marines were the best that Col Sec had, the pride of the military, and it was their duty to protect the Confederation and its people, which included the Confederation HQ where World President Takagi met with dignitaries and members of the various Royal Houses from around the galaxy.

The barracks held only a small contingent from whichever company's turn it was to be stationed there. It was Bravo Company at the moment, or just a small section of it, no more than twenty marines at a time. They rotated every six months depending on the company's duties.

The shuttle landed at the spaceport landing pad where Hawk, Tanya Wilde, Colonel De Boer and the two marines debarked. As they entered the huge building Tanya put a hand on Hawk's arm stopping him and asked, "What happens now, to me I mean?"

Hawk saw her worried expression and smiled to reassure her. Turning to face her he said, "Nothing bad, I promise."

"How can you be so sure? My father has done some terrible things, what's to say some of the blame won't come my way. I'm scared and not just for that but I'm scared because I have no idea what I'll do next."

"Well first off, you don't have to worry about any blame

being attached to you, it simply doesn't work that way, not unless we find some evidence to prove you were party to his actions in some way, an accomplice of some sort either before or after the fact. Considering that you came to us the moment you learned of what your father had done we can safely rule that out. What you do next is quite simple, you come with me to my boss, General Sinclair, and we take your evidence and your statement."

"No, you don't understand, what do I do after that? I have no one and nowhere to go. Since Mom died it's been just Dad and me. Okay, so he wasn't there a whole lot of the time and I mostly had the staff to look after me, but I won't have that now. Dad won't let me return there now; he tried to kill me for Christ's sake. I still can't get over that and I'm rambling again, sorry."

Hawk looked at her, seeing the pain and confusion in her eyes and the bewilderment and fear of an uncertain future.

"You've always had someone to take care of you, haven't you? You've never had to fend for yourself at all, have you?" he asked.

"No," Tanya said almost apologetically.

"Well, you're about to embark on your wildest adventure yet. It's called 'Your Life' and it can be whatever you want it to be," Hawk said, trying to give her spirits the boost they sorely needed.

"That's easy for you to say," she snorted derisively.

"I suppose from your point of view, it is, but it can be for you too. Until your father is apprehended and brought to justice you'll be protected. Your testimony will form the heart of the case so we have to ensure your safety and during that time you can learn what it is to be an independent woman. Once your father has been brought to trial and sent to a penal colony you'll be ready to embark on that adventure I mentioned."

"Will you help me?"

"I will do as much as I'm allowed to, dependent on my duties."

"Will you stay in touch, you know, after, when this is all over I mean?" she asked nervously.

"Do you want me to?"

She nodded her head gently almost afraid in case he declined. "That's settled then, I'll stay in touch," Hawk agreed then caught a disapproving glance from the Colonel who, unnoticed by them, was still close by and listening to every word.

"One step at a time though, let's get this briefing over and done with and then we can all go and get something to eat. You too Colonel, you and your men must be starved, I know I am," Hawk said to get things back on track.

"Now you mention it, I could go for a nice turkey sandwich," De Boer replied with a half-smile, the first time Hawk had seen anything other than his usual dour expression.

"I'm sure we can rustle us all up something like that," Hawk said.

"And a pot of coffee, sir," the marine who had piloted the shuttle added.

"Goes without saying," added Hawk.

"Make mine a cheeseburger, sir, please, and hold the pickle," the second marine said.

"What, a cheeseburger with no pickle?" asked the first marine.

"No pickle," he replied.

"Call yourself a marine?"

"I am a marine."

"Then you'd eat the pickle."

"I don't like the pickle okay, it's no big deal."

"Guys, leave it, we'll order the food when we get to

General Sinclair's office," Hawk said cutting dead any further argument.

Listening to the verbal by-play between these men who had risked their lives to protect hers helped to take her mind off her own fear and by the time they entered the elevator to travel down to the basement sub-levels where the Intelligence Division was situated, she was actually smiling.

NEMESIS WAS a starship that MaxCorp had in the development stage and would be ready for full production within two years after the final rounds of exhaustive tests that would determine her viability as an asset to the Confederation fleet, or so it was thought. In actuality, Wilde had the prototype ready and fully tested.

She was massive, the next-generation carrier and, at over six thousand feet in length and having fifty-five decks she was the largest starship that either the Confederation or the Alliance had ever seen. Able to carry fifty one-man fighter craft housed in drop bays running the length of the craft and with the ability to transport over a thousand troops to a battle zone, she would be an asset to any fleet. Pulse cannons were situated both fore, aft and laterally down port and starboard as well as dorsal and ventral hulls.

Missile tubes were placed alongside these cannons through which she could deliver her load of Sabre, Hammerhead and a variety of other missiles that she carried in the thousands. To defend herself she had not just double hull configuration but triple hull plating and self-sealing bulkheads, which were also protected by primary and secondary shields.

In total, Nemesis was one hell of a threat and OMEGA not only had the only one but also intended to use her.

Rygar and Rover had boarded her before she was about to make her jump to Earth. Wilde had ordered she remain hidden on the far side of Cordoba's moon because the only things they had not yet manufactured were the stealth generators.

Everything else had been rushed through for this deadline but time constraints meant that weapons and defensive shielding were given priority.

Wilde had been on the bridge when Rygar, Rover and the rest of the mercs arrived on board. When they entered they were greeted by the sight of him standing before the huge viewscreen, hands behind his back, as he stared at the scene displayed there.

"Well, we're here, sir," Rygar said when Wilde showed no sign he was even aware of their presence.

Wilde turned around to face them, glanced towards the captain and ordered, "Make the jump."

GENERAL SINCLAIR WAS SITTING behind his large, rather ornate mahogany desk when they entered the office. He immediately rose to his feet when he saw them and came around the side of his desk to greet them, Tanya first.

Standing before her offering her his hand he said, "When Matt informed me of your involvement, Miss Wilde, he never said how lovely you were. It's a pleasure to meet you, my name's General Sinclair. I do hope they took good care of you?"

"Very good care thank you, General," she replied, taking the proffered hand. Before releasing it she asked, "General, what's to become of me?"

"Well, first my dear, we must take your statement and retrieve the evidence from your NI, the call logs of your father and so on so that we may present a full and complete case to the Prosecution Service. Until the case is finalised, and because of your father's recent actions, it may be best if you remain in protective custody until your father is placed under arrest, for your own safety you understand."

"Of course, but what happens after that?"

"I'm not sure I understand but I'm sure we can find the answer to your question. For now, I must insist we continue with the most unpleasant task of building a case against your father," Sinclair said, effectively cutting off any further discussion on the matter. "If you would follow me please, you too gentlemen, then we can get this debrief underway." He led the small group towards the door to his office.

"Sir, is there any chance of us grabbing a bite to eat; I can't remember the last time I ate?" Hawk asked as they left the office.

"I'm sure I can rustle up something," Sinclair replied.

"Make mine a cheeseburger, sir, and hold the pickle," the second marine piped up, then added, "No make that a double cheeseburger with fries, please. I'm starved, sir."

"Again with the 'hold the pickle' thing, some marine you are," commented the first marine.

"Colonel, you have my commiserations on being saddled with this double act," Sinclair said with a half-hidden smile.

"A double act they may be, sir, but they're damn fine marines," De Boer replied with pride.

"I bet they are, Colonel, I bet they are," Sinclair said, his grin more obvious which earned a hasty, "Recon Delta hoorah!" from the double act in question.

As they walked down the brightly lit corridor, Tanya's troubles seemed miles away as she listened to the chatter from the men.

∾

THE NEMESIS RE-ENTERED normal space on the dark side of Earth's Moon. For the time being, they were undetected, not having shown up on any long-range scans from either Earth, the orbiting station or on the Moon itself.

On the bridge, Jonas Wilde stood before the huge viewscreen showing the forward view but could be tuned to show any view from any angle from the starship.

"Have we been detected?" he asked without taking his eyes off the viewscreen.

The ops officer replied, "No sir, but the moment we come from around the dark side of the Moon we'll show up on every scanning station from here to Earth."

"Then we'd better be ready to act the moment we move."

"Aye, sir," replied the ops officer.

Wilde turned away from the viewscreen to face the bridge and the expectant faces watching him. Taking a deep steadying breath he marshalled his thoughts in preparation to giving the command, which, if his plan went as he hoped, would bring Col Sec to its knees and leave the Confederation in chaos. When he spoke his voice was calm and steady and had an even timbre to it, belying the rage built up inside him which was about to be unleashed against the hated Col Sec.

"Captain, deploy your men according to your orders," Wilde said, then turned to Rover and Rygar, "You gentlemen, will have a ringside seat as it were, a reward for your sterling service."

The Captain spoke into the intership com. unit issuing his orders. The fighter pilots were sent to their ships ready to scramble and the gun and missile crews all reported to their respective stations and charged up their weapons systems. The final order was given as Wilde returned his attention to the forward viewscreen.

"Pilot, take us in."

CHAPTER 17

Geneal Sinclair sat at the head of the conference table in his ready room facing the group as they ate the meal he'd had prepared for them and transported from the cafeteria. He thought it would save time if they started the debrief en masse as they ate, foregoing the usual routine of separating them and taking individual reports and later seeing if they matched up to corroborate the overall story. This time he had no doubts that what they said was a fair and accurate account.

While they ate he had a lab tec download all the relevant data for the evidence required from Tanya Wilde's NI. The process was painless and non-invasive, with a link from NI to NI being all that was required.

Satisfied that the events were progressing well and without a hitch, he even afforded himself a wry smile, although that was short-lived as a call from Ops Centre wiped it from his face.

"Sir, we've just received word from our tracking station on the Moon which was confirmed by long-range scanners on Io and our orbiting platforms near Earth. We have an unidentified craft on approach vector. She's not responding to hails, sir, and according to early scans her weapons are hot," said the voice.

Holding up his hand to indicate something was wrong, Sinclair linked the com. channel to the building's com. system accessible to those around the table then said, "Does the craft bear any known recognition codes, markings or energy patterns and does it compare to any known configuration in our data banks?"

Everyone's attention was riveted to the General and the conversation he was having.

"Negative, sir, to all your questions," was not the reply he wanted but it was the one he received.

"Check against any new ships under development," Hawk said. When Sinclair stared at him he explained by adding, "OMEGA has access to the same tec and munitions they provide us with, who's to say a ship under development for us isn't already built and up there now. It could have all sorts of new specifications we don't know about yet."

"I've a feeling we're about to find out," De Boer added.

"How long before she reaches firing range?" Sinclair asked Ops Centre.

"Hard to say for sure, sir. We know nothing about her so we can't be certain what her capabilities are and we won't know until we find her configuration in the database or she comes within our sensor range."

"How the hell did they sneak that one past our sentry sensor posts?" demanded Sinclair angrily.

"I suppose they could've made a precision jump to just behind the Moon where we wouldn't see them. Our SSPs would be tuned to look for craft which we expect to see attacking us, by that I mean they're tuned to seek out and recognise starships from the Alliance, Raiders from various sectors and Outlaws. They're not used to ships coming after us from within our own space," suggested Hawk.

"That will have to be amended as soon as this mess is cleared up. Their range and scope will have to be increased to include all approaching craft of any description that doesn't display the relevant operating codes," Sinclair said confidently. Once the initial shock of the craft's sudden appearance had worn off his usual calm and confident demeanour had returned. He was sure that if this new craft did belong to OMEGA the planetary defences would be able to handle her.

"Operating codes, that could be a problem also, sir. If OMEGA has infiltrated Col Sec as deeply as we think, the codes, in fact, everything, may have to have a complete reboot," suggested Hawk thoughtfully.

The voice from Ops Centre returned to add weight to Hawk's speculation. "Sir we've located the ship's configuration within the folder marked 'Top Secret' subdivision, 'Under Development'. I'm forwarding her specs to you directly."

The ship's specifications were sent to Sinclair's ready room and were shown on the monitor that rose from the centre of the conference table. It had screens on all four sides so that whatever data was shown could be viewed by all who sat around the table.

As the image and specs of the starship were displayed on the screen, Hawk heard Sinclair gasp. Whatever this ship was, the General recognised her and it disturbed him.

"Sir, are you okay?" he asked concerned, for in all the years he'd known the General he'd never seen him react that way.

"Yes I'm fine," was his stilted reply.

"Do you recognise her?"

"It's the Nemesis. She's the blueprint for our new battle

carrier group flagship. We were informed it would be another five years at least before MaxCorp would have a working prototype."

"Seems Jonas Wilde may have pushed the date forward a bit then," added De Boer.

"What're we facing here, sir? What do you know of her capabilities, well those they told you about? If they've got a prototype ready five years sooner than you were told was possible, I would assume that's not all they kept from you," Hawk said.

"Her specs are impressive, at almost six thousand feet she's the largest craft in the fleet. She should have fifty fighters, pulse cannons both fore and aft, as well as down each side and top and bottom, and missile tubes placed similarly. She can carry a thousand marines to the battle zone. They're the things we know about, what else have they packed her with?" Sinclair said.

"There's another way of looking at this, she may not have all her systems online, or at the very least working to full capacity. Think about it, she's in space five years ahead of schedule, so how many corners have they cut to get her here now?" De Boer said, giving them something to think about and hope for the upcoming battle.

"There can be only one purpose for her showing up here like this, they intend to attack. Sir, we need something to counter this threat, and Colonel, I do hope you're right," Hawk said.

"So do I, Matt," De Boer replied, his brow furrowing with lines of deep concern.

"I can't think that Wilde's hatred of me would manifest itself in this fashion," Sinclair said, for a moment lost in thought.

"Excuse me, sir?" Hawk asked confused at the change in topic.

"Years ago Jonas Wilde was under my command, he was Recon Delta and had a promising career, but he began to show signs that he loved brutality more than the Confederation. After a psyche evaluation, he was cashiered out on a medical discharge. He was deemed unsuitable material for a Recon Delta officer. He didn't take it very well; on the day he left he swore revenge on me. I took it as just an idle threat from a man who was embarrassed about his situation, a spur of the moment thing. I never for a second thought he meant any of it," explained Sinclair.

"Well, I guess him showing up with the Nemesis shows he did mean it after all," Hawk said.

"An understatement if ever there was one," agreed Sinclair, then regaining his focus said, "Ops Centre, scramble all fighters and recall the closest starships to Earth, inform them we're under attack. Alert all orbiting defence platforms, bring them up to Battle Stations and do it now before they try to jam our transmissions."

"I'm on it, sir."

"How much of a threat is she, sir? I mean she's not built to function inside the planet's atmosphere surely?" De Boer asked.

"Not that I'm aware, but her fighters are and the planet's surface is within range of her missiles and pulse cannons and I'm not quite sure what his target will be," Sinclair replied, pondering the thought.

"One ship against an entire planet does seem a little one-sided on our part but there must be more to it, there has to be," commented Hawk.

"My Dad never does anything without good reason, he's not impulsive. Whatever he's doing now is something he's had planned for some time," Tanya said, speaking up for the first time since ordering her meal. As all eyes turned to her she added, "Trust me, he'll have a reason for all this."

Hawk said, "We know what his reason is, Tanya." Turning to Sinclair he asked, "Sir, you said his hatred of you, what exactly did you mean by that?"

"When he received his medical discharge he took it personally, he blamed me," Sinclair answered.

"You, personally? That makes a little more sense now," Hawk said as he tried to put the pieces together. He had wondered for a long time what the motives were behind Wilde's actions going right back to the very first time they encountered the original clone. Now he thought he understood it a bit better.

"Sir, I think this whole thing, going back to when I brought that clone here from the chamber, has been about revenge, with you as the focus," he said. Turning to Tanya he asked, "Think back to conversations you've had with your father or you've overheard from him, has he ever bemoaned his time in Col Sec?"

"How do you mean?" she asked not sure where he was going with this, or what it had to do with what was happening right now.

"You know, has he ever said things like 'If it hadn't been for Col Sec I'd be, whatever' or 'If I hadn't spent so much time in Col Sec I'd be...' that sort of thing," Hawk explained.

"A few times, but I don't know how that helps," she admitted.

"It helps us understand his mindset and from that, we can maybe work out his intentions," Hawk said. "Sir, I think he probably blames Col Sec for certain things he sees as not going right in his life, and with you being in command you could be the focus, his main target. In his evaluation was he borderline psychotic with sociopathic tendencies?"

"I believe so, yes."

"Then his interests will be self-centred and he will view himself as being superior to all others. His interests, his opinions and his purpose will be the only things relevant to him and are the only things he'll give precedence to. He's using those pent-up ill feelings and frustration towards Col Sec to fuel this scheme and I wouldn't be surprised if he planned to attack Col Sec itself and, seeing you as the focus, the target will be this building."

"How can you be so sure?" asked Tanya.

"Your father arranged for us to capture one of his clones, probably leaked the Intel to us either directly or via a third party. We duly brought him here to be interrogated. That was probably just a test to see if we'd take the bait and bring the clone back here."

"Why though? That piece of the puzzle has been bothering me from the start," asked Sinclair.

"I have a theory that Wilde arranged for us to capture the clone so we'd bring him back here to see if they could track him. All Recon Delta marines have a tracking chip in their NI, as do all top-level staff at Col Sec, so why not assume that Wilde had the same for all OMEGA staff. I would guess that Miss Wilde here has one too and I'd bet anything that Wilde is going to use that signal to target the Nemesis' weapons."

"Are you suggesting he'd use his own daughter as some sort of laser pointer to paint the target?" Sinclair asked.

"But if he wanted her here why did he try to kill us all before we left Cordoba? It doesn't make sense," De Boer said, unable to see past the small details for the moment and view the larger overall scheme of things.

Hawk took on board what the Colonel said, seeing the rationale behind it, then the truth dawned on him as another piece of the puzzle fell into place.

"It makes perfect sense. If he wanted Tanya here for the purpose I've suggested, what's the best way to ensure she got here? Make us think he was trying to kill her, and knowing she was carrying data vital to the case against him, he knew that we would do everything we could to keep her safe, to the point of bringing her to the safest location, probably in the galaxy – Confederation HQ," he explained with a look that said they were in real trouble.

"Are you saying then that the attack on our shuttle was staged, because it felt damn real to me?" De Boer said still not convinced.

"Oh no, it was real enough, he probably told his men to kill us so it would appear genuine."

"And if they'd succeeded?"

"Oh no doubt it would've slowed him down but I'm sure only momentarily. I feel certain he'd have a backup plan or at the very least an idea he could utilise. He seems very organised, structured almost to the point of being anal, but I wonder if he's had to adapt this plan of his or if this is exactly what he wanted, what he planned all along."

"What's the difference, either way, we're screwed," interjected the first marine.

"Not quite, if this is his plan and it's going along as he predicted it means he's logical, methodical and he's foreseen every step we'll make and he's planned a counter move like a chess grandmaster. If that's so, then we can use that to our advantage," answered Hawk.

"How?" asked the marine.

"By doing something unpredictable, something he can't have planned for," Hawk explained.

"And if it's the second option?" asked the second marine.

"We could have a problem. If he's adapted his plan to changes we've made then it shows he's not only a brilliant strategist but able to think on his feet and come up with solutions to problems as they present themselves. Stopping him could be tough."

"Like I said, we're screwed," the first marine said.

"Not at all, I said it could be tough, I didn't say it would be impossible," Hawk replied optimistically.

Before anyone could say anything further the building began to tremble and they all heard a loud explosion seemingly from a distance but close enough to be heard and felt. They felt the floor move beneath their feet and the walls shake as bits of mortar and plascrete began to shower down on them.

Sinclair looked at Hawk and said, "It's started."

CHAPTER 18

In close approach to Earth, the Nemesis chose a geosynchronous orbit that would place her over Confederation HQ so they could target their weapons onto the building directly. Her primary shields kept her safe from the orbiting platforms that had been manoeuvred into position to defend the planet. A well-aimed Hammerhead missile took out the nearest platform then three more took out the remaining ones. Luckily they were automated platforms so no lives were lost when they were destroyed. That couldn't be said for when the Nemesis turned her weapons towards the planet itself. Once the pulse cannons were targeted at the Headquarters building and began to fire, the loss of life was devastatingly high.

The first salvo destroyed the entire top three floors of the building; two hundred and twenty-four lives were snuffed out in a blink of an eye. The only saving grace being that they died instantly with no knowledge or fear of it happening and no pain when it did. They died mercifully swiftly. That couldn't be said for those who died after that. They all knew it was coming so they died in pure terror and ungodly agony as the building was razed to the ground, one level at a time, slowly, methodically and with absolutely no regard whatsoever for the lives that would be lost in the implementation of this act.

The devastating attack was felt throughout the building right down to the sub-basement levels where the Intelligence Division was housed.

"We need to mount some kind of defence or at the very least get you to a safe location," suggested De Boer.

"And where would you suggest, Colonel? I can think of no safer place than right here, that is until about five minutes ago," Sinclair retorted.

"The Colonel's right, sir. The problem is if they're using Tanya's NI to track and target, no matter where you go they'll find you. We need a way to jam the signal," Hawk said.

Sinclair said, "I've got Tec Division working on that along with other problems since we learned that OMEGA had the same tec and munitions as we do, to try and navigate around that problem and give us some kind of edge."

"Isn't that like shutting the stable door after the horse has bolted, sir?" commented De Boer.

"Hopefully not. Let's go see what they've come up with," Sinclair said.

CAPTAIN JEFFERSON WAS SITTING in the command chair on the bridge of the Valkyrie watching the huge battle carrier approach the Earth as she prepared to enter a geosynchronous orbit over the Confederation Headquarters building.

"Jesus H Christ sir, look at the size of her," exclaimed the pilot.

"She sure is impressive, never seen or heard of a ship like

her before, hope to God she's one of ours," Jefferson said in awe of the monster before them.

"Should we scan them, sir?" asked ops.

"I'm sure Col Sec know what they're doing," Jefferson replied.

"Sir, I'm reading the orbiting defence platforms just went hot and are targeting the new bird and Tiger squadron has just scrambled," ops said urgently as his instruments came alive before him.

"What the..." exclaimed Jefferson as he leaned forward in his seat, his gaze fixed on the forward viewscreen. He watched as the Nemesis fired Hammerhead missiles at the orbiting defence platforms destroying all four then, unbelievably, the huge ship's pulse cannons began firing towards the planet's surface.

"Sir, they're firing on Confederation HQ," ops said.

"What do we do, sir?" the pilot asked urgently.

Jefferson sat back in his chair a feeling of helplessness overwhelming him. His ship was fast and powerful for her size but to attempt to go up against the monster facing them would be like an ant facing off against an elephant, they would get trampled without the elephant even being aware of the ant's existence.

With reluctance, he said, "Against that thing, what can we do?"

THE TEC DIVISION was on the same sub-level as the Intelligence Division so it was just a short walk – a very rushed walk – along a few corridors until they reached their destination.

When they entered the large room it resembled a factory more than a tec lab. There were workbenches laid out along the entire length of the long room, strewn with equipment and devices of all shapes and sizes that were in various stages of repair.

A man wearing a lab coat, the same as all the tec guys working there, came to greet them at the door, a worried expression on his face.

Tall and slim with thinning hair combed across his pate and with ocular implants, he looked every inch the geek he obviously was; yet the straight back and military bearing gave the opposite impression.

"General, what the devil is happening, are we under attack?" he asked in a voice that showed the strain they were all under.

"Yes, Major Purvis, we indeed are under attack and that is why we are here to see if your efforts can help us," Sinclair answered.

"We've made some progress, sir, but I'm not sure how it'll help against an invasion."

"Show us, then we'll decide if it'll be of any use to us."

"Come this way, sir," Purvis said as he turned back into the room and led them over to his workstation. "When you informed me of what OMEGA had in terms of the same tec as us, I went back to basics as it were. If they have Neural Interfaces like us there's a good chance they could access our com. satellites, channels and even the battle com., so like I said, I've gone back to basics. I designed this ear bug which, when placed inside the ear, enables you to communicate with anyone else using the same network. It will be isolated from the usual networks and double encrypted so there will be little or no chance of your com. chatter being intercepted. In time we can have them implanted inside the ear canal for safety reasons. As I'm sure you're aware, placing them inside the ear means they could be dislodged with vigorous activity."

"Impressive," said Hawk. "Anything else?" he added.

"I'm not sure, we've got a few things under development but nothing quite ready."

"We need something to combat that huge ship or something that would help get a team onboard," Hawk said.

"I might be able to get you onboard," Tanya said and they all turned to look at her as if they'd forgotten she was there.

"Excuse me?" De Boer said incredulously.

"I... er... can get you onboard; well I can get you through the shields if they're similar to those at the MaxCorp building where Dad works. I don't know about the locks on the docking bays but then again if they're the same principle as my Dad's office then I can get you in those as well. Why are you all staring at me like I've gone mad?" Tanya said in that rambling, breathless way of hers.

Hawk came over to reassure her and said, "It's okay Tanya, we don't think you're mad, we're just not sure you quite grasp the complexity of the situation."

"Why, 'cause I'm a girl? Listen, my NI allows me access to areas in the MaxCorp building that only top-level managerial staff members have. Dad made sure I could go wherever I wanted if I needed to speak to or see him. Some areas are shielded to keep out those not authorised but I can just walk through them. My NI has a recognition code embedded within it, which negates the security protocols embedded in the shields or locks. Now if they're the same on the ship, and I have no reason to think he'd change them, then I should be granted access," she said, showing she had a firmer grasp of the situation than they had assumed.

"This might work," Hawk said and then turned to Purvis, "I need as many of these com. bugs as you have." Finally to De Boer, he said, "Fancy a trip into the belly of the beast Colonel?"

"Hell yeah!" came the rousing reply from him and the two marines.

"Assemble your team, Colonel, you'll need at least a full squad," Sinclair said. "I'll contact Jefferson on the Valkyrie to stand by, he can transport you onto the Nemesis."

Hawk turned back to Purvis to ask, "Is there any way you could extract those recognition codes from Tanya's NI?"

"I'd have to log onto the NI and search through all the codes written on it, but there's no telling which would be the right one. It could take some time but I'm sure I could do it if Miss Wilde wouldn't mind. I may have to extract the NI for an in-depth search," Purvis said with a thoughtful expression.

"Time is something we don't have, she goes with you," Sinclair said with a tone that brooked no argument.

"I can't ask her to do that, she's a civilian," Hawk argued.

"You don't have to ask, I'm ordering you to take her with you."

"Again with the 'she's a civilian.' You can order me but not her. If she says no then she stays here and we figure something else out."

"What 'something else', there is no 'something else'. We're right out of options, Matt, you know that as well as I do."

"You don't have to ask, I'll go," Tanya said virtually stepping in between the two men whose voices were getting louder and angrier with each new word, or so it seemed to her.

She'd had men fight over her before, well, argue really, they never actually came to blows, but this was different. This was important, life or death important, and not just who she would dance with first. This was how many lives will it save important, and she had no hesitation in saying yes. Was she afraid? Not yet but she was sure that would change sooner rather than later. She was also sure that these men, especially the dishy, tall, broad-shouldered one, Matt, would keep her safe from harm no matter what, she knew that.

So really there was nothing to be afraid of, except fear itself.

Hawk, Sinclair and the rest of them turned to look at her, "What, have I just grown another head or something?" she asked suddenly nervous under their scrutiny.

"Are you sure you want to do this?" Hawk asked, concern causing deep furrows across his brow, his ice-blue eyes intensely boring into her to see if she had the strength to do what would be asked of her if she went along.

"The General's right, you're out of options and short on time. You have to take me along," she replied earnestly. "Do I want to go, quite frankly, no, but I can't allow my father to go through with this, he's done enough harm already and it has to stop."

"Okay then," Hawk said, smiling to reassure her and also feeling quite proud of her for showing some steel, "I don't like it, but it seems we have to go.

Sinclair smiled at her also, like a father who was proud of his daughter's achievements.

De Boer placed a beefy hand on her shoulder and softly said, "Don't worry girl, we'll make sure you're okay, no harm will come to you while we're at your side."

She looked up into his stern countenance and said, "You'd better not let anything happen to me, I've got plans for when this is all over," then leaning into him she whispered, "but don't tell him, I don't want to scare him off," indicating Hawk with a slight nod of her head.

De Boer smiled, the first time she'd seen it and he said, "Don't worry Miss, I'll personally make sure he turns up for whatever you have in mind."

"Tanya, call me Tanya please."

"My pleasure, Tanya."

～

WILDE PACED the width of the bridge watching the forward viewscreen as the Nemesis' pulse cannons fired down towards the planet's surface.

Tanis Rygar, the Rover5 and what was left of the mercenaries, all stood at the rear of the room watching the events unfold on the viewscreen.

"Sir, we have incoming fighters, it's the Tiger squadron based at Col Sec HQ," said ops.

"Launch all our fighters, wipe them out then continue firing at the HQ, raze that building to the ground," Wilde replied coldly. Briefly turning to Rygar he said, "You and your men take two troop carriers full of my new Rover5s and head down to the HQ, make sure they're all dead. I want no survivors, is that clear?"

"Yes, sir," Rygar said, then just as he was about to leave Wilde halted him by saying, "No wait, if General Sinclair is still breathing, bring him here to me."

"What about your daughter, sir, shall I bring her too?"

"Only if she's alive, if she gives you any trouble, kill her."

CHAPTER 19

The destruction of the Confederation Headquarters building was unrelenting. Wave after wave, salvo upon salvo of high-intensity pulsed plasma bolts pounded down, blasting it with each consecutive strike. More and more of the building was blasted away until finally the firing stopped and the once proud edifice that had stood tall for everyone to see, embodying the hopes, wishes and ideals, everything that the Confederation stood for, was nothing more than a burnt-out wreck.

The loss of life was horrendous; hundreds died in the first few seconds of the attack and then more died as the panic set in and escape became the only thought the survivors could think of. Like lemmings, many hurled themselves from sections that had been destroyed, through windows or walls blasted open to the air and to certain death below. Many more were crushed in the mad rush for any exit that seemed a possibility, making it nothing more than a panic-fuelled stampede.

The true death toll would not be known for many weeks, maybe even months, after the attack when all the names could be correlated with the remaining body parts. DNA would have to be used where no recognisable evidence remained. The final count was bound to be in the thousands.

Deep in the bowels of the building Hawk, De Boer, his marines and Tanya Wilde were still with Sinclair when the call from Ops Centre came through.

"Sir, the Nemesis has stopped firing."

"What's happening up there?" Sinclair asked urgently.

"Tiger squadron has scrambled and is engaging Nemesis but they are outnumbered, sir, by the fighters onboard the carrier."

"Where's our backup?"

"Only the Justice and the Legend were within range, sir, and should arrive in five minutes."

"But they're just light battlecruisers, they'll be no match for the Nemesis," Hawk said both shocked and angry at Col Sec's complacent belief in its own invincibility that had left them so undefended against such a formidable enemy. One life lost was one too many and he dreaded to think how many would be lost before this day was done. He wondered if mankind ever truly learnt anything from mistakes made by former generations or were they fated to keep repeating the same ones ad infinitum.

"All the more reason for you to get on board her and do whatever you can to stop this," Sinclair said with finality in his voice, leaving them in no doubt what he meant by 'whatever you can'."

"Sir, we have two incoming craft, Hurricane C230 troop carriers, headed straight for us, ETA ninety seconds," Ops Centre reported.

"This just keeps getting better and better," commented Hawk sardonically.

"Inform the garrison to expect incoming hostiles and to

take whatever steps required to defend this building," Sinclair ordered.

"This is a new development," observed De Boer. "Why send troops down here when they could blast us from orbit?" he added questioningly.

"Does seem a bit like overkill to me," agreed Hawk.

"You're not going to be able to leave by normal exits before they arrive so you'd better utilise the secondary emergency exit tunnels and you should go now," Sinclair said.

De Boer said, "We're still waiting for the rest of my team to arrive so we can be equipped and then leave on the shuttle, sir."

"Contact them and order them to get their asses down here *now*," Sinclair said angrily.

THE GARRISON MARINES from Recon Delta Bravo Company mobilised the moment the attack began. All twenty of them were suited up in battle gear, including the Rapier Mk III battle tec helmet, and were armed with the Sig P996, standard-issue sidearm and the Remm assault rifle.

Hopelessly outnumbered against the approaching OMEGA shock troops they began to mount a defence.

TIGER SQUADRON CAME at the Nemesis from all angles, swaying and twisting through intricate manoeuvres to outfox the defending Nova fighters.

Firing their pulse cannons at both the attacking Nova fighters and the Nemesis when the opportunity presented itself, they fought a desperate dogfight against overwhelming odds, displaying bravery seldom equalled.

The pilots, some of the best that Col Sec had to offer, showed their true worth by destroying ten of the Nova fighters in the first skirmish without even taking a hit, but then greater numbers began to take their toll and Tiger squadron began to lose numbers.

Although they scored numerous hits against the Nemesis, their pulse cannons were no match for the battle carrier's primary shields and again, although they reduced the Nova fighters numbers by over half they found themselves decimated within five minutes. Out of the twelve fighters who took off from the landing field next to Confederation HQ all but one was gone and he made a suicide run against the Nemesis. Taking out two more Nova fighters on his end run he smashed his craft into Nemesis' shields just above the bridge.

Wilde watched impassively as the last fighter came hurtling towards them aimed, so it seemed, directly at him. As the fighter died in the explosion of the collision against the primary shields he turned to ops and said, "Recall all remaining fighters and the moment our two troop carriers are within landing range of their target cease firing against the primary target. They'll no doubt have recalled some starships, so keep long-range sensors on standby. The moment they arrive I want all weapons targeted on them ready to open fire on my command."

COLONEL DE BOER assembled his team from Recon Delta marines who were already in the building; he had no other resources to call upon. There were twelve available, either in the training area or being debriefed, so he split them into two teams. He had six join him at Tec Division and ordered the remainder topside to help with the defence of whatever was left. They were to report to the officer in charge of the garrison on arrival.

They were still en route via the express alternative escape tunnel when the C230 troop carriers came in to land.

The garrison was equipped with a rotating M570 pulse cannon with a missile launcher. The commander had it manned the second they were alerted. Two marines operated it, one to fire the pulse cannon from a seat he was strapped into directly behind the grips with which he would control the huge weapon. Above this control was a screen that he used to target the cannon using computer-enhanced sensor sighting. He could lock onto a target in a variety of ways and be sure he would hit what he aimed at.

The second marine sat below him and, using the same method, would target the missiles that were housed in racks below and on either side of the huge cannon.

They started to fire the pulse cannon as soon as the first C230 was within range. The pulsed plasma bolts lanced through the dust-laden air towards the incoming troop carrier. The first salvo struck the portside engine housing as the two engines tilted into a downward thrust position. The explosion rocked the transport and the pilot almost lost control as the starboard wing dipped drastically as the opposite wing, now minus the main engine, was thrown upwards by the force of the explosion.

Sabre missiles, fired from the ground, streaked towards their target closing the gap almost quicker than the eye could blink.

Seeing their transport was in danger, the Rover5s on board took the initiative and started descending to the ground over two hundred feet below on zip lines.

The second C230 saw the danger awaiting them and opened fire on the ground-based pulse cannon/missile launcher with their own pulse cannons mounted above and below the pilot's station.

Pulsed plasma bolts raked the ground in a deadly trail leading to their target, destroying the plascrete before striking the weapon and destroying it in an explosion which ignited the Sabre missiles making its destructive force at least ten times more than it would've been.

The blast killed the two marines manning the weapon, the six who had just arrived from the remains of the Headquarters building and at least four more who were nearby but not before the Sabre missiles fired from beneath the cannon found their target.

The C230 was blown clear out of the sky killing the crew and the twenty Rover5s who didn't make it to the ground. The remaining C230 came in to hover so that its compliment of fifty Rover5s could descend to the ground. They were given covering fire from the turret pulse cannons and the thirty Rover5s who had exited the doomed first C230.

The remaining fourteen Recon Delta marines stood little chance caught out in the open like that against such overwhelming odds and superior firepower. They were blasted to pieces in minutes hardly slowing the advance of the incoming force of Rover5s led by Tanis Rygar and his mercs.

Within a few minutes of landing, they were entering the ruined Headquarters.

Purvis had supplied Hawk, De Boer, his marines and Tanya with com. bugs as the six other marines arrived. They too were quickly given the com. bugs, instructed on their use and what the intended mission was.

"Sir, the garrison topside has been completely overrun. We now have eighty hostiles en route to your location," Ops

Centre said. Ops Centre was situated on the first sub-level so the Rover5s led by Tanis Rygar would reach them first. Being just one section on that sub-level, the people manning the centre had no idea what purpose the invading force had and so remained at their posts.

"Understood, I suggest you vacate your posts now, seek an exit route that is unoccupied and make your way to the surface," Sinclair offered.

"Not possible sir, the hostiles have split up into teams, they're covering each and every exit tunnel. Seems they've done their homework, sir, and they've come prepared," replied Ops Centre.

"Then lock all the doors and barricade yourselves inside. I'm not sure what their intentions are but arm yourselves just in case. If they want to cripple us they will need to cut all communications with the outside world and beyond, so the defence of your section becomes paramount, at least until reinforcements get here to render assistance. I'm sorry to ask this of you, what's your name son?"

"Lieutenant William Severs, sir," replied the young man, his voice firm and steady.

"Okay Lieutenant, the continuation of Col Sec could hinge on your efforts here today and I know this is not what you and your people signed on for but you know what is needed here," Sinclair said, trying to impart the seriousness of the situation to him and what was at stake here.

"Sir, I'm Recon Delta, as was my father and his father, six generations in fact, so I won't let you down, sir," Severs said firmly, adding proudly, "and neither will my people, sir."

His voice almost catching, Sinclair said, "Good luck then."

"You too, sir. We'll keep this link open for as long as possible and as secure as we can, for now, Ops Centre out."

"How long before the Justice and Legend get here?" De Boer asked.

"Three minutes and counting," Sinclair replied after glancing at the chronometer on his wrist.

"Not before the hostiles reach Ops Centre. Let's hope Severs can hold out otherwise our communications will go out and so will our sensors. We won't know where the hostiles are, what's happening topside or be able to call for reinforcements when they get here, we'll be deaf, dumb and blind," Hawk said to hammer home the situation.

"Is it too late to ask for a transfer to another unit Colonel?" asked the first marine.

"Life in Recon Delta is more than a job marine, it's an adventure, I thought you knew that," De Boer replied with a half-smile. He knew what these guys were like and he knew he could count on them. After serving with them for the past five years they were more than just his team, his men, they were family. They might bitch about it from time to time but he could count on them to get the job done.

"Hell, yeah, sir," both marines replied in unison to which the six new additions nodded their heads in agreement, smiling along with their two brothers in arms.

"If they're after a specific target then once they've reached it and completed their objective they'll bug out, sir. On the other hand, if this is a cleaning exercise then we're all in danger," Hawk said, leaning in closer to Sinclair so the tec guys and Tanya wouldn't hear.

"Which do you think it is, Matt?" Sinclair asked in the same fashion.

"Going by the systematic way they've destroyed everything so far I'd have to say the second option, sir. I think they're under orders not to leave anyone alive. They want to cripple Col Sec, sir," Hawk replied grimly.

Sinclair nodded his head in agreement then contacted Lieutenant Severs at Ops Centre once more. "Contact the Justice and Legend and inform them of the situation. Tell them to send reinforcements down here the second they jump from hyperspace. Also, contact any other craft en route here and tell them if they don't arrive in five minutes or under there'll be nothing to defend," he said.

"Aye, sir, the 'mayday' has been transmitting since we were under attack and I've been in contact with both the Legend and Justice supplying them with constant updates also," replied Severs competently.

"Good work, Lieutenant," complimented Sinclair.

De Boer stepped forward to speak. Whilst Sinclair had been talking to Hawk and Ops Centre he had been in conversation via his NI. "Sir I've been in contact with General Courtney of Bravo Company at Fort Bragg. He's sending reinforcements as we speak. A flight of F260s will be here in minutes followed by troop carriers, that's the best they can do at short notice for a rapid response."

"It'll do for a start and might actually help if we can hold on long enough," Sinclair said. "Good work, Colonel."

"Sir, we're going to have to move, we don't want to get trapped down here," Hawk said. He turned to Purvis and asked, "What weapons have you got down here, Major?"

"Just the usual sidearms, nothing more than a few Sigs I'm afraid," replied the head of Tec Division.

"The test range isn't far from here and only one floor up, so if we hurry we could get there before any of the hostiles reach the lower levels. We need as many weapons as we can get hold of if we want at least a chance of getting out of this alive," suggested Hawk.

"Okay, listen up people, we're moving out now. Leave everything that's not absolutely essential. Have no illusions people, this is going to be dangerous. We're going up against an enemy determined to wipe us out so you must do whatever we say, when we say it. There will be no arguments, questions or discussions. If you want to survive then your lives are in these gentlemen's experienced and very capable hands. Okay, enough talk, Matt and Colonel De Boer, over to you," Sinclair said.

Hawk looked at the Colonel and said, "Okay I'll take point with you two," pointing at the two marines who'd been part of their original team, then continued, "followed by you Colonel with three of the new recruits, then the General, Tanya, Major Purvis and his team with the final three marines protecting the rear. Hopefully, we should be able to protect them and get past the hostiles."

"Which route do you intend to use, Matt?" asked Sinclair, confident in the abilities of his men.

"Once we reach the test range and arm ourselves better we can take the nearest exit tunnel. Whichever we choose we'll meet opposition and have to fight our way past, it goes without saying. I can't see us being able to navigate around them and seeing as they have the same tec as us they'll probably try to tap into our com. chatter via their NIs, so we could use that knowledge to our advantage and keep our real com. chatter private using the new com. bugs."

"Sounds like a plan," agreed De Boer.

"I concur," added Sinclair who continued by saying, "Okay people the quicker we get going the sooner we can reach safety. Let's go!"

The marines checked the battery clips in their Sig P996s then they turned to Hawk, who it seemed had been delegated commander of this deadly situation, trusted to lead them all to safety.

"You heard the man, let's go," he said.

CHAPTER 20

Tanis Rygar marshalled the squad of Rover5s under his command at the ruins of the Confederation Headquarters. Visibility was down to a hundred feet or so due to the dust- saturated air from the destruction of the massive building. Holding up a small palm pad he accessed the Nemesis' sensors via his NI and had the results displayed on the pad's screen. The scans showed all fifteen emergency exit tunnels and, holding up his hand to gain the attention of his squad, Rygar said, "Split up into teams, one to each of the fifteen exit tunnels. Go down and clear each level as you come to it. I want Sinclair and Tanya Wilde alive, to be taken back to the Nemesis with us. Is that clear?" When he received affirmatives from everyone he added, "Okay people, you have your orders, carry them out."

The Rover5 who had been assigned to Rygar when they attacked Hawk and his team in the shuttle on Cordoba, stepped up to him and said, "Wouldn't it be better to set charges at the entrances to all but one of the tunnels, blow and block them then all of us can go down the last tunnel?

They'll be trapped down there and we can just go in and kill them all."

Rygar looked at him thoughtfully, glanced at some of the other Rover5s, then asked, "Are you the one who was with us on Cordoba because I can't tell you apart from the rest of them? Do you have a name?"

"I am simply a Rover5."

"No, that won't do, won't do at all. From now on you're Adam, okay? Yeah, you're Adam. I don't know what the rest of your brothers' names are just yet, but you're Adam and no, it wouldn't be better to dam all the entrances up. All it would do is create work. Wilde wants us to kill everyone we come across. It's much easier to sweep each floor as we go and each tunnel to each floor. If we block the entrance from up here they could hide in the blocked tunnels and we'd have to clear each floor then go back up the tunnel for stragglers; more work. No, we sweep as we go, is that clear Adam?"

"But..."

"No 'buts', do your job. I'm in command, so follow your orders," snapped Rygar angrily, he hated having his authority questioned. He'd had problems like that when he was in the Elysium Alliance as a Black Knight, but since leaving and working for himself, then OMEGA, that problem hadn't arisen. His men knew better than to question him and these Rover5s would just have to learn the same lesson.

Adam looked hard at Rygar with the cold opaline eyes that they all had, giving away nothing. He was about to say something when Rygar drew his Sig P996 and shot him right between the eyes. Adam's head was blown apart by the full power, pulsed plasma bolt at close range in a mist of blood and shredded brain matter.

"I said no 'buts' didn't I?" Rygar said coldly. Turning slowly to look at the other clones gathered around he asked, "Anyone else with any questions, suggestions, anything?"

The clones all stared at him impassively, silently and Rygar holstered his Sig and said, "Thought not, now let's go, we've got a job to do." As they began to move off he added, "What a waste of a good name, now I can't tell any of the bastards apart."

∾

HAWK LED the small group up to the next level as fast as he could, spurred on by the knowledge that if they didn't reach the test range and retrieve some more firepower then their chances of getting out of this ranged from slim to none. The loss of all those lives was something he would just not allow, not while he still had an ounce of breath left in his body.

As they reached the next level they weren't surprised to see it was deserted, all non-essential personnel having evacuated the building via one of the fifteen exit tunnels the moment the alarm had been raised. The computer would have sent out the evacuation order to each NI so there was no need for klaxons or sirens, everyone would know what was happening and where to go. For some reason, this hadn't happened to those in close proximity of Tanya Wilde, a fact that was beginning to dawn on Matt Hawk.

Touching his right ear to activate the com. bug Hawk said, "General Sinclair, what's the security protocol for evacuation procedures?"

"The computer sends out the evacuation order to each individual NI informing personnel of the situation, it's fast and ensures everyone is informed simultaneously which gives people a better chance of survival. Why do you ask?" replied Sinclair, his voice quiet yet distinct in Hawk's ear.

"Because I never got the order and, I suspect, neither did anyone in our group," Hawk stated.

"Now you mention it, I didn't either and until now, it never occurred to me," Sinclair admitted.

"We *were* rather busy, sir. I'm not sure if it's relevant or significant but it does explain why we saw no one as we left Tec Division and why this level is deserted, but it doesn't explain why we or Tec Division didn't get the call."

"What makes you think they didn't?"

"Because the first thing Major Purvis said to you was 'what was happening' and 'were we under attack' remember, sir? If he'd received the call, chances are he wouldn't have even been there to meet us."

"Of course you're right, what do you think it means?"

"I'm not sure, but I'm leaning towards the supposition that if Wilde was using Tanya's NI to target us that somehow he used that proximity sensor to send down a localised jamming signal just so that we wouldn't be warned like the rest. He didn't stop us from using the com. channels though, whether that was by design or beyond the frequency or power I suppose we'll never know. It's just a theory sir, like I said," Hawk finished, bringing the group to a halt, they had arrived at the test range.

"DON'T UNDERSTAND THIS," Rygar said to himself as he viewed the sensor readings relayed to his palm pad. There were a few life signs down in the lower levels, a few isolated in a group on the first sub-level but, apart from that, nothing, the entire lower levels were deserted. He knew warnings would have gone out, that was standard operating procedure for any life-threatening situation but he had thought because Wilde had ordered so many of his troops down here to kill everyone left that there would be more targets, a point he was about to clarify with the man himself.

"Sir, the building is deserted apart from a small group moving up from the lower levels and another in the first sub-level," he said through a com. channel opened via his NI.

"The first sub-level will be where the Ops Centre is and the other group will be General Sinclair and my daughter. Send half your force to shut down Ops Centre and you take the rest and capture General Sinclair and my daughter, the rest you can kill. My original order about my daughter still stands, kill her if she gives you a problem and do it fast Rygar, reinforcements are on their way," Wilde replied not really answering the question that Rygar didn't really ask. Deciding against further probing he chose to take the matter up at a later date and concentrate instead on the task at hand.

Dividing his troops he said, "You lot take Ops Centre on sub-level one, shut it down and kill everyone there, the rest of you with me. The man in charge wants General Sinclair and his daughter alive, the rest are expendable. Let's move out."

As THEY ENTERED the test range again they encountered a totally silent and empty room. Spacious and lengthy, the test range comprised of long aisles with one person-sized booths at one end with a small ledge for the weapons being tested to be placed upon prior to firing, so the user could familiarise themselves with it. At the far end of each aisle were targets placed on a simple hook attached to an overhead rail that ran down the length of the aisle.

Along both walls at the front end where the shooter would stand were an assortment of pistols, rifles and battery clips held in racks lined up like soldiers on parade.

"Help yourselves to whatever you're familiar with or whatever you think you can handle," Hawk said as the marines rushed to the racks. "I want everyone armed with at least a pistol, so if you're not sure how to use it one of the marines or myself will instruct you. Make sure you have at least two spare battery clips for each weapon you choose," Hawk instructed.

Sinclair grabbed a Sig P996 for himself and one for Tanya. "Here you are my dear," he said as he handed her the pistol, "it's quite simple to operate." He ejected the battery clip from the butt, rammed it back home with the palm of his hand, pulled back on the slide on top to prime the weapon, then turned the selector by the thumb position on the butt to 'Full Power'. "See, simple, it has to be for marines to be able to handle it under fire. To use it just point it at the enemy and fire until they fall down," he added trying to make it seem easier than it was so she would feel better about carrying and perhaps having to use a lethal weapon.

Following his lead, she did as she had been shown then once the pistol had been primed she sighted down the barrel holding it in a two-handed grip and at arm's length. "I see what you mean," she said smiling self-consciously.

"Right people, we need to get moving," Hawk said as he strapped on a second shoulder holster holding another Sig P996. He had a Remm Mk III assault rifle slung over his other shoulder. On the belt around his waist were pouches filled with spare battery clips. The pouches had contacts inside connected to a small recharging unit integral in the belt. When the clips were in the pouches they would constantly recharge supplying the modern marine with an almost inexhaustible supply of ammunition.

Looking around at the expectant faces before him he saw people who were looking to him for leadership and guidance to get them through the next few moments and on to safety. Only two men had enough experience to see the situation clearly.

Colonel De Boer understood the chain of command and that in situations such as this only one voice was needed, one leader to give commands and clear directions. In this case, he realised that Matt Hawk was in charge here not because of rank but because it was an extension of an operation that was still ongoing. General Sinclair understood the same and looked on with pride.

Seeing those faces watching him, Hawk knew he couldn't let them down. He would do everything in his power to lead them to safety.

"Okay people, let's move out," he said with calm determination.

∼

Lieutenant Severs had initiated a complete lockdown of the Ops Centre. All three entrances to the circular room were locked securely with force fields in place to ensure no one could gain access.

Another step he took to ensure the safety of the men and women under his command was to arm them all. Everyone was issued with a Sig P996 and, as standard operating procedure, the two security guards, also Recon Delta marines were armed with Remm Mk III assault rifles.

Severs positioned all his personnel in the middle of the centre console so they at least had some cover should the hostiles breach the security measures that were in place.

He had done everything he could, all that was left was to wait and see what happened next.

He didn't have to wait for very long.

Pounding, loud and booming was heard from outside the room as the assault began.

"Hold your positions, people, the fortifications should hold," Severs said. "Only fire if they breach the room. Pick your targets and fire in short, controlled bursts to conserve ammunition," he added.

The pounding continued, increasing in intensity. The doors began to buckle under the onslaught of such concentrated firepower.

Sparks flew out from the doorways towards the interior of the room.

Severs glanced around at his people, at the worried, fearful yet resolute expressions and he knew that even through the fear they would fight, to the very end if need be.

The doors began to glow from the barrage of pulsed plasma bolts. Sparks flew across the room more frequently as the force fields struggled to maintain integrity on the verge of overloading.

Suddenly an explosion rocked the Ops Centre as one of the doors blew inwards, the force fields having failed. Debris mixed with the fiery cloud generated by the explosion blew inwards forcing everyone to duck down behind the centre console.

Before they had time to react another door blew inwards followed closely by the third and final one.

Severs was the first one to come up from behind cover, holding his Sig at arm's length in a two-handed grip he fired off a two-shot double tap at the first hostile he saw. The two pulsed plasma bolts hit the Rover5 high on the chest and throat respectively, the second shot almost severing his head in a mist of blood. He was sent flying backwards to collide with the group of hostiles directly behind him, slowing them down long enough for him to pick two of them off with carefully but rapidly aimed headshots. The Rapier battle tec helmet the hostiles wore was no match for a full-power shot from the Sig at close range so, when the bolt hit, it destroyed their heads, spraying blood, gore and helmet parts.

The hostiles poured into the room in large numbers

through the three open doorways that acted like a funnel and actually gave the defenders time to shoot them. Before they could spread out and use their own weapons, Severs and the two marine guards kept them at bay, each focusing on one doorway.

Helped by the less experienced defenders, Severs and the marine guards shot and killed as many hostiles as they saw entering the room and soon the dead bodies piled up hampering their invasion as they became an obstacle to climb over to get inside, almost a barrier.

From around the doorways, the Rover5s began firing blindly towards the defenders. Remm assault rifles fired on fully auto could send an awesome amount of firepower their way and Severs heard a cry to his left as a colleague was shot and killed.

Severs kept firing, changing battery clips as fast as he could and willing himself to stay calm. Panic at this stage was something he could ill afford or it would spread through the group like wildfire and their defence of the Ops Centre would crumble just as fast.

Suddenly his peripheral vision caught sight of an object hurled into the room. Small, dark and familiar he was aware of it arcing overhead towards the centre of their group. Not daring to tear his eyes away from the hostiles who were still trying to gain access to the room, he lost sight of the object as it passed over his head to drop behind him.

Acting on an unspoken command the hostiles either dropped to the floor or pulled back outside the room and in that moment Severs knew what the object was. He realised what his subconscious mind had been screaming at him and he knew they were all dead.

When the grenade exploded behind the group the shock-wave pulped their internal organs turning them to mush while the shrapnel lacerated and tore at their flesh. Body parts went flying outwards from the blast core as the shock-wave expanded killing everyone behind that centre console.

The assault on Ops Centre was over. Severs, the two marine guards and the seven staff members were all dead along with twenty-three of the forty Rover5s sent to capture it.

The rest of the invading force entered Ops Centre and began inspecting what was left of the defenders; checking for life signs in vain because no one survives a grenade explosion at such close range.

"Sir, Ops Centre is under our control," said a Rover5 via his NI through a battle com. channel.

"Shut it down," replied Rygar. The Rover5 signalled to the rest of the team by bringing the thumb of his right hand across his throat, and they went to work.

Taking small charges of T6 explosive from their belts they placed them around the room on pieces of equipment and then, as one, they left the room walking away from Ops Centre.

Without looking back or giving a thought to their fallen comrades they continued to a safe distance where they detonated the T6 charges by remote.

The ensuing explosions tore through Ops Centre destroying all the equipment and the bodies that had been left there.

The blast cloud blew through the walls and down the ventilator shafts, destroying anything in its path.

The shockwave reverberated throughout what was left of the building and down through the sub-levels below.

"What was that?" Tanya Wilde asked fearfully.

"They just shut down Ops Centre," Hawk replied coldly.

CHAPTER 21

Almost to the second that Ops Centre was destroyed two other things happened.

Firstly, the other fighter craft that had been promised from Fort Bragg flew over the ruined headquarters building then angled it's flight trajectory upwards to engage the Nemesis and secondly, the Justice and Legend emerged from hyperspace on either side of the aforementioned battle carrier.

The two cruisers were dwarfed by the battle carrier, each of them at fifteen hundred feet in length were less than a third of the size of the behemoth, but their smaller size gave them the advantage of greater manoeuvrability and this was needed from the word go for as soon as they emerged from hyperspace the Nemesis trained her weapons systems on them. The captains of each cruiser had only seconds to react and issue the orders that would save their lives and those of the hundreds of men and women on board.

The Nemesis opened fire with her pulse cannons on each cruiser, missing with the first salvo as the targets took evasive action and opened fire with their own pulse cannons.

The fighters joined the fray, swooping in on the huge carrier and firing their pulse cannons as soon as they came within range.

On the bridge, Jonas Wilde calmly strode around seemingly unnerved by this new development.

"Captain, unleash our fighters to take care of those annoying bugs and then deal with those two cruisers if you don't mind," he said sarcastically when the Nemesis' gunners ineffectively fired and missed, again.

"Aye, sir," the captain replied rather nervously. "You do realise, sir, that to launch the fighters we'll have to momentarily drop the shields. We'll be vulnerable to attack during that brief window," he added.

Wilde, his anger boiling to the surface turned on him, "Of course I realise, you imbecile, what do you take me for some sort of rookie?" he barked, furious at the implication.

"Of course not sir, I just..." stammered the captain, unused to being spoken to in that fashion aboard his own ship and in front of his crew, but this wasn't his ship, it belonged to OMEGA and Wilde was the commander of OMEGA so he was in charge.

"Well, I took you to be competent at your job and, as such, I expect you to do the job you are being paid rather handsomely for. Find a way to launch those fighters, now, with minimum risk to those on board."

"Aye, sir," the captain replied, somewhat subdued.

"And Captain, if you're not up to the job I suggest you say so now. Replacing you would be an inconvenience, I admit, but only a minor one. Do I make myself perfectly clear?"

Before responding, the captain glanced at the bridge crew who were furtively stealing glances towards them hoping to catch what was happening without being too obvious. Then when he spoke his voice was calm and steady.

"Yes, sir, perfectly. Alert all remaining fighters, launch in ten seconds. Gunners, lay down suppressing fire against the two cruisers. I want a full missile spread fired the second the fighters launch and the moment they're clear of the bays and past the range of our shields I want them back up again," he said.

Wilde allowed himself a slight smile; sometimes it was beneficial to light a fire under those under your command, he thought, just to spur them on to even greater endeavours.

"Okay people you have your orders, on my mark, mark!" the captain said confident his orders would be carried out efficiently.

THE TWO CAPTAINS of the cruisers knew that the carrier would scramble her fighters to counter those sent against her and so they ordered their weapons to fire the moment they saw them emerge. They targeted the shield generators, as that would be most vulnerable. If they could disable just one of them then the carrier would be more susceptible to damage and the captain may be forced to rethink his motives for being there, and bug out.

At least that was what they hoped; they had no way of knowing what kind of man they were facing.

"SIR I HAVE two troop carriers inbound for the target area, ETA eight minutes," ops said onboard Nemesis.

"Can we target them from here?" Wilde asked.

Before ops could reply, Nemesis was hit by weapons fire from the Legend and Justice. The huge starship was rocked as the pulsed plasma fire and Sabre missiles struck whilst the shields were down for the launch of the fighters.

Explosions destroyed whole sections of the craft as the Legend and Justice had concentrated their fire on just one section.

On the bridge, there was surprise and fear for the first time on the faces of the crew.

"Sir, we've just lost primary shields and most of the secondary too," screamed ops.

Wilde shouted, "What the fuck just happened?"

"They targeted the shield generators while we launched the fighters," explained the captain. "The timing was really quite remarkable," he added with a certain amount of respect for the skill involved.

"Get the shields back up now!" ordered Wilde wide-eyed; this was something he was not prepared for. He had been so confident in the perfection of his plan, backed by the seeming invulnerability of the Nemesis, that the thought of failure never even entered his mind.

The captain walked over to ops, placed a steadying hand on the young man's shoulder and as he read the findings from the sensors said, "Don't worry son, as soon as the last fighter is clear bring the shields back up," his voice calm and steady.

The young officer glanced up at the tall man standing at his shoulder and said, "The primaries are down, sir. The generators were hit by that last strike. I'm reading nothing at all from them and only nominal power output from the secondaries."

"It'll have to do," the captain said.

"But I don't know how long they'll hold or how much they can take, sir," ops said.

"It'll have to do, son," he repeated. He then turned to Wilde and said, "With respect, sir, we have to leave the battle zone to effect repairs. We have obtained our objective of a pre-emptive strike against the Confederation and we have inflicted huge amounts of damage to their infrastructure, we've damaged their capability to retaliate and inflicted large numbers of casualties. If we remain here too long we run the risk of allowing them the time to mount a counter-attack. Already they have sent two cruisers against us, they have reinforced their fighter squadron and more ground troops are on their way. Our numbers are finite. We are only one ship against an entire fleet, which, if given enough time, they could deploy against us. We must not give them that time, we must fall back now."

Wilde looked at him and as much as he hated to admit it, the man made sense and a smile played along his lips.

"Sir?" the captain asked, misinterpreting his reaction.

"Don't worry Captain, I've not gone mad, I was just thinking how glad I was that my decision to give you this command was the correct one," Wilde replied further confusing the captain.

"I agree, Captain," Wilde said laying his fears to rest. Wilde made contact with Rygar; "We have reinforcements heading your way in less than eight minutes. Find Sinclair and my daughter and bring them back with you. The clock is ticking Rygar, so make it fast."

"COME ON, WE HAVE TO MOVE," Hawk said, trying to rally the group looking to him for support. The last thing he wanted was for them to realise just how hopeless he thought their plight was, it would demoralise them to the point where they just wouldn't be able to function and therefore carry on.

"What's your plan, Matt?" De Boer asked.

"I think the only way to go is one floor at a time. Try to get to the next floor without being spotted. If I can find a safe place to hide while they come looking we may be able to get behind them and escape."

"What if they clear every room as they go, you know, toss in a grenade then shoot anything that still moves after?"

"Then we're in trouble, we may be able to get past a small group by taking them out first, but to do that without the rest hearing and coming after us will be tricky"

"Almost impossible," De Boer agreed.

"We have to try though. We've gotta get out of here and take this fight to them," Hawk said.

"I'm with you on that score," De Boer said with a predatory grin.

"Okay people, line up in the formation and let's go," Hawk said as he led them towards the entrance of the exit tunnel.

As the doorway opened Hawk went through first, signalling to the rest to wait behind and be quiet. Holding his Sig at arm's length in the classic two-handed grip he carefully, and as silently as he could, ventured a few feet into the exit tunnel; it was more of a stairway really. It was well lit by lights embedded in the low ceiling and along the walls at regular intervals.

Straining his ears to pick up any sound, he didn't have to wait long. Two floors above him he heard the clamour of boots pounding down the stairway. He tried to count the footfalls, but the echoes coming from inside the stairwell hampered his hearing. He estimated the group to be around eight or ten men, obviously heavily armed. They disappeared through the doorway to the floor above. Waiting with his back pressed against the wall so he could be hidden by the shadows, he realised, once the last hostile had passed through the doorway, that he'd been holding his breath. Releasing it slowly he signalled to the group to come close.

"They've entered the floor above. Now we have a chance to get past them but we have to move quickly and, above all, quietly. If they get wind of us they'll attack us with all they've got and call for reinforcements. Is that clear?" Hawk said keeping his voice low yet powerful enough to convey his message.

His answer was a nod of heads from all around the group.

"Okay follow me, be quiet but be swift," Hawk said and he led them up the stairway.

Quickly and quietly the group made their way up the plascrete stairs. Hawk stayed in front of the group, keeping an eye on their progress and urging them on whilst willing them not to make a sound. His other eye was fixed on the doorway he'd seen the hostiles go through.

Slowly they approached the doorway. Any second he expected to see the squad of hostiles emerge before they had a chance to get past.

When they finally reached the level with the doorway facing them, Hawk kept his Sig trained on the doorway as he ushered the group to go past him, his full concentration focused laser-like on the exit.

Time seemed to stand still for Hawk as the group filed past behind him. His senses were on hyper-alert as he strained to hear anything from the other side of the doorway facing him but there was nothing. No sounds, no vibrations, so no indications of what was happening on that floor which only made the tension and suspense more acute.

Finally, the last person, one of the marines, came past him tapping him on the shoulder to say he could follow on.

Still keeping his pistol trained on the doorway Hawk backed up the stairs after the rest of the group.

He'd told the group to enter the level above where the hostiles were until the said hostiles had moved down one more level, at which time the group could carry on up to the surface, one level at a time, and hopefully to safety.

Although the tension was almost unbearable Hawk still had doubts, thinking that they were getting away too easily.

"This is just too easy," he said softly to himself as he quickly glanced up to see how the group was progressing.

Almost half of them had entered the level above. Just a few more seconds and they would be safe.

A sound alerted him to something happening, something very wrong. The doorway to the level they had just passed was opening.

"OKAY HOLD ON HERE, they'll try to get past us. As soon as they've gone up the tunnel to the next level, we'll have them trapped," Rygar said as he halted half of his team. He was reading the life signs on his palm pad. Rather than chase the group down, he'd chosen instead to allow them to come to him and trap them between the two halves of his team.

Patiently he waited just inside the doorway as he watched the readings on his palm pad go up the exit tunnel, towards the next level. Just as they were almost all inside the doorway Rygar made his move.

"Right, let's go, let's do this right and do this fast," Rygar said as he led them back out into the tunnel.

MOTIONING for the group to move faster, Hawk turned his full attention to the doorway below. Keying his com. bug he said, "General Sinclair and Colonel De Boer we're about to have some company, get ready."

As soon as Rygar came through the door Hawk opened fire with his Sig firing two shots. The first pulsed plasma bolt struck Rygar a glancing blow high on his left shoulder sending him spinning away from the second bolt that struck the wall behind him where his head had been seconds before.

Another figure appeared through the doorway and Hawk's aim improved. Firing a two-shot burst, both bolts struck the clone dead centre in his chest sending him backwards down the stairway in a mist of blood. Even the battle gear they were wearing was unable to stop a full power blast at such close range.

Rygar fought through the pain from his shoulder wound to fire back at his attacker, although his aim was severely impaired. His shots went wide of their mark impacting instead on the exit tunnel stairway walls.

Hawk had to dodge to the left as Rygar's shots struck the wall to his right. He fired again, another two-shot burst at another emerging figure but because of his movement, only one of the bolts struck the target. Luckily for him, the bolt hit the clone in the middle of the clavicle, blasting through his throat and almost severing his head in a savage spurt of blood.

"Move, move," Hawk screamed at the group behind him although the addition of gunfire had spurred them on to virtually fly up the stairs.

Backing up the stairs and firing at anything that came through the doorway whilst trying not to get hit took all of Hawk's concentration.

Plasma bolts singed the air around him, fired by the wounded man who had been the first to emerge at that level. It would only be a matter of time before his wild shots found their mark and his struggle would be over.

A gunshot from over his shoulder startled him until he heard a familiar voice in his ear bug.

"Just a few more feet Matt, hurry, we'll hold them off 'til you get here," Colonel De Boer said, firing his Remm Mk III assault rifle again in a short, controlled burst. The plasma bolts struck another Rover5 as he tried to gain ground on the fleeing form of Hawk. The bolts struck the Rover5 high on his chest stitching a path up from his sternum through his throat and finally destroying the head in a haze of blood and gore.

Hawk saw his chance now that he had backup and he turned and sprinted up the final few plascrete stairs, his arms and legs pumping as he raced ahead of imminent death.

Once through the door he was followed closely by the Colonel, who asked, "What now, Matt?"

"We'll have to reach another exit tunnel entrance on this level, and fast," Hawk replied, his voice stern and full of purpose.

Just as they were getting ready to move, a doorway facing them in the corridor ahead opened and out rushed three clones all dressed the same, full battle gear with Remm Mk III assault rifles aimed at them.

"Oh shit!" exclaimed one of the marines close to the front of the group.

"Freeze, don't move," one of the clones ordered.

Another door opened and then another followed by yet more doors, clones pouring out of each one. Before long they were faced with what seemed an impenetrable wall of man plus firepower.

From the doorway, Hawk came through the group to stand next to Tanya who asked in a very scared voice, "What do we do now?"

Looking at what stood before them and knowing what was coming up behind them he replied, "I'm working on it."

CHAPTER 22

Wilde was pacing the bridge of the Nemesis like a caged tiger, waiting for some word from his troops down on the planet when ops said, "Sir, we have two hyperspace windows opening nearby."

Spinning around he glared at the man and said, "Tell me."

Swallowing hard, ops said, "We have two more cruisers, sir, they're charging their weapons and locking on to us."

Thinking rapidly, Wilde came up with a solution and contacted Rygar down on Earth. "We've run out of time, we're under attack by four cruisers and fighters, we have to leave in the next few minutes if we want to survive. Tell me you have Sinclair and my daughter alive," he said through the com. channel via his NI.

"We do, sir," Rygar replied just as he was about to give the order to kill them all.

"Good, leave now, no questions. Drop everything and bring Sinclair and Tanya here now, you have less than five minutes," Wilde said urgently.

"What about the others, sir?" Rygar asked, halting the clones firing.

"No time, leave them. Just make sure Tanya and Sinclair are alive, now get moving man or we are all dead," Wilde almost screamed at him.

Rygar didn't know how bad things had got on the Nemesis, but now he had some idea from Wilde's words and tone. He was normally cold, efficient and unflappable, so things must be bad.

Wilde turned back to ops and said, "My daughter's NI is coded to pass through our shields so keep them up and keep our weapons tracking those cruisers, stall them for as long as possible. As soon as Rygar gets aboard, jump to our secondary base."

"Aye, sir, but I'm not sure how long the secondary shields will hold out," ops replied.

"We have triple hull plating, if that gets breached close off the entire section. I'm not leaving until Sinclair is on board."

"Aye, sir."

～

RYGAR SINGLED out Tanya Wilde and he knew Sinclair from his time with the Black Knights. Under the threat of certain death from so much firepower, Hawk had lowered his Sig and had urged the rest to do the same. A gunfight inside a confined space against overwhelming odds like that was just plain suicide and Hawk had opted to stay alive, for while life remains, hope endures.

When Rygar grabbed Tanya and went to pull her from the group, Hawk reacted instinctively. He grabbed Rygar's hand in a vice-like grip and twisted it from her arm then punched him full in the face with a straight left that caught him off guard and put him on his back.

Before Hawk could do anything else there were three

clones battering him in the back, ribs and head with the stocks of their assault rifles.

Under such a barrage of blows not even someone as powerfully built as Hawk could cope and he went down, vainly trying to cover up. Once he was on the floor the three clones continued to kick him.

Rygar got to his knees, spat out a wad of blood-red spittle that contained a few broken teeth, then stood up. With a wave of his hand, he called off his dogs and said, "You must be the hero, coming to the rescue."

Hawk looked up at him through pain-filled eyes and his cold stare spoke volumes. Rygar understood that look, had seen it many times from many men. It meant he was a dead man, yet there he stood, alive. This time would be no different he supposed.

"Well, if you're the hero, that makes me the bad guy, but in this version, the bad guy wins," he said with a smirk. Turning to his men he said, "Bring her" indicating Sinclair, "and bring him too," pointing to Hawk who was being manhandled off the floor by two burly clones. "I've not finished with him yet. The rest leave behind, we have to leave now, no time for fun, that'll come later," he finished then led the way to the door.

"You two stay with them and make sure they stay here. Give us thirty seconds then follow on, seal the door after you to make sure they don't follow," Rygar said to two clones standing by the door.

De Boer stood powerless to help the three friends being taken by Rygar and inside he raged with pent up frustration and fury.

A glance from Sinclair told him not to attempt anything for fear it may cost the lives of those innocents present and it was all the Colonel could do to comply.

Rygar led the way, sprinting up the stairs with his men

behind. Hawk was being closely watched even though they had all been stripped of their weapons. Rygar had contacted the team that had taken out Ops Centre and ordered them to rendezvous with him and the rest at the drop site where they would hitch a ride back to Nemesis.

Hawk had a few cuts on his face, one above his right eye and on his left cheekbone, blood trickled from the corner of his mouth, his ribs were bruised from the rifle butt blows and from several kicks and his back was sore, but apart from that, he considered himself to be in pretty good shape considering what could have happened.

What to do about their present situation, now that was the problem? Unfortunately, it was a problem he couldn't resolve at that moment. The situation he was in may have its advantages he realised, once he knew he was to accompany them and not be put to death by the man in charge. Clearly, he was not a clone and Hawk wondered if he was the one who had led the attack on the shuttle and even further back, on the compound? If he was the one then both of them would view this similarly and have scores to settle with the other. The merc would want to get even for Hawk continuing to escape and on the other side Hawk would want revenge for the deaths the other man was responsible for in their first encounter. Again, unfortunately, the other seemed to have the upper hand so Hawk would have to wait patiently for the moment to come when he could reverse that trend.

As they reached the surface, the first of the two Hurricane C230 troop carriers from Fort Bragg was approaching. The C230 from the Nemesis was already on the ground having landed after getting the call from Rygar to come back for the evac.

Recon Delta marines in full battle gear began to rappel down to the ground from the C230 sent from Fort Bragg.

Before any could even reach the ground though, Rygar had organised his clones to fire on them with some success. Two groups of five Rover5s stood on either side of Rygar's team and fired on the marines as they approached the ground. Rygar led the rest of his group including his captured prisoners towards the C230 on the ground which had already started to warm up her engines in preparation for a rapid take off.

The pilot of the first C230, who was hovering so that his cargo of marines could debark, saw the Rover5s firing on the defenceless men on the rappelling lines and knew that if he didn't take action he would lose all of them. Quickly he brought his craft's pulse cannons to bear on the men shooting at the marines and fired. The pulsed plasma bolts struck the ground in a line leading to their target, breaking up the plascrete until it reached the five Rover5s to Rygar's left.

Bodies were blasted to bits by the cannon fire in a shower of blood and gore. With them dispatched, the pilot trained his cannons on the other group firing on the marines. He made short work of them too having found the range, destroying them with a hail of pulsed plasma that sent them flying like their comrades.

As soon as the resistance had ceased the marines began to hurtle to the ground in ever-increasing numbers.

Rover5s began to fall under the blistering fire from both the marines who had landed and the C230 that brought them, giving the second C230 the chance to debark her entire cargo of troops safely.

Rygar saw his transport a scant few dozen feet away and his protection of Rover5s dwindle to dangerously low numbers. Already he'd lost all the mercenaries that had formed his original team before being given command of the clones and now that too was almost gone. Firing his assault rifle from the hip he cleared a path for himself and the three captives along with the eight remaining Rover5s.

Quickly they boarded the ramp of the troop carrier just before her engines were given full vertical thrust making it seem like she almost leapt into the air. The pilot fired pulse cannons at the first troop carrier making her swerve almost into the path of the second, then he fired a brace of Sabre missiles at the second C230 as the pilot of that craft fought to regain control after the near-collision. The C230 carrying Rygar and the rest managed to get clear in the ensuing chaos.

Onboard the escaping C230, Matt Hawk was cheered by the fact the odds against them had dwindled immensely and, although he was still outnumbered by quite a large number, he took heart from that. He was certain an opportunity would present itself soon to thin those odds down even more. He just had to wait, be patient and above all, vigilant so that when it arrived he would be ready to take advantage of it.

COLONEL DE BOER was not going to take this lying down, he was going to do something about it, but as he watched Hawk get beaten and then, along with General Sinclair and Tanya Wilde, get singled out to be taken away he wondered just what it was he could do. Outnumbered and out-gunned he saw little hope in mounting any sort of resistance, and the glance from the General telling him not to put the group's lives at risk was the clincher.

He had run out of options, or so he thought.

The moment he saw the hostiles filing out of the door with their three captives an idea struck him.

Only two hostiles were left behind with orders to wait for thirty seconds then follow on after sealing them in, not a great deal of time to implement his plan but it would have to do. Thirty seconds didn't give him any time to discuss the merits of his plan with the others either, which meant whatever he planned on doing he would have to do it alone.

During the time that the hostiles were leaving, he had managed to position himself at the front of the group facing the two men who had been chosen to remain behind.

A distance of only a few feet separated them from the two hostiles. The other marines had taken their lead from the Colonel and had worked their way to the front of the group and now, like De Boer, were steadily inching forward, crowding the men guarding them.

One of the guards glanced at the chronometer on his wrist and, as the second guard became distracted by the slight movement, De Boer saw his chance and rushed them.

The marines with him were just half a step behind and when he moved they followed by rushing the two clones.

The Colonel slammed into the clone to his right, one hand pinning the assault rifle to the man's chest as they collided with the wall behind taking the other clone with them.

The marines being that half step behind were ready to grab the clones as they bounced off the wall.

The marines quickly subdued the two clones using a savage series of blows, leaving them unconscious on the floor.

"C'mon, we have to move, we've got to help the General and Matt," De Boer said as he opened the door to the exit tunnel. They all left the hallway and ran after the fleeing group who had their friends captive.

223

HAWK MANAGED to get himself seated as close to General Sinclair and Tanya Wilde as possible. The latter two were the real prizes here; Hawk was merely the bonus, a little toy that Rygar planned to have fun with later.

His ear bug was still in place and he heard a familiar voice, "We'll be with you in a few seconds," De Boer said, his voice coming through loud and clear but only to him.

Hawk scratched his right ear keying the ear bug and said, "We'll soon be aboard the Nemesis, General. I wonder what your father has in store for us, eh Miss Wilde?" as he leaned forward to talk to his fellow captives and answer the Colonel's statement.

"Copy that, we'll get to you somehow, just sit tight and keep them safe, De Boer, out," the Colonel replied. Hawk knew there was no need to respond; he would do everything he could to safeguard the lives of the two people with him.

Rygar looked at Hawk and with a sneer said, "Oh you don't need to worry about them my friend. Her father will indeed keep them, entertained shall we say, while you on the other hand…" and he left the sentence to hang in the air.

Tanya asked, "What… what about him?"

Hawk looked at her and smiled then calmly said, "I'm to entertain *him.*"

"I don't know what that means," Tanya said naively, looking firstly at Hawk who sat serenely across from her then at Sinclair sitting next to her.

"Best that you don't my girl," he said, placing a calloused hand on top of both of hers in her lap.

"Don't worry Tanya," Hawk said soothingly, "I'll be fine and so will you."

"How?" she asked in a little voice, trying her damnedest not to show her fear.

"Yes, hero, how are you going to accomplish that little

feat? As the bad guy I have a vested interest," Rygar said, hoping to show the futility of their hopes of salvation.

Hawk looked at him with ice-cold eyes and said, "Simple, first I kill you then I rescue them."

Rygar was taken aback by his blunt, confident words and the manner in which they were delivered, not with passion or histrionics but simply stated as matter of fact. His eyes, the coldness of his stare, chilled him to the bone and he found himself wondering if bringing Hawk along was such a good idea after all. He started to think that perhaps safety might have been more prudent than self-indulgence and decided he would kill him as soon as they were on board. He would do it personally to ensure that it was done right.

Finding he could no longer hold Hawk's stare he had to look away saying feebly, "We'll see."

CHAPTER 23

The Nemesis was surrounded by the four cruisers. The Justice and Legend had each contacted other starships and had been rewarded with the knowledge that the Odyssey and Atlantis would follow as soon as possible and it was they who had joined the battle.

Once the four cruisers were in their relative positions they could circle the Nemesis, evading any fire from her whilst counter-attacking.

It would be almost impossible for the carrier to escape whilst being surrounded by those four cruisers, but Wilde was determined to try. He had come so far and got too close to his ultimate prize to lose it all now. The prize was still his for the taking and he would grasp it with both hands.

THE TROOP CARRIER that held Rygar, Hawk, Sinclair, Tanya Wilde and the remainder of the Rover5 squad, left Earth. At first, the pilot was worried about the fighter craft attacking the Nemesis and having to navigate a way through them, but as they neared their objective he noticed they were busy. That wasn't to say their passage would be easy, far from it. The four cruisers were still attacking and the carrier's shields would have to remain up. Rygar contacted Wilde to inform him they were on approach and was told to come ahead as a diversion would be staged so they could get through the blockade.

Ordering the captain to concentrate all his firepower on one of the cruisers, didn't matter which one, he wanted to cause enough damage to get her to pull out of the attack.

The Justice was targeted and the carrier's pulse cannons were fired and a full spread of Sabre and Hammerhead missiles was sent her way. The amount of firepower unleashed upon the one craft was staggering and overloaded her shields within seconds and she began to sustain heavy damage. Explosions erupted down her flanks and, unwillingly, she had to pull out of the fight until repairs could be completed.

The second a gap appeared in the cordon around the Nemesis the C230 powered through it passing harmlessly through the carrier's shields and straight into one of the flight deck bays.

The Legend, Odyssey and Atlantis closed that gap by altering their courses and firing patterns, battering the larger craft hoping to disable her.

The Nemesis had taken a pounding from the cruisers around her and her armament was quickly becoming depleted, but the news that the prisoners were on board was just what Wilde wanted to hear.

"Captain, hail the respective captains of those cruisers and inform them that we have General Sinclair on board with us and if they do not cease firing immediately, I shall execute him," Wilde said with a satisfied grin.

"Aye, sir," replied the captain who relayed the order to

ops. Turning back to Wilde he said, "Sir, you know as well as I do, Confederation policy is not to negotiate with terrorists, whoever is involved. The most we can hope for is a little time if, and I stress *if*, they wish to verify his presence on board."

"And in that time we make our jump to hyperspace," Wilde replied more calmly now as he knew he had the upper hand once more.

"But what if they don't bother to verify his presence and simply consider him a casualty of war?"

"In that case, the three captains will have to confer with whoever is in command now. My guess is they'll have to contact President Takagi, considering how we just decimated Confederation Headquarters, so either way they'll hesitate and that hesitation will give us the opportunity to make the jump."

"I see, sir," replied the captain, smiling as he saw the simplicity of it. "I'll have the coordinates set and ready to go on your command but I'm afraid that when we open the hyperspace window, being so close to those cruisers, we may drag one of them along with us, sir," he added thoughtfully, working out the calculations required.

"I'm not worried about one cruiser, Captain, I'm sure we can take care of that should the need arise."

"Aye, sir."

"Have Sinclair brought up to the bridge, I want him to witness our victory," Wilde said finally.

AS THE TROOP carrier entered the docking bay the automated docking codes authorised her to land on a specific pad. Once down, clamps engaged from the pad to hold the craft in place securely whilst the pad was raised up to one of the twelve levels where she would be stored until required.

Once on this level, the hydraulic ramp disengaged to allow the pad to be moved along to its allotted storage position along the side of the docking bay where the rest of the craft were stored, leaving the centre section free for incoming or outgoing traffic. The hydraulic ramp returned to the base of the bay where another pad would slide into place. Once the craft was secured in position against the side of the bay by clamps, gantries slid into place to enable the crew to debark.

Rygar and the eight remaining Rover5s debarked along with Sinclair, Hawk and Tanya.

"Your presence is required on the bridge General, you're coming too Miss Wilde, I'm sure your father will be pleased to see you," Rygar said. Speaking to the Rover5s he added, "You two stay here with him, the rest you're with me. Make sure he gives you no trouble. I'll be back shortly to take care of him personally."

Hawk locked eyes with Tanya as she was about to be taken away and he smiled to reassure her that everything would be fine. Then she and Sinclair were gone, being herded along the balcony that ran along the side of the level where they were standing.

The entire docking bay was fully automated which meant that Hawk and the two Rover5s were left alone. This suited Hawk for it would be easier to escape if he only had the two clones present to contend with before he tackled the real task at hand, Tanis Rygar.

Putting his aches and pains to one side he steeled himself for what he had to do, which was to get the better of two heavily armed clones in close-quarter combat. He'd had problems with the Rover5 back at the mall on Cordoba and he'd been up against just the one there, now he had two to face. Taking solace from the fact he had faced one before, knew its strengths and weaknesses and therefore was in a better position than last time, he prepared for the brutal battle.

Rygar led the other group to the end of the balcony then into a large elevator with a clearplas door that closed once they were inside. It took them up to the top where they got out and headed towards the bridge, Hawk supposed, because once the elevator reached the top he lost sight of them.

Hawk decided it was time to make his move; it was now or never.

They were all standing roughly on the same spot where Rygar had left them, having disembarked the C230. The clones were vigilant and watched Hawk all the time. If he were ever going to make this work he would have to divert their attention somehow. As it was, the second he moved they would have him and it would be all over.

"You two are exceptionally alert," he said as he had an idea. "Is that built into your genetic makeup or is it something your father added later? He is your father, Jonas Wilde, well sort of. He is the one who bio-engineered you into what you are; he's the one who set the parameters for the education programme that you absorbed while you were growing in your vat or tube or your mix. Was obedience added, you know, the ability to blindly follow orders?" As he was speaking he was looking at them, first one then the other, he accentuated the dialogue with hand gestures and also slight body movements as he began to creep ever so slightly forward, towards them.

"What I mean is, do you follow orders to the letter? Your boss said to keep me here and that he would deal with me personally. Now, if I tried to escape, obviously you'd try to stop me but, and here's the question, would you shoot me or would you just knock me down. Don't forget, your boss will be back and he's expecting to see me alive," Hawk said smiling at the clones, and then it happened, they glanced at each other and the second they averted their eyes Hawk moved.

Slamming into the two of them he knocked their assault rifles down so they pointed towards the floor with his left arm while he snatched a Sig P996 from the shoulder holster of the one to his right. Regaining their composure remarkably fast they pushed Hawk from them and their combined strength sent him flailing backwards to collide with the railing that bordered the balcony. Glancing down over his shoulder he noticed they were a hundred and fifty odd feet from the bottom of the docking bay, a hell of a drop should any of them go over the railing.

His attention was brought back to the task at hand when he realised the clones were advancing on him and in that instant, he knew he had his answer. They would try to subdue him and keep him alive for their boss, which gave him the advantage of having no such constraints.

Before he could move though they were upon him, pushing him against the railing and bending him backwards with such force he thought his back would break at any moment.

Both his arms were held, and when they thought they had control of the situation they pulled him away from the railing.

Hawk knew what they wanted to do, force his arms up his back and fasten his wrists together with zip cuffs.

As they brought him off the railing there was a split second when the clone passed Hawk's hand across his own body prior to forcing it around Hawk's back to apply the zip cuffs, but in that split second he forgot one tiny detail. That was the hand holding the Sig.

Hawk shot him point-blank three times in rapid succession, the shots striking almost as one. The salvo smashed into the clone shredding his chest cavity in a virtual explosion of blood and gore, the force of which threw him across the balcony. The second clone was shocked by the turn-around of fortunes and in the microsecond, it took for his brain to register, Hawk had brought the Sig around and shot him right between the eyes blowing his brain apart in a mist of blood.

The clone's head was snapped backwards so violently it sent him staggering across the balcony a few steps, his arms cartwheeling as he frantically tried to regain his balance before dropping down to the floor below, dead.

Keying his ear bug Hawk said, "General Sinclair, hold tight, sir, I'm on my way."

"What's the matter with those fools?" Wilde asked angrily as he stared at the viewscreen displaying composite views from around the huge battle carrier. "Has the message been sent? Did they receive it?" he asked as he and everyone else on the bridge watched the three cruisers continue their attack with no sign of it abating. "Are they really willing to risk the life of their leader so readily?" he pondered when a voice answered from the doorway.

"Simple answer, yes."

Wilde turned to face who had spoken, recognising the voice immediately, "Ah General Sinclair, so glad you made it," he said smiling like a genial host greeting an honoured guest.

"How could I refuse such a gracious invitation," replied Sinclair in the same vein.

"Father, what have you done?" Tanya asked, both angry and bewildered at his actions of late.

"I have garnered my revenge against the thing that ruined my life, Col Sec and the architect of it all, General Sinclair. How does it feel, General, to watch everything you've worked for destroyed before your very eyes?" gloated Wilde, his eyes alight with his madness.

"What you destroyed here today can be rebuilt, that's not

going to stop us Jonas, but you will pay for the lives lost here today, you have my word on that."

"Oh I don't think so, you have no idea of the scope of what I've done, what I've achieved, but you will, in time, if you live long enough," Wilde said with the supreme confidence borne from insanity. He turned to the captain and said, "Make the jump."

Before the order could be relayed to the pilot, ops shouted, "We've just lost secondary shields."

The captain turned from ops to rush over to the pilot when the huge ship was rocked by a series of shuddering explosions that were felt rather than heard throughout the massive carrier.

Everyone on the bridge was knocked off their feet and went sprawling across the floor. General Sinclair shielded Tanya from harm, holding and keeping her close to him.

"Sir, the main drive is offline, that last salvo must've taken out the engines, we're not jumping anywhere," said ops once he'd regained his feet.

"The only option now is to give yourself up." Sinclair said, "Surrender now and save any further bloodshed."

Wilde got to his feet and said to the captain, "Get some sort of propulsion online, we need to get away. Prepare to receive borders, they'll try to take the ship by force and I won't allow that." Grabbing a Sig from one of the clones he turned to Sinclair and Tanya, aimed at them and said, "You're coming with me."

He herded them towards the door once more then, to Rygar said, "Organise the troops, Tanis, kill anyone who gets on board," and before Rygar could respond the three of them had left.

Pretending to scratch his ear Sinclair keyed his ear bug then said, "Give it up Jonas, the main propulsion is offline, your shields are depleted and any minute now you'll have troops coming aboard, what will you do then? Do you really think that holding me as your hostage will prevent them from taking this ship or if they can't take it, blowing it out of space?"

Wilde stared at his old commander and said, "They won't do anything while you're on board."

"That's where you're wrong Jonas. I've already given orders that if this ship can't be taken it's to be destroyed with everyone on board, no matter who that may be."

A voice came into Sinclair's ear, "I hear you loud and clear General but it won't come to that, we're gathering to launch a counter-strike as we speak. Just hold tight, sir, we'll be there soon," Colonel De Boer said.

"And did your men understand your order?" Wilde asked.

"Loud and clear, there was no misunderstanding of that, you can be sure," Sinclair replied, then changing tack asked, "What about your own daughter Jonas, don't you want her to be safe?"

Wilde glanced at her with no more affection than a shark shows for its next meal.

"She'll get to see her father's crowning achievement before she dies," he said and then urged them forward with a wave of the pistol.

"I'm sorry my dear, I hoped at least to procure your safety," Sinclair said as they moved forward.

"At least I know where I stand with him," she replied, holding back her tears.

Leaning close to her he whispered, "Don't give up hope just yet my dear, we're not dead yet and I've great faith in the Colonel and Matt, neither of them will let us down, you mark my words."

Tanya gave him a half-smile in reply and she hoped that the general's faith was well-founded for at that moment she couldn't see a way out of this.

~

COLONEL DE BOER had taken command of the troops that had arrived from Fort Bragg and had them organised back inside the troop carriers heading for the Nemesis in orbit around Earth.

The huge carrier was motionless, hanging in space with her engines offline and her shields down, leaving her vulnerable to attack.

De Boer watched as the three cruisers slowly circled her like a pack of wild dogs surrounding their prey, waiting for just the right moment to strike.

Small explosions erupted along the flanks of the great ship, the result of her battle with the smaller craft, and De Boer couldn't help but feel sadness for her, to be reduced to this by such a dishonourable act rather than what she had been intended for, defending the Confederation. Putting those thoughts aside he looked for an available docking bay and once he had located one ordered both pilots to enter.

On approach, he had contacted the captains of the attacking cruisers to inform them of the situation onboard the Nemesis and of his intentions. He instructed them to destroy her after thirty minutes unless they heard from either himself, General Sinclair or Matt Hawk to the contrary. His mission would be a search and rescue one, to locate General Sinclair and Matt Hawk and bring them to safety. Their specialised knowledge of the workings and infrastructure of Col Sec was too important to be allowed to fall into enemy hands. Their secondary mission would be to capture the Nemesis, but if that proved to be impracticable or impossible, they were to destroy her.

Finally, he contacted Captain Jefferson on the Valkyrie who had been watching the battle from a distance with mounting frustration at his inability to render assistance.

"We'll be ready, Colonel," Jefferson said once De Boer had relayed his plan to him.

Confident he had done everything he could at such short notice to secure the success of the mission, De Boer gave the command to enter the Nemesis' docking bay.

CHAPTER 24

Hawk followed the route he'd seen Sinclair and Tanya being taken on to the bridge, but once he reached the level where he lost sight of them he was at a loss to know where they could be. Sure, he had a knowledge of the ships of the fleet and roughly where main sections were, such as the bridge or engineering, but if, as he suspected, Jonas Wilde had left the bridge with his prisoners they could be en route to anywhere on the massive ship and he was running out of time.

Keying his ear bug he said, "General Sinclair, have you any idea where you and Tanya are?"

Sinclair and Tanya Wilde were being herded towards one of the elevators when Hawk made contact.

"Where are you taking us, Jonas, I know this is a big ship but eventually the troops will find us. There is nowhere on board you can hide, you know that, don't you?" Sinclair said in answer.

"Do you honestly think I haven't planned for this General?" Wilde said with a sneer of derision.

"You're taking us off the ship," Sinclair said when it

dawned on him what Wilde intended. "Well it's true what sailors used to say about rats and sinking ships, it works in space too, eh Jonas?" he added.

"Thanks, General, now if you can get him to divulge which docking bay he intends on using, I can head you all off," Hawk said hopefully.

"I suppose you have a special shuttle already picked out for this, one that your troops know nothing about. I mean how would they feel about their illustrious leader if they knew he was leaving them to their fate at the mercy of Recon Delta marines whilst he escaped in luxury?" Sinclair said, hoping to draw the answer out of Wilde for Hawk.

"You are so right, General, if I had time to staff this ship with my Rover5s it wouldn't be a problem, total obedience you see, but seeing as the crew are humans I had to take precautions. I secreted a transport with hyperdrive in a docking bay that wasn't being used. It has a limited range but is sufficient to take us to where I want to go," Wilde replied smugly.

"And your crew bought that, never questioned it?"

"No, I told them it was still under construction. Believe me General there are many systems on here that are not quite up to spec, such as backup generators for the shields. If we had time to outfit her fully there would've been no way your cruisers could inflict the damage they did."

"Thank God your impatience got the better of you then," Sinclair said more to himself than to anyone else.

"Thanks, General, I think I know where he's taking you," Hawk said. Using his NI he accessed the computer and asked for the ship's schematics, specifically docking bays. There were four with only one not being used, and when he had the location of the fourth he logged out saying, "Got you now, Jonas," and he set off for the nearest elevator.

~

TANIS RYGAR LEFT the bridge along with the six Rover5s. He called the rest of the Rover5 contingent, numbering close to a hundred, onboard and ordered them to defend the docking bay when the incoming troop carriers arrived. The other six Rover5s who had followed him from the bridge were ordered to rendezvous with their brothers.

Seeing the clones march off to do battle brought a wry smile to his face as he wondered if using clones like that would be the future of warfare.

Putting that thought away to concentrate on more important matters, he headed towards where he'd left Hawk. There were two things he had to do; first, take care of Hawk and second, get off the Nemesis. It was blatantly obvious that Wilde had deserted them the moment the Nemesis was crippled and Wilde was a fool if he didn't realise he saw through his little subterfuge. So if the great man didn't rate their chances of survival as being too high, then escaping had to be a priority. He would make it the first and only thing on his "to do" list if professional pride, need for revenge, whatever you wanted to call it hadn't got in the way of logic. Hawk had eluded him in the chamber and once again in the shuttle in the skies of Cordoba, he was not going to let him escape a third time. Once he saw him lying at his feet, dead, then and only then could he even think about leaving.

The med patch he'd applied to his shoulder wound had worked well. The bleeding had stopped as the nanobots worked to regenerate new tissue. His shoulder would be as good as new with nothing to show for the wound other than another scar within a few days and, more importantly, the pain had ceased which meant he wouldn't be hindered by it when he reached Hawk.

When he was halfway to where he'd left Hawk he tried to

contact the Rover5s guarding him. When he couldn't get through to them he knew that Hawk had escaped yet again. The man was proving far more resourceful than he thought possible.

Rygar sprinted down the corridor towards the elevator. Frustrated at how slowly the elevator moved, he barely contained his rage. When the doors opened he saw the two dead clones and he released a bellow of pure animal rage.

Where was Hawk? Where was the illusive agent who persisted in frustrating him by surviving? It was a few seconds before he could bring himself back under control so that his thought processes would function to figure out where the man had gone.

He was the hero, right? So he would attempt to rescue the heroine and in this case that meant Tanya Wilde. Having worked that out he knew what to do.

～

HAWK WAS in the elevator on his way to stop Wilde when his ear bug was activated.

"Matt, I'm in command of the reinforcements from Fort Bragg. We're approaching Docking Bay Three in two C230s," De Boer said, his voice crystal clear in Hawk's ear.

"Tread carefully, Colonel, I'm sure Wilde knows you're coming and he'll send whatever troops he has left to try and prevent you getting aboard while he makes his escape," Hawk replied.

"He's going nowhere, the engines are offline," De Boer said triumphantly, misunderstanding Hawk's words.

"No, Colonel, that's not what I meant. He's got a shuttle prepped in Docking Bay Four, it's fitted with a short-range hyperdrive and he's taking his daughter and the General with him. I'm on my way to stop him as we speak," Hawk explained.

"Docking Bay Four is on the other side of the ship, we may not get to you in time," observed the Colonel with some trepidation.

"Don't worry about me, you just see if you can gain control of the Nemesis and if not, just hold those damn clones off me for as long as you can. I'll handle Wilde and get the General to safety, somehow," Hawk said with determination.

"Make it fast then Matt, the captains of the cruisers are under orders to destroy the Nemesis in less than half an hour unless they hear from me, you or the General," De Boer said. He went on to tell him the rest of his plan, finally finishing by wishing him luck and informing him he would try to get to him as quickly as he could.

"Half an hour doesn't give any of us much time but I'll do my best, sir," Hawk replied, feeling the pressure to succeed as a burden on his shoulders.

"Hey, if this was easy, anyone could do it, right?" quipped De Boer, hoping to ease some of the tension without diluting the importance of the mission.

"Yes, Colonel, this isn't just a job, it's an adventure," Hawk replied.

"True, very true. Listen, if we all get out of this alive then the first round of drinks is on me, okay?"

"That, Colonel, I'll hold you to."

"De Boer out."

As the elevator doors opened in front of him he hoped he would have enough time to complete the task before him. One thing he knew for certain, he would not leave this ship without either the General or Tanya and he would do whatever was needed to ensure they got off safely, even if it meant his own life was forfeit. As his thoughts passed over the

General and lingered on Tanya he hoped it would not come to that as he realised that he would very much like to spend some time getting to know her properly.

"THERE YOU ARE," Rygar said, as he saw the blips on his palm pad signifying the position of Tanya Wilde. He had reasoned that the computer would be able to track the particular NI that had the codes, which had allowed access through the ship's shields. After asking the question as to the location of said NI the answer was relayed to his palm pad.

"So Jonas, if you have a way off this ship, I just may hitch a ride with you, or better yet, take it from you," he said as he put away the palm pad. He knew where Wilde was heading, he also knew Hawk would go there too, so if he timed it right he could arrive in time to mop up and then escape. That is, if the ship held together long enough, he thought, as another explosion rocked the massive carrier sending a shudder through it that was felt throughout the entire craft.

As THE TWO troop carriers entered Docking Bay Three, Colonel De Boer instructed each pilot to disengage the automatic docking protocols and remain on manual entry. The tactic served them well for it meant they kept control of the craft and were not secured on a pad, making a stationary target for the defending troops who had appeared on the uppermost balcony.

The clones opened fire with Remm Mk III assault rifles sending down a storm of pulsed plasma at the two craft.

"Take them out," ordered De Boer, and the pilots brought

the two craft up level with the balcony and fired their forward pulse cannons at the clones.

Hovering back-to-back and firing forward as they rotated around in a full three hundred and sixty-degree circle, the C230s sent out a hailstorm of pure death.

The clones continued to fire in a valiant yet vain attempt to protect the ship from invasion and, as he watched them being cut to pieces in the wholesale slaughter, De Boer couldn't help but think what a waste of life it was and that they should give it for such an unworthy cause. On the other hand, was this loyalty, this ability to blindly follow orders, programmed into them at a genetic level? De Boer supposed that was a question that probably would never get answered.

Within five minutes of them entering the Docking Bay, all resistance had been quelled and the two C230s were able to land.

As the troop carriers were preparing to release their cargo of Recon Delta marines, De Boer asked the pilot of his craft to scan for life signs within the Docking Bay.

The other C230 began to unload her cargo when the pilot replied, "Sir, I'm showing a large group approaching the Bay area, almost like they're waiting for something."

"Get those marines back inside the C230," De Boer shouted to the pilot of the other troop carrier. His call was too late as the few marines who had already debarked were cut down where they stood by pulsed plasma fire from the balcony above.

The clones had sacrificed some of their numbers to make the marines believe the defences had been defeated. It was a trap and they had almost fallen right into it.

De Boer had the pilot take off once more and ascend towards the balcony. This time, both forward and aft, pulse cannons were fired along with a few Hammerhead missiles to reinforce the point.

Under this devastating covering fire, the other C230 let loose her cargo of marines who were able to work their way up to the upper balcony and complete the mopping up exercise.

This time they were positive all the defending troops were accounted for and, if they had time to count up all the body parts and collate the results, they would learn that ninety-eight clones died in the action with an added loss of eight Recon Delta marines with three wounded.

De Boer was satisfied that their foothold was secure and they could proceed with the second phase of their operation.

Total time elapsed, twelve minutes.

CHAPTER 25

Wilde smiled as the entrance to Docking Bay Four loomed ahead of them for he knew escape was just a few short steps away.

"Not far now, General, and we'll soon be safe. Well, I will, you, I'm afraid, well you'll be safe too, as long as you co-operate," Wilde said with a smug smile playing across his thin lips.

"We both know that's not going to happen, Jonas, so why fool ourselves?" Sinclair replied defiantly.

"I was so hoping you'd take that position, it will make the knowledge I take from you that much sweeter than if you just gave it up. In the end, you will tell me everything I want to know, it's inevitable. So please, resist all you want, all you can, I implore you; it will make the entire experience so much more enjoyable, for me at least. I'm sure you won't enjoy it at all," Wilde agreed with obvious pleasure.

Tanya looked at Sinclair, put a hand on his arm to make him pause and said, "Don't bother saying anything, General, he's not worth the trouble," then gave her father a look of such contempt it actually stopped him in his tracks.

"Oh Tanya, my dear, I had no idea you felt that way. Well, no matter, this will soon be over and..." Wilde said.

Tanya cut him off by saying, "And what, I'll be dead so you'll make yourself a new daughter, one who approves of everything you do and questions nothing, is that it Dad?"

"What an interesting idea."

"And what would this new Tanya call you, Dad or God?"

Wilde looked at her, studying her almost as if he was seeing her for the first time. Slowly a smile crossed his thin lips and he said, "Very good, I like that, it shows a depth I've not seen before. I must make sure I keep that in the new you, it'll make for some interesting conversations over dinner."

"You're quite mad you know Jonas and this can only end badly for you," Sinclair said.

"Am I, General? That may be one opinion, history may record another," Wilde countered confidently.

"You know what they say about history Jonas, that it's written by the victors and this isn't over yet," Sinclair said.

"We'll see, General, we'll see. Now move, our chariot awaits," Wilde said ending any further conversation.

As they approached Docking Bay Four Sinclair hoped that Hawk would make his move soon for time was running out for them all.

THE CORRIDOR LEADING to Docking Bay Four was curved. As Wilde and his two hostages reached it Tanis Rygar appeared from another direction.

"Hold it right there, Wilde, you're not going anywhere without me," Rygar shouted, his voice booming in the confines of the corridor.

"Ah Tanis, you figured out my little plan then. You're

smarter than I gave you credit for," Wilde replied, surprised to see the ex-Black Knight.

"Tanis Rygar, I read your file when you were with the Black Knights, quite impressive. Tell me, what made you leave the Alliance, was it purely the lure of financial gain?" Sinclair said as he recognised the name.

"I really must get those files updated you know. Did you know we didn't have an image of you on file, anywhere? I must commend you sir on being so illusive," he added, hoping that Hawk was still listening in.

"Thank you, General Sinclair, you on the other hand are in various files with many images available," Rygar replied.

"The price of fame my boy," Sinclair said with a mock bow.

Rygar drew his Sig so quickly he startled Wilde.

"Okay Jonas, before you get any ideas, I'm coming along too," Rygar said as he aimed the pistol at Wilde.

"No need to get aggressive Tanis, your appearance here is fortuitous for both of us. You can help with piloting the transport while I ensure the General here tries nothing foolish to prevent our escape," Wilde said in agreement.

MATT HAWK HAD BEEN JUST a few steps behind Wilde when Rygar confronted him. He had to drop back and hide around the curve in the corridor so he wasn't seen while he listened in to what was being said.

As the group entered the docking bay Hawk came out of hiding and ran to catch up with them. With his gun drawn, he arrived at the door seconds after it closed. Timing was of the essence here and he had to get things just right if he wanted to catch them unawares. He needed to catch them when they least expected it otherwise his plan would not succeed. The odds against him had just doubled so he had to be careful.

Waiting for ten seconds he opened the door and entered.

This bay was the same as the other three with one exception, there was a craft on the pad ready for take-off.

Wilde, the man he now knew as Tanis Rygar, General Sinclair and Tanya were halfway to the sleek transport as Hawk entered, the sound of the doors alerting them.

Rygar was the first to turn around, he spotted Hawk and his mouth formed a satisfied grin.

"I was beginning to wonder when you would show up," he said as he brought his Sig around to aim at Hawk.

Before he could fire Sinclair rammed into him in a shoulder charge that bundled him over, his shot going wild and impacting several feet above the door.

Hawk returned fire but not at Rygar, instead, he fired at Wilde. Caught off guard, the supreme commander of OMEGA shifted his aim from Sinclair for just a second and that movement saved his life, for Hawk's shot missed his head by a mere fraction. Wilde flinched as he felt the searing heat from the pulsed plasma bolt scorch his forehead as it passed him.

Quickly regaining his composure Wilde got off a shot that went wide of the target then, as panic took hold, he turned and ran for the sleek transport, his one thought that of escape.

Rygar got to his feet, looked at Sinclair who gave him a wink, then, as Wilde fired at Hawk, he turned to look at him. When Wilde moved, Sinclair went after him.

"I'll get Jonas, you take care of him," Sinclair said as he pointed at Rygar.

The ex-Black Knight smiled as he watched the General leave and he turned to look at Hawk who stared back at him with those ice-cold eyes.

"It'll be my pleasure," Hawk said.

"Just you and me then, hero. Exactly as it should be," Rygar said as he squared his shoulders in preparation for the meeting he knew must come.

Tanya Wilde stood to the side not knowing what to do or where to go, except that she must watch and hope that Hawk could win the fight.

Rygar came forward with his Sig still in his hand staring hard at Hawk with a sadistic smile on his face. Whatever happened after this, whether he escaped, was left behind by Wilde or captured by the Recon Delta marines, one thing was certain, he would enjoy the next few minutes.

Hawk tried to size his opponent up. He looked strong with good musculature and his gait was evenly balanced which usually signified good coordination. With him coming from a military background, specifically the Black Knights, the Alliance's version of Recon Delta, it meant his training would have been comparable to Hawk's own, so his close-quarter combat skills should not be taken lightly, and he still held his Sig.

He had a feeling though that Rygar would want to test himself. He'd called Hawk the hero and considered himself therefore to be the bad guy, so he would want this to end in a classic confrontation between them, man to man.

Holding the Sig loosely out to his side Rygar said, "We don't need these, you and I, not for this," then he tossed the pistol to the floor and came at Hawk.

"Thought you'd never ask," Hawk replied and he braced himself for the onslaught.

"STILL TRYING TO GET AWAY, JONAS?" Sinclair shouted after Wilde as he chased him on board the transport.

Wilde turned around and saw Sinclair come running onto the vehicle. They were in a corridor that ran almost the length of the craft with doors leading off to various compartments. It led forward to the flight deck where the pilot would fly the craft.

"Well, again General, so glad you could make it," Wilde said as he brought his pistol up. In that split second, Sinclair realised he had forgotten to arm himself, which meant there was only one thing left for him to do.

Hoping he was close enough, and that the surprise would be enough for Wilde not to shoot him in mid-air, he dived full length at him.

～

RYGAR THREW several punches in rapid succession at Hawk, which he managed to either block on his forearms or dodge out of the way of.

A left hook caught Hawk squarely on his bruised ribs forcing him to drop his guard as he winced from the pain. Rygar saw the opportunity and delivered a thunderous right cross straight onto Hawk's jaw snapping his head viciously sideways which he followed up with a left roundhouse kick again to his injured ribs. Hawk almost doubled over from the pain as he took a step backwards and Rygar went into a spinning back kick, which crashed against the side of Hawk's head sending him sprawling to the floor.

Rygar looked at him with contempt and with a sneer said, "Thought you Recon Deltas were supposed to be tough!"

～

SINCLAIR LANDED on Wilde and they both went crashing to the deck. The breath was knocked out of the General and as the two of them lay on the floor momentarily dazed from the impact he forced himself to his knees.

A quick glance at Wilde told him that he too was suffering from the impact and was trying to gather his senses but, more importantly, he still had hold of the Sig.

Hurling himself across the floor he landed on top of Wilde, frantically trying to grasp the hand holding the pistol.

Grabbing the wrist with his left hand he chopped at it with his right sending the Sig spinning across the deck.

Wilde punched Sinclair in the face splitting his lip and was then able to pull himself from under him and scramble to his feet.

Shaking the cobwebs free from his mind Sinclair got to his feet a second later. As they stood facing each other, Wilde asked, "Don't you think we're a bit too old for all of this?"

"Speak for yourself, Jonas, there's still plenty of fight left in me yet," Sinclair replied and he spat out a wad of blood-soaked spittle at Wilde's right shoe. As he looked down at it, Sinclair punched him squarely in the face with a straight right that rocked him back on his heels to such an extent that he landed on his back.

"Too old indeed," Sinclair derided and stepped forward to finish it off. Wilde had other ideas meanwhile, and lashed out with his right foot from his prone position on the deck, catching Sinclair fully in the groin with his heel. The General almost puked from the intense pain as it doubled him over and he collapsed onto the deck in the foetal position, hands clutching his vitals.

Wilde slowly, and with deliberate calm, got to his feet, wiped the blood from his damaged nose then retrieved the Sig from the deck. Standing over the General aiming the pistol at him he said, "Yes, General, too old and now I think it's time for you to retire."

~

HAWK MADE a show of struggling to his feet. "We're tough enough," he said as he stood in front of the sneering Rygar. "Well, I'll show you what tough looks like," Rygar said and he aimed a straight right at Hawk's face.

Having tasted what Rygar had to offer, Hawk decided to join the fight instead of being a bystander. He caught the fist in the palm of his right hand, a hair's breadth away from his face. Calmly he forced the hand down away from its intended target and with a slight smile said, "Okay, when you're ready."

Rygar couldn't believe what had just happened. The man was beaten, and now he was standing there as if nothing had happened. What the hell was going on?

Hawk smashed his left fist into the befuddled expression on Rygar's face sending him staggering backwards.

Shaking his head in disbelief, sending bloody spittle flying from his cut lips, Rygar charged at Hawk in a blinding rage.

Hawk sidestepped to the left blocking a punch with his right forearm, forcing his attacker to keep that arm extended giving him the opportunity to smash his left fist into Rygar's unprotected ribs.

To retaliate, Rygar brought his right fist back, hoping to smash it into Hawk's skull but it swept harmlessly across empty air as Hawk ducked beneath it.

Using a palm heel strike with his right hand, Hawk aimed the blow from his stooped position to come up at an angle of forty-five degrees and impact on the point of Rygar's nose forcing that small strip of bone to travel up at the same angle.

Hawk came up, using the power of his legs and a twist of his hips at the last second to add power to the strike and his hand shot out at almost blinding speed.

Rygar had no idea what had hit him. He saw the hand come towards him, felt a sharp pain from the impact, then his brain shut down as the bone pierced his brain killing him. He fell to his knees, his eyes blankly staring ahead, before falling forwards onto his face.

Tanya rushed forwards, hurling herself into Hawk's strong arms.

"Is, he... er... dead?" she stammered, choking back tears of relief.

"I sure hope so," Hawk replied.

A quick glance told him all he needed to know. "C'mon we've got to get on that transport to help the General," he said, pushing Tanya away just enough so he could look her in the eye, "We can pick this up later, when it's all over."

CHAPTER 26

Hawk entered the transport holding his retrieved Sig out in front of him. In the corridor ahead he saw Jonas Wilde standing over the prone form of General Sinclair aiming a Sig P996 at him. He looked ready to kill the General, which was something Hawk just wouldn't allow to happen.

"Freeze, Wilde, or I fire and at this range I won't miss," Hawk said, his voice stern in the narrow corridor.

"And neither will I, so I suggest you do nothing if you value this man's life," Wilde replied without taking his eyes off Sinclair.

Slowly he raised his eyes from the prone form below him to that of the man challenging him, his aim unwavering. His intense gaze took in the situation with that first second: the tall muscular man with the cold hard eyes holding the pistol expertly aimed at him and just behind him the frightened form of his daughter.

"I take it that you left Tanis out there somewhere?" he asked, already knowing the answer.

"Yep, he won't be joining us, ever," Hawk replied. He

knew he would have to wait and see what Wilde was going to do. There was no way he was about to shoot Wilde, not in front of his daughter and besides if he did shoot him he didn't want to risk him shooting the General in a reflex action. He would just have to allow this scene to play out and see where it took them.

"You're not going to do anything stupid now are you, whoever you are, and risk me shooting the General here," Wilde said. When no reply was forthcoming other than the intimidating stare he added, "No, thought not, now here's what's going to happen. I'm going to keep this Sig trained on the General here as I back away towards the flight deck and you'll continue to do nothing because if you do..."

"Let me guess, you'll kill the General, how original," Hawk interrupted sarcastically.

"You won't goad me into doing anything foolish you know, that's because I hold all the cards," Wilde stated calmly.

"Now you're beginning to sound like a bad comic book villain," Hawk said, wishing that Wilde would move his pistol away from the General just enough so he could take the shot and end this, but that wasn't going to happen. Whatever Wilde had become since leaving Col Sec he hadn't forgotten his training and he kept the Sig aimed unerringly at his target as he backed away down the corridor.

The moment Wilde went through the door at the bottom of the corridor Hawk holstered the Sig and rushed to the aid of the General who was still curled up in agony on the deck.

"Why didn't you take the shot?" Tanya asked from the doorway. As she moved forward the door closed behind her and they all heard the sound of the engines firing up.

"Excuse me?" asked Hawk as he knelt by Sinclair's side.

"Why didn't you shoot him, my father, when you had the chance?" she reiterated.

"Because he's your father," Hawk snapped back.

"Well, you should have," she replied tersely.

Hawk looked at her not knowing what to say and before he could think of something, anything, Sinclair said, "Yes, you should have," in a voice that was gravelly and still full of pain.

"Well, I couldn't," Hawk said finally, softly, for he knew his failure to act could have cost them all dearly.

"Matt, if you get the chance again don't hesitate, shoot. You have to stop him," Tanya said and Hawk looked at her to see if she meant it.

Could he shoot him? Well of course he could shoot him, he'd done that more times than he cared to recall, but could he kill a man in front of his daughter? No matter what that man had done, no matter how many lives he'd taken or would take, should he be allowed to continue? That man was still her father and seeing him shot dead in front of her would have an untold effect on her.

During this mission, he'd grown closer to her and now he found himself thrust into an intolerable situation. He wanted, more than anything he could imagine, to try and build a relationship with her, but how would that be possible should he take the action she told him he must and that he *knew* he must?

Simple answer, it wouldn't be possible.

He would do what he knew he had to do to safeguard the lives of Tanya, the General and the possible millions of other lives put at risk by her father's actions should he continue down the path he was on. He would kill Wilde at the first opportunity and he would never see her again, for if he did all she would see would be the man who had killed her father.

Glancing at her he simply nodded his head and said, "Okay."

The transport lurched off the pad, spun on its axis horizontally then powered out of the open docking bay out into space. Almost immediately a hyperspace window opened and the sleek craft shot through it seeming to stretch out to infinity then vanish, the window collapsing in on itself as it closed.

Inside the transport, the inertial dampeners prevented the passengers from being splattered across the bulkheads but they were aware of what had happened.

The internal speakers came to life as the intership com. unit was activated and they heard Wilde say, "Well, gentlemen and daughter of mine, we have made our escape from Earth and within a few moments we'll be met by more of my men so please make yourselves comfortable while you can."

Hawk helped Sinclair to his feet supporting his arm, which the General yanked away from him angrily.

"I do hope your inability to act earlier hasn't cost us dearly, Matt," he said fairly spitting the words at Hawk.

"We're not dead yet, General, so just hold tight," Hawk replied with altogether too much confidence for Sinclair's taste.

"Hold tight?" Sinclair muttered as he watched Hawk grab hold of Tanya and brace her against him, almost as if...

A sudden explosion erupted in the rear quarter of the craft throwing it into a spin.

Hawk held Tanya tightly as the three of them went sprawling across the deck of the corridor.

"What the hell just happened?" Sinclair asked as he leant against the bulkhead.

"I'll explain later, sir, now I've got to get to Wilde," Hawk said as he headed towards the flight deck, gun drawn and ready to use.

Once within sight of the door, he started to blast away at the locking panel at the side which, after being hit by a couple of pulsed plasma bolts, burst into flames and blew apart opening the doors.

Hawk entered the flight deck, his Sig held out in front in a two-handed grip moving from left to right as he swept the small room for his target.

Jonas Wilde was just pulling himself back into the pilot's chair as Hawk burst into the room. He saw the tall agent over the back of the chair and quickly reached for his Sig and fired.

Hawk caught the movement in his peripheral vision and dived into a roll just as Wilde snapped a frantic shot at him.

Rolling straight into a crouch and still holding the Sig, Hawk returned fire at the pilot's chair, his first two shots striking the back smashing it to pieces, but Wilde had already moved.

Quickly searching for Wilde and at the same time aware that his present position was unprotected, Hawk dived for cover just as Wilde fired another couple of shots at him, each bolt striking the deck where he'd been just moments before.

Seeing the muzzle flashes gave him a better idea of where his attacker was and in which direction he was moving. He fired a snapshot off at where the muzzle flashes had been then anticipated where the next ones would come from and aimed there.

Wilde appeared from behind a workstation to the left of where Hawk had last fired.

Seeing him just in time Hawk quickly readjusted his aim slightly and fired again.

The pulsed plasma bolt struck Wilde in the centre of his forehead exploding his head in a spray of blood and gore.

Wilde was sent flying backwards hitting the deck hard. He was dead before landing.

Rising to his feet, the Sig aimed at the ceiling, Hawk's eyes never wandered from where Wilde lay. He knew the shot was good after seeing the result of the impact, but at this late stage in the game, he was taking nothing for granted. As that thought was running through his mind a warning siren echoed throughout the ship.

"What's that?" asked Sinclair from the doorway to the flight deck.

Hawk was searching the controls for any sign of what it could be and then saw a digital readout with a warning light flashing above it.

The readout was counting down.

"Somehow a self-destruct has been activated, must've been wired into Wilde's life signs," Hawk said as an explanation.

"You mean he was fitted with a biomonitor?" Sinclair asked.

"Yes, all the top executives at MaxCorp had them fitted to keep an eye on them should they fall sick or be injured," explained Tanya from behind the General.

"This one must've been tied into a self-destruct, probably one on board the Nemesis too," Hawk said as he looked around for a way to terminate it.

From the door, Sinclair asked, "How long do we have?"

Calmly Hawk looked at him and replied, "One minute twenty-nine seconds."

Putting an arm around Tanya's shoulders to comfort her Sinclair said, "I'm sorry, my dear."

"For what?" Hawk asked then he keyed his ear bug and said, "Captain Jefferson, when you're ready sir, make it quick please, we have less than a minute before this ship blows."

"Jefferson, on the Valkyrie?" Sinclair said in surprise.

"Who else do you think attacked us, sir? I'll explain fully once we're aboard the Valkyrie, right now we need to move."

The three of them quickly left the flight deck and headed towards the docking hatch where a green light was flashing showing that the Valkyrie had docked and ready for them to board her.

Opening the hatch Hawk bustled the other two through, then followed closing the hatch after him.

"Okay Cap, take us away from here as fast as you can," Hawk said through the ear bug com. The Valkyrie was moving away on full thrust as Sinclair asked Hawk, "How long?"

Hawk glanced at his chronometer and said, "Any second now."

The shockwave from the blast struck the escaping craft but luckily her shields were able to protect her so she sustained no damage.

By the time the trio reached the bridge, it was all over. Captain Jefferson rose from the command chair when he saw them enter and stood to attention.

"Officer on deck," he said and the rest of the bridge crew did likewise.

"As you were, gentlemen," Sinclair said and as they returned to their duty posts he asked, "Now would someone please explain to me what just happened?"

"Simple really, sir, when Colonel De Boer was en route to the Nemesis he contacted me and I gave him a sit-rep. He'd already alerted Captain Jefferson that he may be needed to help evacuate us from the Nemesis, but when I told him of Wilde's plan to escape he told me he would gain control of the Nemesis and make her captain tell him the location Wilde would be escaping to, then pass that on to Jefferson so he could jump ahead. It was the Valkyrie who attacked and disabled us after we escaped from the Nemesis," Hawk explained.

"Congratulations Captain, you did good work. Please relay my thanks to the rest of your crew. Contact Colonel De Boer on the Nemesis and tell him to get a ship here ASAP to investigate the wreckage of that transport. I want the entire area searched thoroughly, if Wilde had a base out here anywhere I want it found and destroyed," Sinclair said.

"Right away, sir," Jefferson said.

"Now, we head home and start to rebuild."

"What about Tanya, sir?"

"I'll do what I can to ensure she is looked after. There will be no charges brought against her, she was completely innocent of her father's actions and therefore is free to go on her way. I'll see about freeing her father's assets for her personal use so she is financially solvent when she begins her new life, that's the least we can do after all we put her through."

"Thank you, sir," Hawk said. He looked at her; she was standing slightly apart from them. It was already starting, he thought, the distancing herself from him after he had killed her father.

"Sir, Colonel De Boer reports the Nemesis secure and the Odyssey and Atlantis are en route here to begin the investigation of the wreckage site and start the search for the hidden base. They'll be here in less than an hour," ops said.

"Why the delay?" Sinclair enquired.

"They're waiting for more marines to arrive from Fort Bragg and Ford Trenton, sir. He says that he wants a full battalion ready to go if a ground assault is called for."

"That's fine, just tell him that time is at a premium here and we don't want to give them time to evacuate. If they're here I want them found and dealt with. I won't have them coming back to bite us on the ass again because we were lax."

"Aye, sir, relaying message now."

"General, Matt and Miss, would you care to wait in my quarters until it's time for us to leave? It's not much, as you can imagine, but at least you can relax for a while," Jefferson said.

"Thank you, Captain, most generous, but I see no point in

us waiting around. If a base is nearby we're ill-equipped to do anything about it and we would only be subjecting ourselves to needless danger. This location has been forwarded onto Earth and cruisers are en route so let's just leave it to them, shall we. Our time can best be served back on Earth."

"As you wish, sir," Jefferson replied then turning to the pilot said, "Take us home."

CHAPTER 27

Upon arriving back on Earth, General Sinclair met with Colonel De Boer for a quick debrief of the actions up to and after the taking of the Nemesis. Once he had all the available facts he set about securing the area.

The Nemesis was placed away from shipping lanes with a ship stationed nearby as guard to prevent any unauthorised access, while a repair crew went to work restoring her systems and extracting data from her computer logs. There was still so much about OMEGA they didn't know and needed to know if they were to combat it, should it still prove to be a viable threat.

Work on the Confederation Headquarters building was started, clearing the site and identifying all the remains.

This had to be done first before it could be made safe. What to do after would be a decision for when all the dead had been properly identified and their relatives notified of the tragedy.

Hawk took Tanya to a safe location until everything had

been settled and he left her in the capable hands of two Col Sec agents with orders to keep her safe, twenty-four seven. That having been done he returned to Col Sec HQ to continue his work.

Colonel De Boer returned to command the marines who went on the Atlantis and Odyssey to search for any signs of a hidden base in the area near where the transport exploded with Jonas Wilde on board. There was a solar system close by with at least five planets that could have a hidden base. None were E class planets but that didn't preclude them from being host to a structure that could sustain life. On the one hand, it would be a good idea to have a base on a planet where no one would think to look. On the other hand, it would make the task of locating it that much harder because nowhere could be discounted from the search area.

It would take weeks for the search to be completed so De Boer asked for more ships to help out on a rotating pattern. His request was granted with two more cruisers being added to the roster allowing downtime for the crew and marines.

Sinclair had to report to President Takagi on the present status of events.

"Glad you could come, General, please take a seat," Takagi said as Sinclair entered the President's Oval Office at the White House. No longer the home and residential headquarters of the President of the United States of America, it was now home to the World President and office to EarthGov. The Confederation was run by a council whose head chairperson was the World President, with smaller matters, more personal to Earth alone, being run by EarthGov.

"Thank you, Mister President, hope you don't mind but I asked Matt Hawk to accompany me as he led the operations against OMEGA and was involved at every level," Sinclair replied before taking a seat before the large mahogany desk.

"Not at all, I'm sure his input will be most valuable and help me to understand this terrible situation a little better," Takagi said, his face a mass of worry lines as concern was etched across his normally serene features. A slightly built man in his early fifties, he was remarkably fit due to his daily regimen of karate exercises. His inky black hair was swept back from a high forehead. Deep brown eyes looked at the two men before him, the epicanthic folds accentuating his Asian heritage.

As the two men sat down heavily in the offered chairs Takagi took in their dishevelled appearance, their blood-stained faces and said, "My God, you look like hell. Can I get you anything, a drink? When was the last time you two ate a decent meal or slept?"

"Not sure, sir, we've been a bit busy, as I'm sure you're aware," Sinclair replied with a sigh as he suddenly realised just how exhausted he felt.

"Of course, so let's make this brief so that you can both get some well-earned rest," Takagi said.

"I'm afraid that may not possible for some time yet, sir," Sinclair started but the President held up his hand to halt him.

"That's not up for discussion, General. I cannot afford to have you making mistakes because you're fighting fatigue at the same time as you're fighting OMEGA, so you General Sinclair and you, Matt Hawk will go home from here and get at least eight hours sleep. Do I have to make that a Presidential Order?"

"No, sir," Sinclair replied with a half-smile.

"Now then, where are we with this whole situation?" the President asked.

"Okay, what we know so far is that Jonas Wilde operated a group known to us as OMEGA. Somehow he was siphoning assets from MaxCorp to fund it. Using the same assets that MaxCorp was providing Col Sec with, he made OMEGA the viable threat that it became.

"Apparently Wilde had an unlimited supply of money to fund this organisation. He probably cooked the books so that the money appropriated for certain projects was overestimated making the budgets larger so that he could supply both Col Sec and OMEGA with the same items."

"Do you think Maxwell Eisenhower was aware of what he was doing?" Takagi asked bluntly.

"Up to this point we have no way of knowing either way and until we can get to question him I'm afraid that question will have to remain unanswered, sir."

"I understand, but please make that a priority," insisted Takagi.

"I assure you Mister President that it is one of many priorities I have at this time, sir," agreed Sinclair.

"What else have you learned of this group?"

"Not only was it extremely well funded but it had operatives implanted inside Col Sec itself. At this point, we are not sure how deep that infiltration has gone but it's something we are actively investigating. We also know that they had a cloning operation that was really quite impressive. As far as we know it had two levels of clones each called Rovers. The basic model was a normal humanoid model that we presume was built for administrative duties at the managerial level. The other model, the Rover5, was the military version. Matt has more insight on these than I do, sir."

"And what have you learned about these Rovers, Matt?" asked Takagi.

"The basic model is your average team leader, sir, intelligent, articulate and intuitive all built around the same matrix, much the same as the Rover5s except in the latter's case physical attributes had replaced mental acuity. So far we are not aware that they share any memories or experiences but it's something we are working on. How far their individuality extends once they're activated we're not sure either. We do know the Rover5s were genetically engineered to be stronger and faster than the basic model and with a higher pain threshold that made them quite tough to kill. At this point in time, we don't know how far this cloning operation extends or even where it is. We think it must be secreted somewhere in one of the many MaxCorp research facilities probably under a false name to keep it hidden from prying eyes and until we talk to Eisenhower, we won't know. Wilde had an alternate base where he could have a similar operation going," Hawk explained.

"How's the search for that coming along, General?" Takagi asked.

"We've been working for two days straight with rotating shifts, three cruisers on, one off. It's a slow process, sir, and if it's there we'll find it. We do know that no ships have been seen leaving the area, so either they're dug in deep and hoping we don't find them or biding their time to make a run for it."

"Or they could be planning to fight to their deaths," suggested the President with a dour expression.

"No, I don't think so, sir. I tend to gravitate towards the first thought that they're dug in deep and are waiting for us to pass them by. We've dealt them a major blow, sir. We've captured the Nemesis, killed their first attack force along with their commander-in-chief. They'll need time to regroup and rethink their strategy, e.g. do they appoint a new leader and continue or do they disband and go their separate ways? Either way, they'll need to keep their heads down until they decide. To act now without clear leadership would be suicidal for all concerned."

"Okay, I see your point," agreed Takagi. "What about Confederation Headquarters, what's happening there?"

"We're still in the process of clearing the site, making it safe and identifying the dead, sir. Again it's a long process."

"Of which I'm totally aware and my sympathy goes out to the families of those who lost their lives but I must be practical here and point out something we are all aware of and that is that we have to carry on, so I suggest that Col Sec be moved to a temporary location along with Confederation Headquarters until a more permanent solution can be found," Takagi insisted.

"I've already made provisions for Col Sec to be relocated in our underground base at Area 15, sir. I would suggest that the Confederation Headquarters be moved to the Capitol Building here in DC. It can be renovated and refitted to the needs of the residents and, with the modifications to security I can provide, it can be functioning within the week at most, a few days if they work around the clock. In that way, sir, business will revert to normal more quickly. We can extend the existing structure to accommodate the extra staff much quicker than if we had to start from scratch with a whole new building."

"Very good, I'll get my team on that right away," Takagi agreed gratefully.

"Sir, one more thing," Sinclair said almost reluctantly.

"Yes, General, what is it?"

"Sir, we've learned a valuable lesson from OMEGA, in that we shouldn't place all our eggs in one basket. MaxCorp supplies a staggering quantity of our munitions, equipment and tec to Col Sec which gave OMEGA the opportunity to become the powerful threat it is," Sinclair explained.

"You said 'is', do you think they still are a threat?" Takagi asked leaning forward in concern. He was just beginning to feel they had the situation under control and now this!

"Until I have positive proof that Jonas Wilde is dead, the base is found and destroyed, that Maxwell Eisenhower was not involved and that Col Sec has no more moles, I can't be certain of anything, sir. I'll proceed under the assumption that they are still a threat," Sinclair answered as concisely as he could given the information he had to work with at the time.

Takagi sat back and steepled his fingers under his chin as he contemplated what had been said. Finally, he spoke, "I see, please continue."

"With your permission, sir, I would like to contact Rand-Corp with a view to them supplying Col Sec. I do not wish to sever ties with MaxCorp until we have other suppliers who can step in to supply our needs with the volume we require and to our exacting standards. Besides, it'll give us a chance to keep an eye on MaxCorp to see if they still have ties to OMEGA," suggested Sinclair.

"You suspect Eisenhower then?" queried the President.

"Let's just say I find it hard to believe they could hide an operation as huge as this from the man in charge. Even if they could, they must have someone else in place now that Wilde has been revealed as commander-in-chief, to carry on their work. Rooting out all the moles in a group as insidious as this will take some time, sir," agreed Sinclair.

"I take it then that you want the contact with RandCorp kept on the quiet?"

"Initially, until they've agreed and I'm certain they can meet our needs and standards. Once we've seen some samples and tested them, the rest of the operation can be handed over to admin. I know it sounds a bit OCD, sir, but until I'm confident the security aspect has been covered I'd prefer to take charge."

"I understand General, and as always you have my trust and the support of this Office."

"Thank you, sir, I appreciate it."

"I also trust that because Captain Hawk is here you wish him to continue as the lead in this investigation."

"I do, sir."

"I agree also, it would be a waste to remove him to other duties in favour of someone else when he is so familiar with the details of this case. Is there anything else gentlemen?"

"No, sir, not at this time."

"Then I'll let you get back to it as I know you are extremely busy men."

"Thank you, sir, as are you," Sinclair said as he and Hawk wearily got to their feet to leave the room.

"Good luck gentlemen and keep me informed, and get some sleep," Takagi said as they turned to leave the room.

As they left the White House in the armoured ground car, a Grand Voyager 600s manufactured by MaxCorp, Hawk relaxed into the lush leather upholstery and sighed, "You know, a shower and eight hours uninterrupted sleep sounds just about right," he said as he rubbed his tired eyes.

Sinclair looked at him and said, "I agree. Make sure you're well-rested Matt, because we're meeting Able Rand at ten tomorrow morning."

Glancing at the chronometer on the dash in front of him he noticed the time, twenty-three hundred, and he said, "Doesn't that guy ever sleep?" meaning the President.

"Oh, about the same as us, I guess," Sinclair said.

"You mean never while on duty, right?"

"That's right."

Matt leant back on the headrest and said, "Okay, nudge me when we're at my hotel," then he closed his eyes and was instantly asleep.

Sinclair listened to Hawk's breathing slowing as he sank into a slumber and wondered how he could do that, fall asleep at the drop of a hat wherever he was. It was an ability many agents cultivated over time but one he had never been able to grasp. Instead, he sat back and looked through the side window watching the lights of the city pass by, pondering at what lay ahead and hoping the steps he was about to put into place would help prevent another tragedy from taking place.

Only time would tell.

CHAPTER 28

The Grand Voyager 600s was at Hawk's hotel by nine the following morning. He had managed to get some sleep after a hot shower to wash away the grime and blood accumulated during his recent efforts against Jonas Wilde's OMEGA.

Having been awake for at least an hour he had time to shower, get dressed and have a breakfast of a bacon and mushroom omelette with coffee delivered to his room. Dressed in combat trousers, a casual shirt and his favourite leather jacket he left the hotel. As per regulations, he wore a soft leather holster beneath his left armpit that held his Sig P996, although he didn't think he'd need to use it this time. As he got into the rear seating section he saw General Sinclair looking relaxed in a dark blue pinstripe suit.

"Good morning Matt, hope you slept well," the General said as Hawk sat next to him.

"Yes, thanks sir, and you? You look rested," Hawk replied.

"I managed to drop off thanks, now down to work," Sinclair said, wasting no time. "According to our file, Rand-Corp is run by Able Rand and has been for the last thirty-five years. He took over from his father when he deemed young Able ready to take the reins. It's been passed down from generation to generation for the past six hundred years. His son and daughter, Joshua and Jessica, are his chief officers and help him run the business.

"It really is a family concern. RandCorp is as big as MaxCorp and just as powerful. They already supply us with atmosphere processing plants for terraforming, most of the ships of the Independent Space Agency, the Colonial Line of cruise ships and they build some of our cruisers such as the Legend. Their weapons are of the best and only lost out on the contract to supply Col Sec to MaxCorp due to the latter offering the lower bid, something that Able Rand himself complained about. He claimed that somehow, someone at MaxCorp got wind of Rand's bid and undercut it by one per cent."

"I remember hearing about that, it caused quite a stir," opined Hawk.

"Yes, nothing was ever proved either way but even to this day it's rumoured that Able holds a grudge."

"Has that got any bearing on why you want to offer him this deal?"

"It will give him the chance to prove something he's maintained to this day, that his weapons systems are superior to those supplied by MaxCorp and this time the price is not an issue. If they're as good as he says and he can supply the numbers we need in the given time frame, the deal is his."

"Well, seeing as OMEGA has the same systems as us and was using them to kick our asses, a change might give us the edge we need."

"My thoughts exactly. Here's the data file, upload it to your NI and get to know the corporation and the players involved. I want you fully briefed by the time we enter Rand's office," Sinclair said as he passed him a palm pad with the data file encoded within. Using his NI Hawk connected with the small device and uploaded the data file directly to his NI where it would be stored and where he could access it at will, similar to a memory.

The rest of the journey was completed in silence.

When they reached their destination the Grand Voyager 600s pulled up outside the towering edifice that was Rand-Corp. The two passengers got out while their vehicle was directed to a parking area in the basement of the building where it could wait until summoned.

Sinclair and Hawk walked through the front entrance where they were scanned and their identities verified. Only because they were officers of Col Sec were they allowed to keep their weapons.

Once this process was completed they were escorted to the penthouse where Able Rand's office was situated and their meeting would take place.

The decor in the building was tasteful and conducive to a good working environment with few distractions, but when they reached the penthouse it was obvious more money had been spent on a few of the finer little luxuries that would make the working day just a little more comfortable for the higher echelon.

Able Rand greeted them in his private office and as they entered he got to his feet and came around from behind the large mahogany desk. Tall and slim, he exuded an air of raw, undefined power. His hair was a dazzling white and worn brushed straight back from a high forehead over piercing brown eyes. He had an easy smile that brightened his face and a smooth, unblemished complexion that belied his sixty-three years of age.

"Gentlemen, I'm so pleased to see you, but somewhat puzzled by the urgency of your request and intrigued by what this could be all about. Please, take a seat so you can explain," Rand said extending a hand out first to General Sinclair then Hawk. They were both slightly taken aback by his straightforward approach and by the strength of the man's grip in the firm handshake.

"I must thank you for seeing us at such short notice, I'm General…"

"There's no need for introductions General Sinclair, I know all I need to know about you sir, and this must be the intrepid Captain Matthew Hawk, former Recon Delta marine recruited by General Sinclair himself to work for him in Col Sec's Intelligence Division. There's more but I think I've made my point. You may call me Able, all my friends do," Rand said cutting the General off.

Hawk glanced at Sinclair and smiling, said, "I prefer Matt, and how can you be certain we'll be friends, if you don't mind my asking?"

"Just a feeling I've got, gut instinct and it's almost never let me down," Rand replied. "Now tell me, gentlemen, what can I do for you?"

Sinclair sat on the luxurious two-seater sofa by the wall to the right of the desk. "Okay Able, what I'm about to tell you is classified and must remain that way. You must have heard of the attack on the Confederation Headquarters building."

"Who hasn't, it's been on every news channel."

"Well the group responsible is called OMEGA and it was run by Jonas Wilde."

"The same Jonas Wilde who works for that snake in the grass Maxwell Eisenhower?"

"Yes, and we think he was siphoning funds from MaxCorp to fund OMEGA and using that company's assets, which they were providing us with, to use against us."

"Eisenhower must be behind it too, there's no way he would allow Wilde to work something of that scale right under his nose. That bastard hasn't had an original idea for years. A fact he's so paranoid about that he has moles in every major corporation in the galaxy. I'm sure he has one here, I've just never been able to figure out whom, but when I do I'll skin the fucker myself."

"Why would you think he has a mole here?" asked Hawk wondering if it was merely sour grapes over losing over the contract to supply Col Sec.

"He has to have one, how else would he win that contract with what he had. The weapons he'd offered to supply Col Sec with were faulty; they had a glitch in the power modulator that caused the battery clips to overload when used on sustained fire. Two weeks before the deadline to submit samples they suddenly had a breakthrough and solved the problem giving them the opportunity to submit the Sig P996 to you," explained Rand.

"That could happen surely," Sinclair said, clearly not convinced.

"You're right, it could happen, but the design they had wasn't for the Sig P996, they were developing the Tokarun T90. They stole the Sig from us; they had to change most of their production matrixes to fit the new model. If I remember rightly, they were late getting the bulk order to you."

"That's right," Sinclair agreed.

"Every major new development they've come up with within the last decade has come from us and we can't seem to plug the hole," Rand said angrily.

"In that case, I'm not sure it would be wise to ask what I came here to ask," Sinclair said and got to his feet.

"I can assure you General that security here at RandCorp is second to none. I know to say that after divulging what I just have would seem a tad laughable, but I can assure you that although the leak may still be unplugged, we've made it more difficult to hack into our systems. We are in fact in the process of attempting to pinpoint the leak so we can plug it permanently."

"Able, we need an alternative to MaxCorp, one that can give us the edge against OMEGA and not someone who freely gives them the same. Col Sec can't afford another Nemesis incident and neither can the Confederation," Sinclair said in disappointment.

"Excuse me, Nemesis?" Rand asked.

"Yes, that was the starship that attacked us."

"The bastard stole that as well," Rand almost screamed.

"Well, that just proves my point."

"General, I understand your doubts and I sympathise with you. Perhaps if I show you something we've been working on it might persuade you to reconsider and maybe loan us Matt here to help plug the leak."

Matt Hawk said, "Can't hurt to look, General."

Sinclair looked at Hawk then at Rand and paused, with a sigh, he said, "Okay, let's see what you've got."

CHAPTER 29

"You won't be sorry I can assure you, gentlemen. What I'm about to show you will rock your world," Rand said as he led them through the door from his office. Pointing to his private elevator that was at the end of the hall Rand smiled as a tall, elegantly dressed man was just leaving an office close by.

"Maguire, can you inform Josh and Jess I may be late for lunch, there are some things I must attend to," Rand said as the man turned to face them.

"Certainly, sir," the man replied and Hawk placed a hand on Sinclair's arm as he knew that he, too, had recognised the voice.

Rushing past Rand, Hawk strode up to Maguire, his Sig already drawn and grabbed Maguire by the throat, slamming him against the wall and placing the muzzle against his forehead just above and right between a pair of familiar opaline eyes.

"Give me one good reason why I don't splatter your brains all over this wall Maguire, or should I call you Rover?" he snarled through gritted teeth.

283

"Matt, what the hell do you think you're doing?" Rand asked as he made to go up to him and pull him off his employee. Sinclair put a restraining hand on his shoulder stopping him and as he turned to look at the General he asked, "What the hell is going on here Sinclair?"

"That man is a clone, one of many made by Jonas Wilde to use in the employ of OMEGA, he's a Rover. There's your leak Rand, right there," Sinclair replied releasing his hold on him.

Rand looked at the man being pinned to the wall by Hawk and Sinclair could see him working things out in that sharp mind of his, seeing if it was at all possible. Maguire looked from Hawk to Rand and the fear that was present when he was grabbed, slowly drained away to be replaced by utter calm.

With a smile, Maguire said, "You got me."

"Why?" Rand asked.

"I'm a clone, my allegiance is to my master, and it's pre-programmed at birth. I do as he orders," replied the Rover who then calmly touched something on his wrist. Both he and Hawk were suddenly enveloped in a bright light that seemed to expand and fill the hallway and then, just as suddenly, collapsed in upon itself.

Rand and Sinclair were momentarily blinded by this and turned away to shield their eyes. When they turned back to where the light originated, the hallway was empty.

"Oh no!" Rand exclaimed with obvious dread.

"What?" Sinclair asked.

HAWK WAS LYING on the ground when he opened his eyes. All he could remember was the blinding light that surrounded him and the Rover. A light so bright, so intense he could actually feel it, and that sensation was pain. All-encompassing pain that blotted out all thought, all emotion; a pain so deep he swore it reached down into his bones. Then, when the light collapsed in on itself, he blacked out to wake up here, wherever 'here' was.

At first, he couldn't move, not a muscle. Wherever he'd travelled to, the pain had come with him and it even hurt to move his eyes. Gradually the pain began to recede and he found he could breathe once more. Taking a slow, calming breath he began to assess his condition mentally to see if the pain was a marker of some deeper damage.

Furtively he looked around him, hoping not to draw attention to himself or to the fact he was awake, at least not until he was sure he could move. The first thing he wanted to do was have a serious talk with that Rover and find out what the hell just happened but until he was certain he could at least stand without falling over, he guessed that would have to wait.

"Ah, you're awake," said a voice he recognised from somewhere behind him and therefore out of sight. From what he could see from his position on the floor he was in a huge, dimly lit chamber, so he was guessing it was closed down or at least not used very often.

"I'll bet you're feeling terrible, I know I did the first time I used it," said the clone. Suddenly overhead lights were turned on and the chamber was bathed in bright light that made Hawk wince as thousands of needles were thrust into his eyes probing towards his brain, or at least that's what it felt like.

"They say it disrupts the neurons in the brain almost short-circuiting it as it affects the body at a cellular level. I don't really understand all the technical details but they also say it causes cellular degradation each time it's used with a cumulative effect. After three times the effects are irreversible. Death is inevitable, a slow and painful death by all accounts. No one has survived more than five trips using the device," explained the clone.

"Well that explains what just happened, sort of, how about telling me where the hell we are?" Hawk said as he gathered his strength to stand and face the clone. As he got to his feet and unsteadily turned towards the clone he took in some more of his surroundings. There was equipment around him, but he had no idea what it could be used for and when he laid eyes on the clone he noticed a change. The skin on his face looked pale, almost translucent, and there were dark circles beneath his eyes; those opalescent eyes that all the clones had in identical faces, which had given him away.

He looked ill and as if he'd aged a decade in the blink of an eye.

"How many times have you used the device?" Hawk asked, but he thought he already knew the answer.

"That was my third, I'm a dead man walking," Maguire said with a half-smile.

"Oh, you became that the moment I saw you," Hawk replied sourly.

"Very good Mister Agent Man, but seeing as how I'm going to die anyway I've got nothing to lose, so do you think it's wise to piss me off?"

Hawk looked around the chamber searching for something.

"What?" Maguire asked angrily.

"Oh nothing, I was just trying to see if I could see anyone who gives a fuck," Hawk replied coldly.

"Oh very good, I must try to use that."

"Make it fast then, dead man walking, remember?"

"Not before you though," Maguire said and he brought up Hawk's Sig and fired.

~

"Okay Rand, you'd better damn well explain what the hell just happened here," Sinclair said angrily. Rand was staring at the space where Hawk and the clone had stood seconds ago.

"That damned fool," Rand managed to say finally.

"What? Say something damn it," ordered Sinclair his anger reaching boiling point.

"He's used the SUT, the damned fool," Rand replied as if that explained everything.

"What the hell is a SUT and why do you keep insisting he's a damn fool? Talk to me Rand," Sinclair said trying to get Rand to focus. Clearly what had just happened had rattled him and was unexpected on so many levels, but now more than ever he needed the man's help.

Seeming to gather his wits Rand looked at Sinclair and said, "I'm sorry General, the SUT, or Single Unit Transporter was, or is, just that, a transportation device for a single unit, one person, but we abandoned it because it proved too unstable for the user. It disrupts not only the binding of cells to each other but also the entire nervous system. Anyone using it, their brain sort of short circuits, that is bad enough but something we thought we could work on and eradicate in time, until we learned of the cellular degradation. No one using it more than five times lived, after the third, possibly the fourth trip, depending on the subject, the effects are irreversible."

"Oh my God, so where has he taken Matt? C'mon, think man," Sinclair shouted. He needed to move, to do something, anything, in order to help Matt.

"I'm not sure. No, wait, you said he's a clone, right, and he works for Jonas Wilde and that OMEGA group thing?"

"Yes, a clone, we need to stop him. He may be able to lead us to where they are, and now that Wilde is dead we have to stamp them out."

"Well, before you do that General, come with me. I think I know where he's gone."

$\sim$

HAWK SAW the Sig come up and adrenalin flooded his system giving him the strength to move. Not expecting to be able to evade the shot, he dived into a roll anyway and the pulsed plasma bolt passed under his right armpit grazing his already bruised ribs but at least he was alive, which was more than could be said for the clone once he got his hands on him, he vowed.

Maguire had aimed directly at him, firing at him as he stood there, and he knew of no man alive who could dodge a shot like that, but he also knew why he had missed. The slight tremor in his hand threw his aim off; the effects of cellular degradation had begun.

Still fighting the effects of travelling via the SUT, Hawk felt a little disorientation lingering throwing him slightly off his game. Putting a hand to his ribs beneath his right armpit he felt the blood oozing through his shirt from the wound. He had to finish this quickly before loss of blood became a factor. Looking up from the ground where he'd landed after being shot, he saw Maguire bringing the Sig onto him for another shot.

There was a desk close by and he frantically hurled himself behind it just as Maguire fired. The shot blasted away the corner of the desk and Maguire, sensing victory, fired again and again destroying more and more of Hawk's cover with each shot. Soon there would be nothing left to hide behind. He had to do something – but what? He realised he was having trouble thinking clearly, obviously another effect of the SUT, but what could he do? He couldn't move or he'd be shot, he couldn't stay there for much longer either and he had nothing to fight back with. He was trapped and rapidly running out of time and options.

RAND RAN to the private elevator with Sinclair hot on his heels. Once inside he ordered it to take them to Sub Level 5 and then he called security and ordered an armed team to meet them on arrival.

"Okay, Rand, do you want to tell me where we're going or should I cover my eyes and act surprised?" Sinclair was getting fed up with being kept in the dark like this and he realised this must be what it was like sometimes for those who worked for him and a wry smile escaped.

"Glad you're enjoying yourself, General," Rand said after spotting the quickly disguised expression.

"Just anticipating what Matt will do to that clone."

"Trust me, General, he'll be in no fit state to do anything, not after his first trip. I doubt he's even conscious."

"You obviously don't know Matt Hawk very well; he's got the constitution of an ox and the strength to match."

"I hope you're right, sir, because he'll sure need it. Okay get ready, we're almost there."

OVER HALF the desk had been destroyed by shots from the Sig and Hawk could tell Maguire was getting closer in anticipation of the kill.

There was only one thing Hawk could think of doing and that was to take the fight to him. Seconds ago he wouldn't have had a clue what to do, but now as the fog around his mind began to clear, he knew exactly what to do.

"Just a few more shots, just a few more steps closer", he thought.

Grabbing hold of the underside of what was left of the desk, Hawk thrust up with his legs and pulled up with his hands hurling the desk at the oncoming clone.

Maguire wasn't expecting any resistance from Hawk and when the desk came at him it caught him off guard and he momentarily panicked. He threw up his hands to ward off the incoming missile and therefore stopped firing.

Hawk continued his momentum and followed the desk towards the clone. By the time Maguire had deflected the desk Hawk was within striking range. He had run and dived through the air at him and they collided with a bone-crunching impact and Hawk's momentum took them both off their feet to crash to the floor.

They rolled on the ground and Maguire suddenly found himself on top. He couldn't believe his luck and before Hawk could react he'd smashed the butt of the Sig against the side of his head.

Unable to defend against the blow, Hawk braced himself as best he could, but still, it rattled his teeth and for a second stars flashed before his eyes.

Maguire pushed himself away and looked around, momentarily disorientated by the fight. Seeing what he needed he moved off in that direction.

Shaking off the effects of the stunning blow, Hawk got to his feet faster than the clone thought possible and was after him once more. Forgetting he still had the Sig in his hand the clone began to run towards his objective, which looked to be a computer terminal over by a huge piece of equipment, the purpose of which was a complete mystery to Hawk.

Reaching the terminal, Maguire realised he still held the Sig and brought it around to fire at the onrushing Hawk who, on seeing the movement, once more dived full length.

He caught Maguire across the chest with his arm and took the two of them down again but this time, instead of landing in a heap, Hawk managed to roll clear then come up on his feet at almost the same time as the clone. Maguire still had the Sig in his right hand and as he tried to bring it up, Hawk kicked it away with his right foot in an outside crescent kick. This move knocked Maguire's arm across his body as the kick connected and he watched as the weapon was sent sliding across the floor.

Hawk planted his right foot on the floor after landing the kick and followed through with a left cross to Maguire's chin, which snapped the clone's head around so viciously Hawk thought he may have killed him.

Maguire went sprawling on the floor from the tremendous blow to his jaw, actually following the path of the Sig. He managed to reach out and grab it then bring it back around to fire a series of shots at Hawk.

Instead of finishing the fight as he'd hoped, the punch not only prolonged it also gave his adversary the advantage again.

Seeing the pistol in the clone's hand again, Hawk dived for the nearest cover he could find just as a salvo of pulsed plasma bolts strafed where he'd been standing.

He landed hard on his shoulder behind the huge piece of equipment he'd been next to and hoped the energy from the shots would not cause this thing, whatever it was, to explode.

Searching frantically for anything he could use as a weapon he noticed that the shots being fired at him were very erratic, almost none of them were hitting the target. He wondered if this side effect of travelling through the SUT would affect him too and if so, how soon.

All that could wait though, now he had more important things on his mind, like how to survive the next few minutes.

There was a cessation of gunfire then almost silence; the

only sound was Maguire working at the computer terminal. Hawk had no idea what he was doing, then another sound invaded the silence, that of equipment powering up. No, more like an engine, and he was right behind it.

~

RAND AND SINCLAIR braced themselves to move the moment the elevator came to a halt. The doors opened with a soft hiss and were immediately greeted by two large men with pistols drawn and aimed at the ceiling.

"We've secured this level, sir. No one's getting in or out through those doors," said the largest of them who was obviously in charge. Both men wore battle vests with various pockets filled with spare battery clips and other equipment, similar to vests worn by Recon Delta marines. Leggings of the same material with patch pockets on the side of the legs were also worn with padding covering the knee area. Military-style boots adorned their feet while a helmet of a design unfamiliar to Sinclair protected their heads. The blast shields were down so their faces were hidden from view.

"Very good, now let's get in there before he gets out the other way," Rand replied as the two guards went before them.

"Other way? You should've sent guards to cover every exit," Sinclair said angrily, he didn't want Maguire to escape due to the incompetence of internal security.

"There's only this one door, General," Rand replied, further confusing him.

"Then what the hell are you talking about? Oh, you mean escape using the SUT?"

"No, I'm betting by now he's having trouble even thinking straight. He won't dare use the SUT again, not if he's about to do what I think he's about to do."

"Okay, now you've lost me again," Sinclair said, his frustration mounting.

"Don't worry, General, you'll see what I mean soon enough," Rand said, not explaining at all. "Okay guys, let's get that door open," he added ordering the guards to move in.

～

THE SOUND from the huge machine was devastatingly loud and Hawk wondered what it did. One thing was obvious; apart from making a lot of noise, it used an awful lot of power.

Peering around the side he could see Maguire standing about twenty feet away from the machine, staring intently at it, the Sig held loosely by his side.

Catching sight of Hawk watching him Maguire brought up the Sig and fired at him, but his hand was shaking so badly by this time that the bolt went wide of its mark by feet rather than inches.

Quite suddenly there was a sound like a huge thunderclap that originated from the machine and reverberated around the huge chamber. The look of satisfaction and relief on Maguire's face was palpable.

Hawk knew then that whatever Maguire had set out to do, was done.

～

OUTSIDE THE CHAMBER RAND SAID, "That's gunfire," and then when he heard the thunderclap he said, "We've run out of time, get that door open, now."

"What the hell was that sound?" Sinclair asked.

Rand turned to him and said, "It's started."

CHAPTER 30

Hawk knew he had to do something, anything, to stop the clone from doing what he was about to do, even though he had no clue what it was. Taking into consideration that Maguire worked for OMEGA, whatever he intended was bound to be extremely bad.

On his side was the fact he was feeling stronger each second as the effects from the trip were wearing off faster than he thought possible, considering how bad he'd felt at first. Also on the plus side was that the same effects seem to be worsening for Maguire. On the downside, though he was still unarmed and pinned down by Maguire and, as ineffective as his aim was, there was still a danger from a lucky shot.

All that went through his mind in a flash with no obvious solution. Then, when he peered around the huge machine and saw Maguire walking towards it, he knew whatever he was planning to do would have to be done now.

Behind Maguire, the door to the chamber began to open and as he turned to look, Hawk made his move.

Thrusting off the ground with his powerful legs, renewed strength returning to him with every passing second, he powered towards Maguire. Head down, arms pumping to gain maximum speed, he ran at the clone closing the distance between them with each ground-eating stride.

With Hawk just a few feet away, Maguire turned back to face him and braced himself for the impact.

As he got closer to Maguire, Hawk saw two things in his peripheral vision. On his left where the door was, he noticed figures entering and two of them looked like Rand and Sinclair, but on the right, amazingly, the front portion of the huge machine had vanished to be replaced by what he could only describe as an energy vortex. Before he hit Maguire in a running tackle he wondered what the hell it was.

Without realising it, seeing the energy vortex made him slow down and instead of bowling Maguire over they collided but remained on their feet.

Striking the side of Hawk's head with the Sig gave Maguire control again. Stars burst before Hawk's eyes as they grappled in front of the vortex.

Hawk refused to let go as Maguire pounded on him with his fist and the butt of the Sig. Inch by agonising inch he dragged the Col Sec agent with him towards the energy vortex and as they got closer, although he had no idea what it could be, instinct told Hawk to stay clear.

Through the door, four men entered the chamber and saw Hawk and Maguire struggling at the edge of the massive vortex. It was almost large enough to drive an ATV through, and Sinclair gasped in awe at the magnificent sight, breathlessly asking, "What in hell is that?"

"It's the Gateway."

"To what?"

"C'mon, we have to stop them," Rand said, cutting off

further questioning as he motioned the armed guards forward.

Maguire looked up through pain-filled eyes, saw the guards approaching and with one last blow to the back of Hawk's head made his way towards the vortex.

Hawk felt the blow strike his head and almost blacked out. Feeling his strength leave him, he collapsed to his knees and knew it would be so easy to just stay there, to give up.

Maguire felt Hawk's grip slacken and he knew that victory would be his and OMEGA's in just a few short steps, once he'd reached the vortex.

To give up was not in Hawk's nature though and as he saw the clone move off towards the vortex he was filled with a grim determination. It fuelled his limbs with power and with a strength he couldn't imagine was possible he got up from his knees and ran at Maguire. This time there was no distraction and when he struck the retreating clone in a flying tackle he had the advantage. What he didn't consider though was the momentum he'd gathered by the time they collided. Without thinking he struck the clone with such force that both of them went straight into the vortex and vanished.

"NO!" screamed Sinclair in horror.

Rand turned to him and said, "Come on, we can't let them escape."

Sinclair stopped in his tracks, looked at Rand and said, "What?"

HAWK AND MAGUIRE collided on the edge of the vortex and Hawk's momentum carried them both into it, through it and out the other side to land on the floor of another chamber somewhere else entirely.

297

Immediately lights came on illuminating the huge chamber, the twin of the one they'd just left.

The vortex was still active behind them as they rolled on the floor and, although Hawk was aware of having travelled somewhere, he didn't know how, just a sense that he'd moved, but this time there was no disruption to his nervous system. He could think clearly.

Maguire got to his feet and aimed the Sig, which somehow he'd kept hold of, straight at Hawk's head.

"Don't move Agent Man, as you can see my hand isn't as steady as it should be. I'm dying but I can assure you, not before you," Maguire said with a sneer, but the pain in his eyes told the truth.

"Why don't you let me help you, perhaps our medical staff can find a cure," Hawk pleaded, hoping to buy some time until he thought of a way of overpowering him.

"There's no cure for death and anyway, I gladly give my life for OMEGA. It's my purpose in life."

"Ah yes, the blind obedience factor, I've seen this before in other clones, just before I killed them."

"You won't get that chance here, I can assure you."

"Then get on with it, why the delay?"

"I don't want you to die without seeing my victory."

"Which is?"

"I download all the data pertaining towards this project, the Gateway Project, then upload it to OMEGA's servers and then we'll have the capability to…"

"Yada, yada, yada, yeah okay, cut the crap. Why now, why not before, why wait until we were here?" interrupted Hawk.

"You give yourself far too much credit Agent Man. You think all this was for your benefit? To what, rub your noses in it, so to speak? Don't be so naïve; this project is about to go online tomorrow. This base will be fully operational by then and the staff will arrive at eight am. This was the only opportunity I had to gain access to the codes required. You just happened to stumble into this by accident. Your distraction of Rand actually gave me the chance to do this," explained Maguire.

"Bullshit, you don't want me to see all this," Hawk said as he watched the clone concentrate on something.

"I've downloaded all the data," Maguire said.

"You're so fucked up you can't multi-task any more, you can only concentrate on one thing at a time," Hawk said and he lunged forward grabbing the extended arm holding the Sig at the wrist, turning it away from him. Then he smashed his fist into Maguire's face snapping his head back with an explosion of teeth and blood.

Twisting the Sig from the clone's grip he quickly aimed at him and fired. The pulsed plasma bolt struck the clone in the centre of his forehead exploding the top of his head in a spray of blood, bone fragments and pulped brain tissue.

"Say hi to Jonas for me," Hawk said as he stood over the lifeless corpse.

A sound behind him alerted him to movement. Turning he saw four figures rushing through the Gateway.

"Cool, isn't it!" Hawk said when he saw the expression on Sinclair's face. "Oh don't worry, Maguire is over there, very much dead," he added when he saw Rand's worried expression.

"What happened?" Rand asked.

"He was going to download all the data to this Gateway Project and upload it to OMEGA's servers. I'm assuming he was using his NI so I shot him in the head before he could upload it," explained Hawk.

"Why now? What is this Gateway Project and where the hell are we?" Sinclair asked, just wanting some answers. He felt he'd been kept in the dark for long enough.

"I'm sure Mister Rand can fill us in with all the details but

Maguire told me our distraction gave him the chance to gain access to the codes before this base goes online tomorrow morning, is that right, sir?" Hawk replied, inviting Rand to offer some insight.

"Yes, this base is due to go operational tomorrow and I must thank you for preventing what could've been a tragedy," Rand said.

"Just where the hell are we?" Sinclair asked finally.

"On the Moon, General, or rather several miles beneath her surface," Rand said and he watched their expressions as the news sank in.

"But... well... er... the Moon you say, but we were..." Sinclair was at a loss for words.

"What General Sinclair is trying to say is, how?" Hawk said putting the question forward they both wanted to be answered.

"Quite simple really, we came through the Gateway which in layman's terms is a hyperspace window or tunnel, if you prefer, one opening here, and the other on Earth."

"Before we go any further, is there any way to verify that Maguire didn't upload any data off this base?" Hawk asked. Although he was fascinated by this new project he was more concerned that the technology didn't fall into the hands of OMEGA and was bastardised into a weapon to be used against the Confederation.

"I can check to see if any transmissions left the base," Rand said, going over to the computer terminal Maguire had accessed earlier.

"As far as I can tell, he managed to download the data but no transmissions of any kind were detected emanating from this base by the sensors," Rand said after running a diagnostic on the sensor logs to check they hadn't been tampered with.

"Are you sure? Could he have relayed it through another

transmitter or piggybacked it onto something else?" Hawk persisted wanting to be sure.

"I can assure you, Matt, nothing left here. There were no transmissions within five miles in any direction from here so you can relax."

"Just how big is this base Rand and what's it used for?" Sinclair asked, suspicion growing in his mind.

"It covers over five square miles, has twenty levels and it reaches almost ten miles down from the surface. We're on level eighteen by the way and it's used for, or I hope it will be used for, the security of the Confederation."

"I don't follow, how can it be used for the security of the Confederation?" Sinclair asked still suspicious but now confused too.

"You planned on handing this base over to Col Sec tomorrow, didn't you?" Hawk said.

Rand nodded his head and said, "When we all learned of the attack on Confederation Headquarters by an unknown terrorist force as the news channels put it, I decided that this base would be ideal for whatever you need it to be. When it was on the drawing board I originally planned to use it for Research and Development, and the Gateway Project was five years into development by then anyway, all the major tests having been run here."

"I thought you said it was going operational tomorrow?" Sinclair asked still not quite clear on the details surrounding this base.

"General, we've been operating out of this base for the last three years, we moved the Gateway here then so we could really test it. The day of the attack I shut the base down and withdrew my people. If you hadn't come to see me I would've asked to see you sometime next week. How do you think you got an appointment to see the CEO of one of the top five megacorps at such short notice, even President Takagi has to book a couple of days in advance?"

"That explains how you knew we'd be friends, you already envisioned us working together," Hawk said.

"A bit premature, I admit, but here we are," Rand agreed smiling.

"Tell me more about Maguire, the Rover," Hawk asked.

"Rover?"

"It's what Wilde called them."

"Okay, well he's been with us for about ten years and for the last three years he's been an executive assistant to the board, consisting of myself and Josh and Jess, my two children. So he was a clone, what gave him away?"

"His eyes, and they all look alike, like identical twins. The moment I saw him I knew he was your mole. I'll lay odds on there being one in the executive offices of every major business in the Confederation. General, if that's true then this has just gained another dimension," Hawk said, a worried look crossing his face.

"Then it's just as well you have this new base of operations, isn't it?" Rand said.

"What are you looking to gain out of this?" Sinclair asked pointedly.

"I'm a patriot, General, but I'm also a businessman. This base is yours for the Confederation to use. All I ask is fair consideration on any of the tec and munitions contracts up for grabs. My corporation can provide the best you could ask for and more at a fair price. You said yourself you need an alternative to MaxCorp, which has been supplying both you and OMEGA. I'll even bet they kept back some of the upgrades to give OMEGA the edge and, judging by the Nemesis attack, I'm not far wrong."

"I'm afraid you're right, I can't disagree on that point," Sinclair said.

"Do we have a deal then?" Rand asked.

Offering his hand Sinclair said, "We do indeed, Able."

"Great, wait 'til you see what else we have for you," Rand said, smiling broadly as he accepted the firm handshake to seal the deal.

CHAPTER 31

The rest of the day went smoothly with Able Rand giving them a tour of their new base and explaining how the Gateway worked. Then they enjoyed a relaxed lunch after which they returned to their respective jobs.

Sinclair and Hawk returned to New York to organise the movement of staff to the new base and whatever else it entailed.

RandCorp supplied Col Sec with new com. units until upgrades for all NIs formerly supplied by MaxCorp could be implemented. Basically, they were similar to the ear bug supplied by Tec Division but with a greater range that could reach anywhere on a planet, with encrypted audio and muscle flex operation. That meant there was no need to key the ear bug any more, it was now possible to activate it by a certain muscle flex, similar to clenching the jaw. They toyed with the idea of voice activation but how to differentiate between a call and normal conversation was a problem. Keyword activation was thought of but that would mean it being on constantly, monitoring all conversations, and choosing which words could activate and end a call? Finally, it was decided that manual control would be best. The new unit fitted much better as it was smaller and more comfortable so the wearer was hardly aware of it and there was no impairment to the hearing when it wasn't in use.

New sidearms were also issued, the Sig P999, a smaller more compact version of the P996 with only one setting – maximum. This gave a full load of twenty shots with the same range as the earlier model. Being a full three centimetres shorter and weighing almost a hundred grams less, it fitted well inside the custom-made holster beneath an agent's jacket where it would be unobserved.

Hawk tested the new Sig on the firing range at Fort Brag as he underwent debriefing and put in some light training. After getting through three battery clips he felt as if it was almost like an extension of himself and he gladly replaced the larger, bulkier P996.

Sinclair contacted President Takagi with an update on the OMEGA situation and the new deal he'd struck with Able Rand. He was sitting in his office in Col Sec HQ at Area 15 when he made the call through a secure video link.

After the briefing, Takagi said, "And what are your thoughts General?"

"My thoughts, sir?"

"As to the validity of Rand's offer of the base and other supplies."

"The base is extremely well equipped, the standard of which we're just not used to from MaxCorp. The arms already supplied to us are excellent. Matt has given the new Sig P999 a thorough testing and it's received his go-ahead. He's already adopted it as his personal weapon of choice and I've given Recon Delta the green light for a change over to it. The com. units are working fine and will do so until we can upgrade the NIs with new tec from RandCorp and then

OMEGA won't be able to track or eavesdrop on our operatives. I've seen the new Cobra battle tec helmet already and on first inspection, it seems an improvement on the Rapier. Again Recon Delta is giving it the run through as we speak and we should have a full report on it by the weekend."

"I take it then your thoughts are favourable at this point?"

"Yes, sir."

"Where are you on OMEGA?"

"We've contacted every megacorp in the Confederation with details of Maguire, the Rover. We've forwarded them his ID, his DNA, voice pattern, fingerprints and retinal pattern. Any one of these would be enough for them to recognise a clone if he's there. I've ordered him to be detained by their security staff until we can send someone to pick him up and for his access to any databases to be terminated forthwith."

"Very good."

"Sir, I would ask you to contact your counterpart in the Alliance and suggest they do likewise. OMEGA failed here with us because Jonas Wilde held a grudge against Col Sec and me personally. There is nothing to say that if we don't smash them they won't try to get the Alliance to do their dirty work, turn the cold war hot once more."

"I see your point, General. You have my word; I'll get right on it. What do you intend to do about Maxwell Eisenhower?"

"As soon as Matt returns from Fort Bragg I intend we drop in and see him."

"Keep me informed."

"As always, sir."

"It's been three weeks now, General, since the attack, how's the recovery operation going for the bodies at the site?"

"It's going well, sir. They've recovered enough to identify over thirty thousand people whose loved ones have been notified. All the remains have been recovered now and the identification process goes on and should be completed as per schedule, the site is being rendered safe as we speak."

The memorial service will go ahead as planned then I presume?"

"Correct sir. Matt and I will be back from Cordoba by then and the search for the base will be complete also, it'll go ahead on time as planned, sir."

"Good, maybe people can get some closure then."

"Yes, sir, let's hope so."

"Have your people identified Jonas Wilde in the wreckage from that transport yet? Three weeks seems an awful long time with the technology available to them."

"They managed to locate a trace of DNA which they ran tests on but they couldn't get a positive ID from it, claimed the sample was too degraded from exposure to the vacuum of space. Another sample was found and multiplied so they'd have enough to test, but every test came back with the same result, that of cellular degradation."

"Are you saying what I think you're saying?"

"I'm afraid so, sir. The only way that all the tests could show that level of degradation was if the sample was taken from a clone."

"Dear God!"

"Yes, sir, Jonas Wilde is still alive."

MATT HAWK LEFT Fort Bragg and drove to where he'd left Tanya Wilde under the protection of two Col Sec agents, both recruits from Recon Delta as he himself had been.

Armed with the knowledge that the man he'd killed was a

clone and not Tanya's real father, he was faced with a real dilemma. Should he tell her the truth or not?

Should he allow her to think that her father was dead, that he'd killed him and in that way find some closure and move on with her life, probably hating Hawk for depriving her of her last parent, regardless of the kind of man he had been?

What happened though if she learned the truth? She would hate him for lying to her.

If, on the other hand, he told her the truth he would be consigning her to a life of continual fear. A fear that one day he would return for her again.

During the long drive to the safe house, he pondered the question: what to do, what to tell her? As he pulled up outside the building he had come to the decision that it would be best to tell her the truth, she deserved that much at least and if she required his help he would give it freely.

The safe house was in a secluded area outside of New York's sprawling metropolis. The street it was situated on had few houses and the owners liked to live private lives away from the prying eyes of the public or the lenses of the news channels on the GalaxyWeb. As a result, when he pulled his ground car up at the massive gates at the bottom of the tree-lined driveway, identified himself with a retina scan, then entered, no one gave him a second glance.

The house was quite large having five bedrooms, two bathrooms, two lounges, a large kitchen and a dining room. The entrance hall was open plan, in that a stairway led to a circular balcony, which fed the rooms upstairs. It was positioned centrally giving access to all the rooms on the ground floor. To the rear of the house was a large conservatory that overlooked the impressive lawns.

Hawk parked the ground car, a nondescript Maxim cruiser, one of the many pool cars available to Col Sec agents, on the white gravel forecourt in front of the house. The door slid into the recess in the coachwork allowing him to exit the vehicle and stretch his back and legs. The long drive had been almost intolerable with his six feet six-inch frame squashed into the cramped interior of the Maxim. He loved to drive but these pool cars were a nightmare for him and he hadn't had the time to pick up his own vehicle, an Alpha GTV9000, a two-seater sports coupé that was his dream car and an absolute beast to drive.

The front door to the safe house was situated centrally leading to the entrance hall and as he approached it opened.

Cameras on top of the gateposts, which gave an unobstructed view of the street in both directions for several hundred feet, watched his approach. Other cameras on the roof of the house picked him up as he entered through the gates and walked up the drive to the house. Not only did the cameras watch him they also scanned him so the agents knew he was coming, if he was armed and what physical condition he was in, right down to a skeletal scan.

"Matt, long time, no see," greeted Mike Gregory, one of the two agents tasked with babysitting Tanya Wilde. Slightly shorter than Hawk at six feet three, he was still an impressive size and in good shape. He kept his light brown hair cut very short, almost down to the scalp, somehow accentuating the hazel eyes, which sparkled as his easy smile told Hawk he was pleased to see him.

"Mike, man, how long's it been?" Hawk replied as he walked up the two stone steps to the front door to give his friend a bear hug, as they slapped each other on the back.

"Got to be years man since we were last in Delta together," Gregory said, as they separated to look each other over.

"We're still in Delta Mike, once a Recon Delta marine, always a Recon Delta marine, you know that," Hawk said smiling.

"True, so very true, it gets hard sometimes when you get stuck with a babysitting gig like this though."

"That lady is one very important lady. I can't go into details but she ties in with the recent events at HQ."

"You mean the attack?"

"Yep, can't say any more, it's classified, but this is more than just a babysitting gig."

"Should've known really."

"Not really, it was on a need to know basis, you know how it is. Anyway, you're looking good. Listen I just need to see her, and then we can catch up before I head off again, okay?"

"Fine, she's in her room, bedroom number one. Maguire has just taken her evening meal up to her, she's not feeling too well."

Hawk's blood froze at the mention of the name.

"Who?" he asked, filled with a feeling of dread.

"Maguire, new guy, only arrived today. Carter was given this gig with me originally but he has gone on compassionate leave. Apparently, his wife died yesterday, an accident at home or something," Gregory explained.

"What's this Maguire like?" Hawk asked.

"He checks out, Matt. What's this about? I know you, what's wrong?"

"His eyes, tell me about his eyes," Hawk insisted.

"Strange you should mention those – opaline green."

Hawk was past Gregory in a flash, running up the staircase, his legs pumping to power him forward. He'd already drawn his new Sig P999 and pulled back on the slide to prime it. He was already halfway up the stairs before Gregory had time to draw his own weapon and follow.

On his way up, his eyes searched for the right bedroom and the one to the far left was the only one with the door ajar; that had to be the one.

Reaching the top of the stairs Hawk turned to the left and reached the bedroom in a few strides. With a kick from his right foot, the door was smashed open, almost coming off its hinges and the sight before him chilled his blood even further.

Standing before him in the centre of the room at the foot of the king-size bed was Maguire; his arm outstretched holding a Sig P996 to the forehead of a terrified Tanya Wilde. Those distinctive opaline eyes stared straight at Hawk as he burst into the room, his own gun aimed straight at him.

"You must be Matt Hawk," Maguire said.

"Didn't I kill you already?" Hawk replied hoping to put the clone off his stride.

"Oh, very good, calm in the face of impending danger, but in this case that's easy I suppose, seeing it's her and not you that the gun is aimed at," Maguire said calmly with a trace of derision in his voice.

Tanya's eyes were pleading with him to help but at the moment there was absolutely nothing Hawk could do but see how the situation panned out.

"Put the gun down," he said calmly not wanting to precipitate what the clone was obviously here to do.

"Can't do that, Matt."

"How?" Hawk asked, hoping to learn something at least before the shit hit the fan and he killed his only lead, the one thing in this situation he was certain of.

"Oh, we still have contacts inside Col Sec. I found out who was guarding Tanya here, had to be Carter, Gregory out there has no one, been a loner most of his life. Recon Delta is his family, but Carter, he had a wife, lovely creature. I killed her so I could replace him. I knew you'd come to visit; you had to, seeing as how you showed such affection for her, coming to her rescue like that. Oh, how it must've pained you to have to kill her father. What would she have thought of you? But on discovering you didn't really kill him, you had to come and give her the news. Well, I have a message from Daddy, and I had to wait for you to arrive, Matt, it's a message for you both. Daddy says that you've been a naughty girl Tanya and you must be punished."

With that, never taking his eyes off Hawk he fired the Sig. Tanya's scream was cut short as her head exploded from the pulsed plasma bolt fired at point-blank range. Blood erupted over the bed as she was sent flying backwards, arms outstretched to land on her back, bouncing slightly on the mattress before settling down.

She died instantly.

Hawk caught all this; even though the second Maguire fired he too fired a rapid double-tap. The two shots struck the clone's head almost as one in a mist of blood, throwing him to the far side of the room to land in a crumpled heap, killing him stone dead.

Gregory rushed in to verify what he already knew, that the shooter was dead, while Hawk went to the bed.

Tanya, or what was left of her, was unrecognisable. The shot had destroyed her lovely face, her head was nothing but the lower half from the nose down, just a jumbled wreck of tissue and mashed bones covered in a patina of her own blood.

"Matt, what the fuck just happened here man?" Gregory asked from his position by the dead clone.

"Classified Mike, that's all I can tell you," Hawk replied, his voice deep and dark, full of rage. Turning away from the gory remains on the bed he left the bedroom and headed for the staircase. With a clench of his teeth he activated his ear bug and said, "General, we have a problem."

CHAPTER 32

On his way out to the cruiser, Hawk told Gregory to hold the fort until the clean-up squad arrived and then he left with no further explanation.

It was just a short drive from the safe house to the nearest spaceport where a sub-orbital shuttle was waiting to take him to Area 15 where General Sinclair would be waiting for him. The shuttle was one of a fleet that was loaned to Col Sec for private use in cases such as this, when military transport was unavailable or logistically infeasible. It was a small, sleek dart of a craft that had all the luxuries of a much larger passenger shuttle. The Cessna C210, nicknamed the Silver Dart due to its sleek profile and swept-back wing configuration, would get Hawk to Nevada in a fraction of the time a commercial flight would and in a lot more comfort. That fact, however, did nothing to improve his mood and he doubted anything would until he crushed Jonas Wilde and his insidious group, OMEGA.

"Can I get you anything?" said a voice at his side. He was so wrapped up in his thoughts, dark thoughts full of blood and revenge; he failed to notice the flight attendant until

315

she'd spoken. When her words finally registered he turned to look at the bright-eyed young woman with the beaming smile.

"I'm sorry, I was lost in thought then," he apologised, his voice still dark and full of menace.

"That's okay, sir, rough day was it?" she asked.

"You have no idea," he said trying to hide the pain and anger he was feeling. The need to lash out was almost overwhelming and it wasn't this young woman's fault, so he had to control his urges.

"Can I get you anything to eat then, I always find a hot meal helps me to unwind after a tough day, you know, refuel for the next day, give you the strength to fight on."

"You know, I am hungry, I can't remember the last time I ate, so bring me whatever's on the menu please."

"Anything to drink, sir, the wet bar is quite impressive."

"It has been a rough day so bring me a large whisky, I don't care which just as long as it's a single malt."

"Coming right up, sir."

"Excuse me Miss, but what do I call you?" Hawk asked once he'd finished ordering and she was about to leave. He found talking to her had actually helped his mood somewhat.

"I'm Lieutenant O'Neil, sir, and your flight crew are Captain Wright and Lieutenant Commander Sanders," she replied courteously.

"Thank you, Lieutenant O'Neil," he said with a brief smile. "You ought to do that more often if you don't mind my saying, sir?"

"Excuse me?" he asked, not sure what she meant.

"Smile, sir," she replied then turned and walked towards the rear of the shuttle to fill his order.

He was taken aback by her comment and he glanced around his seat to watch her leave. He was surprised to see her glance at him over her shoulder just as she went through the door.

Her smile was genuine and he had to admit she certainly was easy on the eye and, despite his earlier dark thoughts, he found himself smiling.

When she returned with his glass of Jameson Gold Reserve she said, "Your meal will be along shortly, sir," and was gone again.

He took a sip of the amber liquid savouring the creaminess and honey sweetness as it lay on his tongue, before swallowing it and allowing the warmth to spread through him up to the peppery finale as he began to finally relax.

On his drive from the safe house, he'd called Sinclair to give him a sit-rep and was told to stay on the Cessna where the General would join him once he arrived at Area 15. From there they would go directly to the Legend, which had returned from the search for the illusive base. They would dock with the cruiser and proceed to Cordoba and their meeting with Maxwell Eisenhower.

Everything was set in place; all that seemed to be required of him was to go along. With nothing left to do but wait, he sat back in the plush padded seat to savour his drink until the meal arrived.

His meal was rack of lamb with roast potatoes and seasonal vegetables embellished with mint flavoured gravy, and was quite superb. As he ate his mind wandered over what Maguire had said, the message that was for both Tanya and him and was to be delivered personally. Maguire must've known that it was a suicide mission, still more evidence of the blind obedience programmed into the clones, but the message wasn't what he said but rather what he did. Look at the lengths I will go to, to deliver this message, even though it will cost me my life. Look at how easily we can reach you even though you think you are safe.

The message was clear. How were they supposed to fight and defeat an enemy with resources and resolve like that?

It was clearly meant to demoralise them but in fact, it had had the opposite effect upon Hawk. He was now more than ever determined to see this through to the bitter end, and he was sure General Sinclair would feel the same.

Before he knew it the Cessna was landing at Area 15, a bleak military outpost in a remote part of the Nevada desert. From the ground it appeared to be a few low buildings dotted here and there, the real base stretched several miles underground and covered more than five city blocks.

General Sinclair boarded and Captain Wright soon had the sleek Silver Dart airborne once more. He wasted no time getting to and docking with the Legend, barely giving Sinclair time to get comfortable before he and Hawk were being led up to the bridge where they met another old friend.

"Nice to see you again, Colonel," Sinclair said as he saw the figure of Colonel De Boer standing next to Captain Walker Townsend, commander of the Legend.

"Nice to see you too, sir, and you, Matt, but it's not good news I'm afraid," De Boer replied.

"Go on," Sinclair said.

"We covered the entire area twice with no signs of any base being there at any time. We ran every test, every scan we could, sir, and still came up with nothing."

"I've a theory about that," Hawk said. Something had been bothering him about Wilde's escape plan and, with the results now in, it was time to air his thoughts.

"Go on, Matt," Sinclair urged.

"It's been bothering me, sir, that Wilde used a transport with a limited range on the hyperdrive. Why? Was it because their base was that close? The search proved that not to be the case, so another alternative would be that he was rendezvousing with another craft for the second leg of the journey, which I feel is doubtful. He already had a hyperdrive so why use two ships for one journey, seems pointless? The only other alternative is that he programmed the nav-comp for another jump and we stopped it before it could be completed."

"You know that can't be verified don't you, the ship was totally destroyed in the explosion? Even if we could find enough of the flight recorder to test, chances are the data would be corrupted beyond recognition," De Boer said.

"Yes, I know, but it's the only explanation that makes any sense."

"I tend to agree," Sinclair said, then turned to Townsend and asked, "How soon before we can make the jump to Cordoba, Captain?"

"We're ready when you are, sir," Townsend replied in his huge bass voice that seemed to fill any room he occupied.

"At your discretion then, Captain, I'm eager to get this over with," Sinclair said with grim determination.

When they arrived at Cordoba, General Sinclair, Matt Hawk and Colonel De Boer met at the docking bay to board the Cessna.

"Are you ready for this Colonel? This time I can assure you there will be no stalling. I've gained a Presidential Warrant to proceed and question Eisenhower," Sinclair said before they boarded.

"I've been waiting a long time for this, sir, and despite your warrant, I'd still like to have a few of my men present, just in case it doesn't go quite as planned," De Boer replied.

"Good idea, Colonel. Have them ready, we leave in five minutes," agreed Sinclair, turning to enter the Cessna.

"Are you alright, Matt?" De Boer asked when he saw the dark look in his friend's eyes. He wore an expression that warned of impending violence and it worried him that he may be close to breaking point.

"I'm fine, which is more than I can say for Eisenhower if it's proven he's involved in all this," Hawk replied coldly.

"Matt, take a step back my friend. Don't take this personally, be the professional we all know you to be."

"I didn't make it personal. Jonas Wilde did when he sent one of his damned clones to kill his own daughter in front of me. He was told to wait until I arrived, told him exactly what to say before shooting her in the head knowing full well I would kill the shooter no matter what happened. If that's not making it personal I don't know what is."

"Okay, I see your point but please think before you act. Don't let him cloud your thinking so you blunder headlong into making a mistake you'll live to regret."

"I'll do my best, Colonel. All I can see at the moment though is that poor girl's terror as she lay there waiting to be killed, knowing there was nothing I could do to help but praying I would try anyway. That's an image I'll take to my grave," Hawk said and his haunted eyes told the truth of it.

De Boer had nothing to offer and watched him board the Cessna. Once he was alone he contacted four of his marines and ordered them to get there in less than five minutes.

Once everyone was on board Captain Wright took the Cessna out of the docking bay and headed towards the planet they were orbiting.

The endgame was about to be played.

CHAPTER 33

Captain Wright took the Cessna down to Cordoba's main spaceport and put her down on a pad reserved for private charter users. A ground car had already been ordered, one of the fleet of Grand Voyager 600s that Col Sec used was waiting for them as they left the craft. Their driver was a Col Sec operative stationed at the embassy there, named John Todd.

General Sinclair, Matt Hawk, Colonel De Boer and the four marines, Privates Wilkerson, Davies, Moore and Shaw piled into the rear compartment of the vehicle settling themselves down in the comfortable seats.

"Where to, sir?" Todd asked once they were all buckled in.

"MaxCorp Headquarters please," Sinclair said without preamble.

"Okay, sir, we're on our way," Todd replied.

"What armaments does this vehicle contain son?" De Boer enquired.

"Agent Todd, sir, and she has standard firepower, pulse cannons front and rear, missile racks to either side with six mini Hellfires to each rack and reinforced coachwork with

321

blast shields. Are you expecting trouble here, sir? I only ask because when I saw those Recon Delta boys back there I assumed this wasn't purely a social call."

"You're right, Todd, this isn't a social call but we're not expecting any trouble. However, if we do run into any, it's best we go in fully prepared, don't you agree?" Sinclair added.

"That's just what my Daddy used to say, sir, be prepared. Yes, sir, General," Todd replied with a smile.

"You know who I am?"

"Yes, sir, General Sinclair, head of Col Sec Intelligence Division. So this is big, right?"

"You have no idea, Todd," Hawk said and Todd closed the screen between him and the passengers to give them some privacy and as it closed Todd couldn't help but wonder what the hell he was getting involved in. Concentrating on his driving he tried to put those thoughts out of his mind. He was there to do a job and that's what he would do.

A little over an hour later they pulled up at the front of the huge MaxCorp building. The seven passengers got out and Sinclair said to Todd, "No matter what happens, you stay here."

The concierge came running down the steps from the foyer waving his arms at them telling them they couldn't park there as it was reserved for VIPs only.

Sinclair halted the irate man with a hand placed firmly on his chest. "We are VIPs, sir. General Sinclair of Col Sec and party to see Maxwell Eisenhower. I believe you'll find he's expecting us," he said calmly, yet firmly.

The concierge looked first at Sinclair then at each of them in turn as if he was sizing them up. Finally, he waved them on up to the front entrance of the huge building.

"Do you get the impression we're not that welcome?" Hawk said as they made their way into the building.

"About as welcome as a fart in an elevator," Wilkerson commented which brought a rousing, "I heard dat!" from the other three marines.

As they entered the foyer Hawk expected the same stonewalling treatment they received the last time they were there, several burly, armed security guards reluctant to let them pass without the proper authorisation.

This time though the foyer was virtually empty and they could get to the elevators without any trouble.

The ride up was smooth and fast and the elevator deposited them on the Penthouse level where Eisenhower had his office. They got out, again expecting some form of resistance from security, but their passage to the huge office was uneventful.

"Secure the area around the office," Sinclair said to De Boer who immediately began issuing orders to his men via hand signals. "Matt, you're with me. Let's go pay Maxwell a visit and give him the bad news," he added, then opened the office door.

Inside the door was another office where Eisenhower's aide sat, almost like a sentinel guarding it's master, except that the desk was unoccupied along with the room.

"You know, General, I'm starting to get a very bad feeling about this. We've hardly seen a soul since we entered the building and those we did see avoided us like the plague," Hawk said as he paused before the door to the office of the CEO.

"I've been getting the same feeling too, Matt," Sinclair agreed activating his ear bug. "Colonel look lively, this could be a setup. Any sign of trouble and you come get us, okay?"

"Copy that, sir," De Boer said from the corridor. He had already deployed his men to what he considered to be the best positions; he just wished they had come with more fire-power than just standard-issue sidearms.

"Well, we've come this far, let's not back out now. I've waited far too long to deliver this message and it's cost too many lives for it to go undelivered, especially when we're so close," Sinclair said.

Placing his hand on the butt of his Sig in preparation for a quick draw should the need arise, Hawk said, "Okay, sir, let's do it."

The door opened as they approached revealing a large office tastefully decorated in warm colours. A rich, thick carpet on the floor, pictures on the walls from contemporary artists and large drapes hanging by the window that covered an entire wall, giving the occupant a spectacular panoramic view of the city below. That occupant was seated behind a large mahogany desk that had just one item on it, a computer monitor.

"Welcome, gentlemen, I've been expecting you for some time now," Eisenhower said calmly.

"Thank you, I've wanted to meet you too, but the illusive Maxwell Eisenhower is hard to pin down, so I took the direct approach seeing as my agent here had so much trouble the last time he called," Sinclair said as he watched the man seated before him. He certainly was a cool customer; there was no sign of stress, just an outward visage of serenity.

"I must apologise for the last time you called, my second-in-command Jonas Wilde was playing some sort of game that I was totally unaware of. He actually ran a criminal organisation out of this building, funded by my corporation without my knowledge, can you believe that?" Eisenhower said exasperated at the consequences.

"Actually, sir, no, I can't. I find it extremely hard to believe, so much so that I am hereby cancelling all Col Sec contracts with your company, effective immediately," Sinclair said coldly.

"I see," Eisenhower said slowly rising to his feet. He

started to slowly pace across his office observed by Sinclair and Hawk.

"You don't seem perturbed by my statement, in fact, it's almost like you expected it, which again, I find hard to believe. I mean, it's not like you lose multi-billion credit contracts every day now is it?"

"But you're wrong, General, I did expect it but you have no proof that any of what happened can be tied to this corporation."

"Please don't insult my intelligence."

"And don't insult mine either," snapped Eisenhower almost snarling at Sinclair in uncharacteristic rage. "As far as I'm aware, Jonas Wilde was killed escaping from you, was he not?" he added.

"Yes, but we have the Nemesis and we can prove she was built at one of your shipyards and then there are the clones. As we speak, an operation is underway to round up all the 'Maguires' that you planted in all the businesses around the galaxy. You can't deny they're yours; they all have your eyes. Oh, and as for Wilde, he was a clone too. Very clever of him to have us think he was dead so he could carry on with his work from behind the scenes undetected, or was that your idea?"

"His idea? Do me a favour, he hasn't had an original thought for a decade or more," said a voice off to their left, a voice they both recognised.

"Jonas, I was wondering if you'd show up here," Sinclair said without even looking at the man who emerged from the hidden doorway that had slid silently open just after they had entered. The dark interior of the secret room had kept Wilde hidden in the shadows as he listened to their conversation.

Hawk spun around towards the voice his Sig suddenly appearing in his hand, but Wilde was standing just behind the General with the muzzle of his own Sig pressed against Sinclair's temple.

"I wouldn't if I were you, Matt," Wilde said with a smug smile. "You know if this was a game of chess, I would have checkmate," he added basking in his own success and imagined glory.

"Well, this game isn't quite over yet," Hawk said through gritted teeth. He was determined that Wilde was going down but he couldn't risk anything yet as long as he had a gun to the General's head.

"You overestimate your position, Matt, I hold all the cards."

"And what do you intend to do now then? You have to know that the second you move away from the General, I'll kill you. There's no escape Jonas, five marines are guarding the exit, which leaves just you in here, alone with me. You are going to die you know," Hawk said calmly and coldly with a determination that chilled even Sinclair.

Smiling, Wilde said, "I'll just have to take the General with me then." Backing away towards the passage he'd entered through, Wilde pulled Sinclair with him.

"Where are you taking him?" Hawk asked, hoping to stall him while he thought of a way to stop him once and for all.

"To the roof where I have a transport waiting. I intend to gain all the information I can from him to use against you. I tried to capture you all when I was on the Nemesis, or rather my clone did, but you insisted on being troublesome. Well, this time that won't happen because I've rigged the entire top floor of this building with J10 explosives. The blast will destroy everything and everyone up here, even Max there, but he doesn't matter, he's a clone and I'll have another one ready to replace him by the end of the day in time for the press release. He'll tell the news media that you came up here and questioned him, but he was able to escape in his personal transport before the suicide bomber, who had infiltrated your group from RandCorp, blew him and the top of this building to smithereens.

"Genius isn't it?" Wilde said excited at his own plan and how he could kill two birds with one stone, cripple Col Sec and discredit his biggest rival RandCorp at the same time.

"Max is a clone you say?" Hawk asked.

"Yes, he's been in place since just before the attack with the Nemesis."

"Then you won't mind if I do this," Hawk said, then spun around and shot Eisenhower right between the eyes. The clone was sent flying, his head shrouded in a mist of blood from the plasma bolt.

Wilde was shocked by the sudden action, an action that seemed pointless. It had no effect on the outcome other than surprise but that surprise gave Sinclair the opportunity to ram his left elbow deep into Wilde's solar plexus winding him. Spying his chance, Hawk fired the second his boss was clear.

The shot missed Wilde's head by a fraction as it came forward from the blow to the stomach.

Feeling the shot almost graze the top of his head Wilde turned and ran down the passage closing the door behind him.

"C'mon we've got to get out of here before it blows," Hawk said grabbing the General by the shoulder and virtually dragging him to the door.

Instructing the marines to follow they sprinted for the elevator. They knew they had some time, Wilde wouldn't detonate the explosives until he was well clear but just how much time they had was an unknown. They would have to trust to luck on this one.

The elevator doors opened and they piled in quickly ordering it to go the ground floor, express speed.

～

WILDE CURSED his luck as he ran through the passageway and out onto the roof. Why couldn't he have seen that play coming? He'd had them where he wanted them, it was a done deal, and then Hawk went and turned things on their head with that idiotic play of killing Eisenhower.

As he climbed on board the transport, started the engines and lifted off the roof climbing into the clear sky above the city, he warmed himself with the knowledge that they wouldn't survive the blast as he pushed the button on the remote detonator.

The blast was enormous, spreading outwards blasting all the windows out around the building and actually lifting the roof off and throwing it into the air, only to rain down in fragments onto the unsuspecting bystanders below.

～

THE ELEVATOR WAS ALMOST to the floor when the blast destroyed the top of the building. The seven occupants were hurled around the interior of the small box as it danced on the cables, smashing up against the sides of the shaft before dropping like a stone for several feet as the cables snapped. Safety measures kicked in the second the cables snapped and clamps came out from the sides of the shaft to act as external brakes stopping it before it could impact against the floor below.

Sinclair and the rest breathed a huge sigh of relief when they realised they were still alive. Not out of the woods yet though, as they opened the doors manually and sprinted down the last few flights of stairs to the foyer where panic reigned. The last few employees who had remained in the building to give it the air of a normal working day were all rushing for the exits.

"Let's get out of here before people start asking too many questions. We can release an official report when we get to safety," Hawk said as he ushered Sinclair out of the building.

The Grand Voyager was where they'd left it, now covered in ash from the debris but luckily it had sustained no damage. They were soon on board and heading back to the spaceport and the Cessna.

The rest of the journey was uneventful and they had time to reflect on what had happened by filling in De Boer and the marines on the action inside the office that they had not been privy to.

They reached the Cessna and were soon back on board the Legend where they went to the bridge to find Townsend waiting for them.

"Eventful trip I take it, sir? It's all over the news channels on the GalaxyWeb," he said.

"Very eventful and we need to get the truth out there before Wilde has the chance to put his spin on it. Contact the local Constabulary and all the news channels. Inform them I'll have an eyewitness report for them in five minutes. I'll use your ready room if I may?"

"Help yourself, sir. I'll contact you when they're ready."

"Thank you."

As he headed for the ready room he turned to Hawk and said, "We've a chance to land a vital blow to Wilde and OMEGA here. We can deprive MaxCorp of their CEO and therefore cut off Wilde's source of revenue. I want you to stay out of the statement though, so you'll still be able to work from the shadows. That would be nigh on impossible if your face was plastered all over the media. I'm already the face of Col Sec so I'll take it from here."

In the ready room, alone, Sinclair had time to marshal his thoughts and organise what he needed to say; what must be said and what must not. He knew that this would be rushed although it mustn't appear to be for the sake of his credibility, but he had to get the truth out before Wilde had the chance to muddy the waters. He understood that what he was about to do would affect the lives of those honest, hardworking employees of MaxCorp who had no knowledge of, nor took any part in OMEGA, but this was for the greater good and he could not allow himself to be swayed by his sympathy towards them.

When he was informed the news channels were ready for him he began by introducing himself and saying that what he was about to tell them was his eyewitness report of an incident that happened earlier and he would not be taking questions. They would get their chance to ask whatever questions they wished at the official press conference at a later date.

He kept the details concise telling them how the explosion today was a direct result of the investigation into the attack on Confederation Headquarters on Earth over three weeks ago. He told how the attack was perpetrated by a criminal organisation called OMEGA, which was run by Jonas Wilde one of the chief officers of MaxCorp. He then went on to say that Wilde had sequestered funds from MaxCorp to finance his schemes and when they went to question him about it he killed Maxwell Eisenhower and somehow set off a previously primed explosive charge, unfortunately dying in the blast too. He told them the Constabulary would carry out a full investigation assisted by Col Sec.

Finally, he told them of the sorrow he felt for the families of those who had died, adding that the memorial service for those lost during the attack on Confederation Headquarters would take place at the site of the attack at ten am two weeks from Sunday next. Thanking everyone for their time he ended the call.

That statement would air live on the GalaxyWeb and he hoped finally that they had dealt a lethal blow to OMEGA. Sitting down in Townsend's chair he contemplated what he'd done. With the news of Eisenhower's death, Wilde couldn't replace him with a clone, robbing him of the greatest resource he had, the bottomless pit of finance he'd enjoyed from his involvement with MaxCorp. Also, his announcement that Wilde was dead too meant he couldn't appear in public anywhere.

In one swift, bold move Sinclair had deprived Wilde of his funding and severely limited his ability to travel. All in all, considering their previous losses, he could rate this one a massive win.

By the time the Legend had made the jump back to Earth the news of the event and its massive ramifications were common knowledge throughout the known galaxy, not only throughout the Confederation but also the Alliance and the few non-aligned worlds. Wherever the GalaxyWeb reached, so did Sinclair's statement.

For the first time since learning of OMEGA, he felt they had them on the run.

President Takagi was pleased with the outcome and the steps Sinclair had taken to help rebuild Col Sec. The addition of RandCorp was a pleasing and welcome bonus and the assets they could provide were both plentiful and gratefully received. The President told Sinclair to take some time off as he'd earned it, to which he replied that he would organise leave for all those involved once the memorial service was over. The service would give them what they all needed, time to grieve, and would also provide something else that would help them draw a line under the entire event, and that was closure.

EPILOGUE

The day of the memorial service arrived, along with a low-pressure weather front that pushed along layer upon layer of moisture-laden dark clouds that added to the sombre mood.

A huge, three-metre fence had been erected around the site where only a few short weeks ago had stood a proud building, a symbol of everything the Confederation stood for, which was cut down in that savage attack by OMEGA.

OMEGA, a name everyone had grown to know and despise since Sinclair outed them on the GalaxyWeb, could no longer hide in the shadows as they had been thrust headlong into the public awareness.

This day was not about them though, not about the cowards who attacked innocents but rather the victims of that attack and remembering them from better days.

A podium had been set up in front of the fence close to where the entrance to the huge building once had been and it would be from there that the various speakers would deliver their eulogies.

Thousands of mourners flocked to the site and by nine-thirty am the entire area was just one massive, heaving crowd from all walks of life, come together with one purpose, to say farewell and give respect to their loved ones.

General Sinclair, Matt Hawk and Colonel De Boer all arrived in full dress uniform. President Takagi, resplendent in a black suit took to the podium to deliver a short speech. The weather, which had taken a turn for the worst with slanting rain drenching the crowds, wasn't even a consideration; they would have attended no matter what.

He spoke of that day being one of remembrance for those lost and a day that would live in infamy, as one such day over five centuries ago was remembered when the people came together to unite against a common enemy.

With no more political posturing, he surrendered the podium to a succession of religious leaders who in turn would lead services for members of their denomination.

The services would go on for almost half the day as everyone's beliefs were catered for. As it was drawing to a close Sinclair looked at Hawk who had been silent throughout the entire proceedings, a dark expression firmly in place.

"Are you okay, Matt?" he asked as the three of them sheltered beneath a huge umbrella from the pouring rain.

Matt glanced at the General and said, "I just can't get it out of my mind, sir, how Tanya was killed."

"Then I would say that the message was not only delivered but understood," Sinclair replied.

"How so, sir?"

"Well, you said it was a message for both of you; to Tanya that she couldn't go against her father and to you, how did you put it, 'look at the lengths I will go to deliver this message'? How are you supposed to fight someone with these sort of resources and this kind of resolve and the moment you made that connection, the message truly had been delivered?"

Understanding came into Hawk's eyes then as he said, "The purpose of terrorism is to terrorise."

"That's right and as soon as that thought, that doubt takes root in your mind, they've scored their first victory. You change the way you approach the fight, you change things you normally wouldn't change, you're put off your stride, another small victory and so it goes on."

"Yes, I see, sir," Hawk said his face relaxing a little as some of the tension left him.

"What we have to do is continue as normally as we can, take the fight to them. You thought about their resources, well I've stripped them of those. We have them on the defensive for the first time since this conflict began and we'll continue to do so until we win."

"Look at that, it's stopped raining," De Boer said as he tilted the umbrella back so they could see.

The service was over and the crowds had begun to disperse. In the distance, Matt thought he saw a face he recognised, a face from not so long ago, someone he had helped and called friend. The hair was a little longer, a goatee added, but as it was only a fleeting glimpse he couldn't be sure and he soon forgot about it.

His thoughts returned to the present and what Sinclair had just said. Sinclair was right, now was the time to rebuild.

The fight would go on.

ABOUT THE AUTHOR

Jan Domagala was born in Staffordshire, England to a working class family where at school he discovered the joys of reading. Jan was a big fan of sci-fi books but would read almost anything he could get his hands on. His mother took him to join the local library as soon as he could read and from that day on, if it had words on it, he'd read it.

In the early 70's there wasn't much choice for employment where Jan lived so he ended up in an apprenticeship in screen printing for the ceramic industry. In the early years of his apprenticeship he had the pleasure of a trip on the schooner Captain Scott, a training ship as part of the crew. They sailed around Scotland and even up as far as Stornoway in the Outer Hebrides.

Jan is still in the same trade after a forty year career, but his passion is and has always been writing. After several abortive attempts, he started the Col Sec series, which is an action-adventure series set in the twenty fifth century.

Jan is currently working on the next book in the series.

Join Jan by subscribing today!
http://eepurl.com/dLM3gk
Follow me on BookBub! https://www.bookbub.com/authors/jan-domagala

And on Facebook: https://www.facebook.com/ColSecSeries

www.ingramcontent.com/pod-product-compliance
Lightning Source LLC
Chambersburg PA
CBHW020932260626
47169CB00006B/1678